Caught in Us

By

Layla
Hagen

Dear Reader,
If you would like to receive news about my upcoming books,
sales and giveaways, please sign up for my author mailing list
HERE: http://laylahagen.com/mailing-list-sign-up/
Also, if you sign up, you will receive a FREE electronic copy
of my full-length romance Found in Us (retail price $3.99)

Lost Series

Lost (Lost Book 0.5: prequel novella to James and Serena's story)
Lost in Us (Lost Book 1: James and Serena's story)
Found in Us (Lost Book 2: Jessica and Parker's story)
Caught in Us (Lost Book 3: Dani and Damon's story)

**Author's note: the beginning of this story takes
place before the beginning of the previous books
in the series, but it will fall into time order by the
end of the book.**

Caught In Us
Copyright © 2015 Layla Hagen
Published by Layla Hagen

Published: Layla Hagen 2015
Cover: Cover it! Designs. https://www.facebook.com/CoverItDesigns

Chapter One: Dani

Any senior worth her salt has three goals before graduation.

One: stack college acceptance letters.

Two: snatch a prom date.

Three: lose her v-card.

Midway through my senior year, the first one's in the bag; the other two have disaster written all over them. My best friend, Hazel, is in the same boat. I arrive at our English class with one minute to spare and saunter to my place next to her.

Blue-eyed and with dark brown hair she keeps up in a bun, Hazel is almost a head taller than me, though she's as skinny as I am. We're both wearing baggy t-shirts with our favorite bands to disguise our utter lack of curves. We kept waiting for them to appear all through high school, but it looks like that ship has sailed.

At eight o'clock sharp, Ms. Evans, our English teacher, enters the classroom. She looks around with wide, fearful eyes, as if bracing herself for an hour of Hell. I smile at her encouragingly. It's her first year teaching, and her youth hasn't done her much good. She doesn't have any experience exerting her authority, which often results in mayhem, or her being the butt of underhanded jokes. Insecurity is something overconfident teenagers prey on. She's barely seated at her desk when the door swings open and someone comes in. I've never seen him before. He pauses in the doorway, holding a yellow slip of paper in his hand. He must be a new student. Changing schools in the middle of the senior year isn't common.

I study his appearance carefully—my brother, James, always tells me I'm too perceptive for my own sake. New Guy is a contradiction. He looks more man than boy, and he's possibly the most handsome man I've come across. His black hair is messy and unkempt, as is his two-day beard. I gulp, not wanting to admit to myself how good that looks on him. It makes his full lips stand out, and it's immediately apparent to me that he has the habit of biting his lip—like me. The recognition that we have this in common shoots a tide of warmth through me. I continue with my inspection to his broad shoulders and toned chest and arms. He's wearing a black shirt with long sleeves. I flinch when I notice how calloused his hands are. His jeans are as black as his shirt, though ripped, appearing not only old but also giving him a disheveled air. I can tell he's going for a devil-may-care attitude. He wants to pass himself off as someone who couldn't care less what happens around him. Yet his shirt is perfectly buttoned up, and his shoes laces are symmetrically tied. Boys are careless with these details. He's a perfectionist. My eyes peruse his luscious lips again, and an unexpected shiver grips me.

There is a shift in the third row, and murmurs from the popular group—Anna, Ella, Sherry, and Deb—break the silence. Murmurs turn to giggles as they vie for New Guy's attention. Anna even goes as far as walking to the girls in the first row, pretending to borrow a pen. She winks at him. New Guy doesn't even glance in her direction, nor does he acknowledge any of the giggling girls.

That's a plus point for him because the girls are popular for a reason: they're stunning. Even boys who've known them forever aren't immune to their charms.

The effect they have on new guys ranges from hungry stares to downright ridiculous behavior, like flexing muscles to show off —yep, I've seen it firsthand. New Guy continues to look uninterested, even bored. He walks to Ms. Evans, who seems thoroughly confused. When she reads his paper slip, her face lights up.

"Excellent. Principal Charleston told me you'd start today, Damon. Would you like to introduce yourself to the classroom, maybe say a few words about yourself?" She looks at him with hopeful eyes. I silently beg for him to be polite—he'd be the first guy in our year to show her some respect. That would earn him another plus point in my book.

All my hopes come crashing down when he opens his mouth.

"You also want me to pirouette or roll a ball on my nose?" Then he walks off to the only free seat in the last row, leaving Ms. Evans stricken.

"Jerk," I murmur under my breath.

"A hot jerk," Hazel says. My jaw drops as her pearl-white complexion acquires a reddish hue. In our twelve years of friendship, she has never expressed herself so openly about a guy, much less about a jerk, no matter how good-looking. Hazel and I met in first grade, when both of us weren't nerds yet, just socially awkward. Luckily, my parents own a chocolate factory, so I showed up with a mountain of chocolate that first day, giving out bars to everyone who wanted some. Those bars said what I wanted them to: I suck at making conversation, but have some chocolate. Turns out chocolate is thicker than blood, because Hazel and I became best friends from that first moment.

We're usually on the same page, but not today apparently. I shake my head then concentrate on poor Ms. Evans, who starts the lesson with a trembling voice, almost tearful.

For the next hour, I can't help stealing glances at Damon every few minutes. Long lashes caress the skin under his eyes as he blinks lazily, as if the class is boring enough to put him to sleep. I study the curve of his strong jaw. The vein in his neck betrays his apparent boredom. It pulses like it's about to explode. Explode with what? Annoyance? His oversized ego? Both?

His dark green eyes look up at me as if he can suddenly hear my thoughts. My heart stops when we lock gazes, his intense green eyes making the nerve endings in my entire body shimmer. I involuntarily cross my legs and look away from him, biting my lip. Maybe I shouldn't judge Hazel so sharply. He makes an impression.

"He's not even taking notes." I work as much disgust in my voice as I can. "He must think that's so beneath him."

"I wouldn't mind if he borrowed mine," Hazel says under her breath. I glower at her.

I'm usually a coward, but I despise people who act like jerks just because they can. Also, poor Ms. Evans doesn't deserve this. For the remainder of the class, I work up my courage to walk up to Damon during the break and give him a piece of my mind.

I never get a chance to talk to him. Anna, Ella, Sherry, and Deb corner him after class. They put a lot of effort into getting his attention. They usually only have to smile and play with their hair, and any guy is at their feet. Now they're just making fools of themselves, and not getting anywhere. Well, they do. By the end of the break, Damon doesn't look bored anymore. He looks pissed.

Trig and Biology go in similar fashion. Both teachers have the unfortunate idea to ask him to introduce himself. His answer leaves Mr. Smith stricken in Trig. Damon doesn't bother to answer at all in Biology.

I detect a disturbing pattern. The ruder he is, the more sighs and ohs the girls let slip. What the hell? My only hope is the other guys in class will take his ego down a notch. They're all throwing him unfriendly glances as it is.

***

Since it's the warmest end of January ever, Hazel and I sit on the roof during lunch break, each of us enjoying a tuna salad with extra Parmigiano. The roof is above the cafeteria and serves as a terrace in spring and summer, but it's unused now. I had planned to corner Damon at the end of Biology, but he skidded out of the room before I even rose from my seat. He might have vanished into thin air, because he wasn't in the cafeteria when Hazel and I bought our lunch. From below us comes chitchat about prom—dresses, hair, nails, boys. I can't believe it's already a topic of discussion. Prom is in May.

Hazel and I listen in silence while we gulp down our lunch, and then Hazel asks loudly, "Have you decided when you'll leave for London, Dani? Will you spend the summer here?"

We have an agreement not to discuss prom since it's going to be a sad night for both of us. We'll probably keep each other company—or skip it altogether. Everyone else has dates already, but no one asked us.

Mom insists I don't have a date because I make no effort to look beautiful. She used to be a renowned, highly-paid model in her youth. She secretly hoped for a daughter with long legs and beautiful features she could send on the runway. Instead, she ended up with me, a nerd. To my mother, that's a disease. In high school, there's no greater crime than not being beautiful, or at least very pretty. My mom and my classmates agree.

I love my parents, but they're toxic. Luckily, my grandfather set up a trust fund for me when I was born. I'll get access to it when I turn eighteen and move to England—my mother's birthplace—for college. I already received my acceptance letter to Oxford. It's conditional on achieving high grades, but I don't worry too much about that. Surviving prom worries me more. I try to put on a brave face when Mom questions me about it, but I can't deny it—being invisible sucks. I try not to dwell on it.

"Depends. If James has time to vacation with me this summer, I'll move in September. If he doesn't, I might leave right after school ends and settle in."

"Aren't you nervous? About leaving?"

"A bit," I admit.

"Well, I am very nervous. I can't believe we won't go to college together."

I melt on the spot and put an arm around Hazel. "I'll visit often," I promise, though I know it won't make much of a difference. We won't be there to experience each other's firsts, the way we have for the last twelve years. First college class. First frat party. First kiss. I shudder lightly as the image of Damon's lips pops in my mind. What has gotten into me?

"I still don't understand why you want to leave. We have some of the best colleges around here," Hazel says. I don't understand myself why I want to move overseas. I guess it's because I never felt at home here, much as I wanted to. Somehow, I don't think the answer to feeling home is moving to a foreign place, but I have to try. "Come with me to Stanford, pretty please," Hazel insists. My father and brother went to Stanford, and it's the closest college, so it would make sense to attend it.

"You haven't gotten your acceptance letter yet," I joke.

"I will," she says. I know she will. If there's something Hazel and I are confident about, it's our brain. We know what we're worth. We've excelled at every subject in school, except for Trig, but that didn't have any influence on my acceptance to Oxford, and I expect it won't have any on her acceptance to Stanford. I spend the rest of the lunch break reassuring Hazel that everything will be just fine in college.

Before going to the first afternoon class, I stop by the restroom, hoping to clean off a stain I got on my t-shirt from dropping an oily salad leaf on my left boob. It takes me a few good minutes of rubbing to realize I won't be able to get it off. I give up, swing the door open, and break into a run because I'm already late for class. I collide with something hard head-first.

"You," I bellow when I realize I haven't collided with something. I've collided with Damon, jerk extraordinaire, who currently has a self-satisfied smirk the same size of his giant ego.

"Well, well, well, this is new. No girl tried to hit on me by literally hitting me before."

His comment throws me off-balance, and in the few seconds it takes me to pull myself together, my cheeks catch fire. "I'm not hitting on you; I just didn't see you," I say. His smirk widens. "I'm not hitting on you," I repeat. "Not every girl in this school thinks you're the eighth wonder of the world."

"So you just crashed into me." He jams one hand in the pocket of his jeans, leaning against the wall.

"Yes."

"Then move out of my way."

Stubbornly, I keep my stance, avoiding looking at his lips or eyes. Something about his eyes unsettles me. Maybe it's their intensity, or the fact that I'm afraid he might read my thoughts and discover I find him hot. So ridiculously hot, in fact, that my breath becomes uneven.

In a fraction of a second, he wraps an arm around my waist, turns me around, and pins me against the wall. He presses his palms against the wall on my sides, effectively trapping me. His chest is closing in on me, his hot breath blowing against my temple.

"Mmmm...not the eighth wonder of the world, huh? The racing pulse, the blush in your cheeks, care to explain them?" He lowers his head until his lips are only inches away from my cheek. I try to push him away, but when my palms grope at his chest with that intention, an electrical impulse heats my skin, cutting my breath short.

"You pretentious douche. You annoy me; that's all."

"Annoyance looks good on you," he offers, then takes a step back, freeing me. "Are we done here?"

"Yes, but first I'd like to tell you that you're a jerk."

"You just did that. I take douche to be a synonym for jerk. Excellent vocabulary, by the way."

"Why did you have to be so rude today?"

"You're the one who hit me. People have the habit of blaming everything that goes wrong on me, but I wasn't the one crashing into you. Can't blame me this time."

"I didn't mean me. You were rude to every teacher."

"Who are you?" Disbelief colors his features as he gives me the once-over. "Wonder dork, defender of the teachers?"

"You suck." I chew the inside of my cheek to hide my mortification. No guy has called me a dork to my face. Then again, boys treat me as if I'm non-existent when they don't need my notes or homework. Still, being insulted isn't an improvement over being invisible.

"Thank you. Now, we're both late, so—"

I step in front of him, blocking his way again. "I'm serious." Before I realize what he's up to, his arms are around my waist again, hoisting me up in the air. Every inch where our bodies connect instantly heats up as if his skin ignites me.

"Don't touch me," I stammer, pushing him away after he puts me down again.

He fixes his piercing green eyes on me, his head slightly tilted to one side. "What's your name?"

"Dani."

"Well, Dani, here is some friendly advice: don't throw yourself in a man's way if you don't want to be touched."

***

I arrive to class panting and with my cheeks flushed. Hazel stares at me questioningly as I sit next to her, but I shake my head. Damon is here, too. Damn it, how many classes do we have together?

My thoughts keep flipping to what happened earlier in the corridor. I'm mortified and baffled at my reaction to him. No guy has ever affected me like this. I risk a glance at Damon after he tells Mr. Brown off for asking him to introduce himself. His gaze is focused on me. I feel the heat on my cheeks deepen, which pleases him endlessly.

"Why are you and Damon engaging in a battle of stares?" Hazel whispers, not taking her eyes off her notes.

"I cornered him in the corridor to tell him what a jerk he is."

"No offense, but you look like the cornered one."

I don't take any offense, because she's right. Damon leans back in his chair, looking more relaxed than he had all day while I'm a heavy-breathing mess.

Chapter Two: Dani

I blush all the way home. Our house lies in a residential area a few hours from San Francisco and looks like a modern palace. My mother's main job is attending charity functions and redecorating the house. It used to be a cozy nineteenth-century villa, but slowly, Mom turned it into a soulless glass and wood shell. She kept adding wings, even though it was just the three of us living in it. My brother, James, was sent to boarding school at a very early age.

It's so easy to feel alone inside.

Thoughts of what happened at school vanish when I see James's car parked outside the house. He arrived early today. Smiling, I burst through the front door.

"James," I call, yanking off my shoes and my bag. "James."

"We're in the dining room," Mom's voice booms. James walks out of the dining room and toward me, flashing a grin. Tall, with broad shoulders, short dark hair, and vibrant blue eyes, my brother is quite the looker. When he was in college and going through his rebel period, he looked like a total hunk. Now, he dons expensive clothing and a groomed appearance worthy of the successful business man he is. He looks very attractive. James totally inherited the best of Mom and Dad. Unlike me. With my brown eyes and hair and petite frame, I am utterly average.

However, the fact that I still look like a midget next to James has its perks. I can still hop in his arms, and he can carry me around effortlessly. I immediately jump him.

We're like a bull in a china shop, trotting down the long corridor. A dozen expensive paintings line the walls, giving it the appearance of a museum. When James visits us, it feels like home.

"You know, you should stop doing this," he says, but his strong arms sustain me, as always. "You're not ten years old anymore."

"I'll always be your younger sister, which entitles me to cuddling forever," I say. He laughs softly, hugging me tightly to him. "Can I come to your place tomorrow after school and stay for the weekend? We could do a movie marathon?"

"Sure. You can come anytime; you have a key, after all." He puts me down, but still keeps an arm around me in a half-hug. "But how about spending some time with kids your age? And by that, I don't mean nerding out with Hazel," he adds. I glower at him because that's what I call my time with Hazel, but secretly I'm pleased that James pays enough attention to what I say that he remembers it. "Go out with a group of girls. Do something fun. Or here's an idea, how about going on a date with someone?"

"Girls at school don't like me, James. I'm supposed to be into Vogue, and some other ridiculously named fashion magazines. Not to mention that I should be looking like a runway model. That would probably help in the dating department, too. I'm into fantasy books and comics, and I look...like myself."

James opens his mouth, no doubt to tell me I am in fact very attractive, I just don't know it. Like the good brother he is, he has to say this by default. I interrupt him, not in the mood to go through this again.

"Don't say anything."

Mom and Dad await us stoically at the table when we enter. The dining room is sizeable, the twelve-person table occupying most of it. It's Rococo, or Baroque, or something. Mom's newest acquisition. She scoured nearly every antique shop on this coast to find it. Mom and Dad sit at opposite ends. Beatrix and Anthony Cohen used to love each other passionately. They met when Mom was at the height of her modelling career, in her native London, and had a whirlwind romance, ending up married six months after they met. She quit her career afterward, because Dad was too jealous and impossibly controlling. Somewhere along the years, their love burned to bitter ashes.

As usual, they avoid looking at each other. This is the one day every week when they are forced to eat in each other's company, because James visits. I almost always eat alone in the evenings, in the kitchen. Sometimes our cook stays after schedule, so I don't have to be alone. Mom and Dad mostly eat out. Separately. I very much appreciate that at least every Thursday, they make an effort to be together in one room and behave in a civilized manner. I don't understand how their relationship can survive on nothing but coldness. When I get in a relationship, it will be the exact opposite.

As we eat the appetizer, salmon tartare, Mom drinks her first glass of wine while asking James if he'll be around for her yearly themed charity party. Mom throws multiple parties every year, but the themed one she hosts every spring is the highlight. This year, the theme will be nineteenth-century Venice, which translates to extravagant dresses and masks.

I always had misgivings about this party-throwing occupation of hers, deeming it shallow, but it does raise a lot of money. The party is still months away, but Mom has worked all the details out already.

"Put Parker on the guest list," James tells her.

"Parker is here?" I ask excitedly.

"Yeah, we'll be working together for a few months."

"Let's go out to dinner, the three of us," I say.

"Sure."

Parker is our cousin. He lives in London and visits a few times a year. Like me, he's not much of a talker, but I like being around him. He's a good sport and has a perfect British accent. Mom has an accent, too, but it's faded since she's been living here for more than twenty years.

Then Dad contributes his part to the evening's chatter. I almost know by heart how the conversation will go. He asks James how his company is doing, and after James briefly recounts his latest achievements, Dad heavily hints that he could use James's brain at the chocolate factory. James politely declines, and then my parents go silent. When I was little, I used to adore the chocolate factory, even dreamed about taking it over one day, but as I grew up, I started resenting it for keeping my father away from me.

"Mom, there is an event at school in two weeks on Friday. Do you have time to come?"

"No," she says automatically. I try not to appear too disappointed. "I have to prepare for the Steel's charity gala that weekend."

"You can just come for an hour or so." I know for a fact that preparation means long hours of shopping followed by more long hours at the spa. Would it kill her to do something with me, just this once?

"No," Mom repeats. I sink lower in my seat, pushing the last bits of salmon around with my fork. Well, at least I can count on Hazel's mom to be there, and she's the funniest person I know.

With the serving of the main course, the evening belongs to James and me. Mom and Dad could leave the table for all the attention they pay to what is going on.

"Anything new at school?" James asks.

"A new guy came today. I've never seen a more arrogant jerk; he treats everyone like they're beneath him. He didn't bother to take notes in any of the classes and is rude to everyone, including teachers."

James laughs. "That's a passionate speech. Falling for the bad boy already?"

I choke on my orange juice, spewing some on Mom's beautiful tablecloth. Thankfully, she's too preoccupied gulping down her third—or fourth—glass of wine to pay any attention. I glance quickly at Dad, who focuses on his steak, lost in thoughts of his own. They probably concern the chocolate factory, as usual.

"What's his name?"

"Damon Cooper."

"I didn't know Cooper sent his son to your school," Father says in surprise.

"He's a snob. He probably learned it's the best school around and sent him there, hoping he'll be accepted if his son goes to a decent school," Mom says. "As if anyone wouldn't know Cooper is a leper."

"Didn't you just start working with him a month ago, Dad?" James asks. "He must have some redeeming qualities if you chose him as one of your suppliers."

"The only redeeming thing about him is his low prices," Dad retorts.

"Always cheap," Mom says. "He made his fortune from gambling, and now wants to appear like a serious business man."

I know there is more to their disgust with Cooper than this. Now that I think of it, I remember Dad ranting a few weeks ago when James came to dinner about this Cooper guy, but I can't remember what he was saying.

"Just make sure you keep away from his son. I can't imagine he's anything less than a leper like his father," Dad says. What a shock to hear him take an interest in anything happening in my life.

The real shock comes when Mom says, "Exactly. Your father is right."

Afterward, they both finish their course in silence. I'm still stunned. My parents rarely talk to each other, much less agree on anything. Naturally, the fact that they both agree I should avoid Damon at all costs makes me want to do the exact opposite.

Chapter Three: Dani

Eager to get out of the house the next morning, I arrive early at school. I'm looking at about forty-five minutes to kill on my own. Glad I brought a book with me, I decide to hang out at our usual lunch place. On my way to the rooftop, I pass by the principal's office and hear two voices inside.

"You are going to respect our teachers if you want to stay here."

I wince, coming to a halt in front of the door. The principal never shouts.

"Maybe I don't want to stay," Damon says in a defiant tone.

"Your father insists—"

"What did he bribe you with?"

"You will show me respect, boy." After a long pause, he continues. "You could do well here. Your old grades are good. Better than good, actually. Someone who had to deal with so much and still got mostly A's has perseverance. You could get very far, Damon. It depends on what you will use your perseverance for."

Another long pause.

"Anything else?"

"No, that will be all," the principal says in a defeated tone.

I realize a split-second too late that Damon will exit the office. I pad back, looking for a place to hide. Too late. Damon bangs the door open and darts out. He's wearing black today, as well. I catch my breath. Something about his bright green eyes completely unrattles me. Were they as impossibly beautiful yesterday? They couldn't have been...I can't imagine being angry at someone whose gaze impacts me this way.

When he speaks, I remember just how angry this boy can make me. "Among all your defects, you also like to eavesdrop?"

I clench my fist, pulling myself to my full height, which doesn't amount to much. "I was just passing through here."

"And then you heard my sweet voice and couldn't help listening?"

"N—no," I stutter. "I just—"

He crosses to me fast. Before I blink twice, his arm snakes around my waist, plastering me to him.

"Let me go."

His lips curl into a satisfied smirk. "This is the second time in two days that you've been in my arms. I think you like it here."

Hunching his shoulders, Damon lowers himself until we're eye to eye.

"You're delusional." I'd sound more believable if my voice wasn't so breathy and undependable. "Get your hands off me."

"I will as soon as you admit you were eavesdropping." He's so close to me that the whiff of hot breath accompanying every word lands on my lips. It makes my knees weak and the inside of my mouth dry.

Determined not to give him satisfaction, I spit, "Fine. I was. And you know what?"

"Oh, I'm dying to know."

"This whole arrogant, bad-boy image, always dressing in black and rebelling against your father is very passé."

He drops his arms, his eyes growing cold. "You know nothing about me."

"Oh, the misunderstood bad boy. You're turning into a walking cliché by the second."

"So are you. The rich girl who thinks she's better than everyone else. Someone dressing like you has no business giving fashion advice," he says. His comment stings, but I don't let it show.

"I think I'm better than everyone else? You look at everyone around here like they're scum, you frustrated moron."

"Frustrated?" There is a hint of surprise behind the coldness in his tone.

"Yeah. Only frustrated people enjoy taking their feelings out by being rude to others like—"

"Oh, not this again. Go bore someone else with your defense of spineless teachers. Why don't you go hang out with the principal since you both seem to enjoy the subject so much?"

I purse my lips. "If you hate it so much here, why don't you leave?"

"I can't." He fixes his backpack on his shoulder, his hands twitching along the strap. "If I had a choice, I would be out of California in a second." He shakes his head. "Have you ever felt so trapped in your skin you were sure you'd asphyxiate?"

The desperation in his question catches me off-guard. His bright green eyes bore into mine, demanding honesty, so that's what I give him.

"Yes. It's a feeling I wake up to most days."

I'm expecting him to mock me, but he just says, "For your information, I'm not wearing black to make any statement. I'm mourning someone."

"That just makes half of the things I said to you awful," I babble. "I'm sorry."

"You think just half of the things you said to me were awful? In this case, you're awful," he says, but with a smile. Then he bursts out laughing. Not in a mocking way; in a heartfelt, cheerful way.

I still hear his laugh echo in the corridor as I make my way to the rooftop.

***

As usual, I get too engrossed in my reading and am almost late for class. Sitting next to Hazel, I take out my books when Damon appears in front of our desk.

"You dropped your phone in the hallway," he says politely.

"No, I didn't." I look in bewilderment as he drops my smartphone in my hand. Damon smiles mischievously, walking over to his desk as Ms. Evans enters the class. Wouldn't I have noticed if my phone had fallen on the corridor during our altercation? Not really...I was too preoccupied with him to notice anything else. My skin heats up at the memory of his closeness. I swivel to ask Hazel something and find her staring at me with curious eyes.

"Do you have anything to share about your morning?"

"I read a book," I mumble.

Ms. Evans starts talking about the Bronte novel we had to read when I receive a text.

You should take better care of your things.

The sender appears only by number, not name, but I know who it is. Sure enough, one glance in Damon's direction confirms my suspicion. He's not looking at me or his phone, but lifts the corner of his lips. It dawns on me that I might not have dropped my phone at all. He must have taken it from my pocket.

And you shouldn't steal other people's things, I reply.

Hey, you were eavesdropping, so don't go all saint on me. You were the first offender.

I smile, overcome by a strange giddiness. I can't believe he stole my phone, or that he got my number, or that he's texting me right now. I'm grinning like an idiot. It's the first time a guy has written to me and not asked for my notes or something similar. Given our less-than-friendly interactions yesterday and this morning, this is a surprise. Sometimes it takes a healthy fight and a familiar pain to gain a friend.

"After the battle of stares yesterday follows the battle of messages?" Hazel murmurs, smiling. "Bad boy is showing quite an interest in you."

"No, he's not." Something light settles in my stomach.

"I heard a junior tried very hard yesterday to make him ask for her number and failed. He must be very interested in yours if he got it on his own."

"This doesn't mean anything." The lightness grows, the giddy feeling bubbling up inside me.

"Maybe not." She leans in conspiratorially. "Maybe it does."

When Ms. Evans announces she'll question us about Wuthering Heights, I have the feeling Damon might take this opportunity to display the same unpleasantness as yesterday.

Be nice if Ms. Evans asks you something, I type quickly. Please.

He doesn't type back, and as Ms. Evans begins to ask questions, I brace myself. She deliberately avoids asking him anything, though. Then she asks Beckett what his opinion is about the motives behind Heathcliff's behavior. He stares at her with a blank face, clueless.

It's Damon who answers. "Heathcliff felt out of place. He didn't belong to their class, and everyone else never let him forget it."

Ms. Evans' eyes widen, but all she says is "Do you think that justifies him?"

"No. That's no justification for being a dick to everyone," Damon says nonchalantly.

Ms. Evans flinches. "That language doesn't belong in the classroom, Damon." Her tone is firm. I'm proud of her. "I'll let you out of the questioning round because you're new, and I gave this assignment a week ago."

Damon's lip twitches, and I can tell he's about to say something obscene back. I sit up straighter, staring at him intently. He catches my eye and winks at me. I instantly flush, dropping my gaze to my hands.

"I had to read the book in my junior year," Damon replies. Ms. Evans nods, and then continues questioning Anna. I think about something the principal mentioned today... Damon scored mostly A's at his old school. My assessment was spot-on yesterday. Under the mask of carelessness hides a perfectionist. Someone who is clearly smart. As Ms. Evans instructs us to look up a certain passage in the book, I shift in my chair, holding my copy in my hands and pretending to flip through its pages. In reality, I am sneaking glances at Damon. Who was he before he came here and whom did he lose?

Thank you for not being rude, I text him under the desk. I receive an answer almost immediately.

Ouch. That sounds like something you'd tell a dog. I'm not a poodle; don't try to train me.

I write back quickly. You're definitely not a poodle. More like a pitbull. I hear those are hard to train. Whatever they do, it's because they want to.

There is a pause in which I wait breathlessly, and then my smartphone vibrates. They also tend to attack their owners.

My fingers almost snap as I hurry to reply. I don't believe that. They just have a bad reputation. Don't believe everything you hear. It's all appearances.

Another short vibration. Ms. Evans looks at me, so I just chance a quick glance at my phone. So what should I make of your Linkin Park t-shirt?

Frowning, I text back as best as I can while pretending to pay attention to Ms. Evans. What's the harm in liking Kinky Fuck?

Damon's next message confuses me. Is that an invitation? I read what I wrote before, and shame washes over me.

Abandoning all pretense of paying attention to the teacher, I write It was autocorrect. I meant Linkin Park. OMG, I'm so sorry.

He doesn't write anything back, and when I look at him, he appears on the verge of bursting out laughing.

The bell rings and Damon walks out to his locker, where Anna follows him.

Chapter Four: Damon

Someone corners me during the break. I feel the presence behind me without even looking up from my locker. I've had more than enough occasions to sharpen my instincts.

"Hi," a girl's voice calls behind me. I take my time closing my locker before turning around to face her.

"Hi, Anna," I answer. She's been pestering me since yesterday, and I couldn't give less of a damn. She's as close to the cheerleading type as it gets. Tall, blonde, huge tits. She has the attitude to go with it, too. She knows she's beautiful and expects everyone to fall at her feet. This time, she chose the wrong guy.

"Black suits you, Damon." She tries to purr out my name, but to me it just sounds like she's swallowed an egg. Still, I'm sure enough idiots have fallen for it. "Let's go out sometime."

"Why? You don't know anything about me other than my name." Her face falls for a split-second, but then she flashes a smile. Persistent girl. I can tell she has no idea what answer to give because she thinks her beauty doesn't require one. As if to make a point, she pushes her chest forward, twirling a few strands of hair between her fingers. Everyone from the classroom storms out, their voices filling the space.

I spot the girl from this morning in the crowd, the one I texted. Dani. Blondie also sees her, giving her a short once-over then dismissing her with a self-indulgent smirk. This seals it for me.

"So, I know a nice cafe nearby. We could go after school," Anna says.

"No. And a word of advice: start working on your personality; you have a lot of catching up to do. Your ass and boobs aren't as good as you think." I purse my lips. She backs away like I've cracked a whip in front of her. I take off, swinging my backpack over my shoulder. I can still see Dani, even though she's far ahead of me on the corridor. I smile as I remember the shade of pink her skin turned when I was texting her. She seems so pure; it's a sin to flirt with her. But something's hidden deep beyond that innocence—passion. I don't think she even knows it. I do. I saw it in the way she talked to me this morning, how her eyes sparkled. It was almost worth it riling her up just to see her like that. I wonder how she'd spark if I did something else to her.

I shake my head, musing how this girl can have this effect on me. It's the first time since Mom died that I feel anything else except pain and anger. I've been in Hell since the funeral, and I can't make anyone pay for it, though I'll keep trying. That bastard calling himself my father deserves it. My fingers twitch, forming into fists as anger swells up inside me anew. Then Dani turns and smiles brightly at me, and that anger is replaced by another equally consuming sensation...my cock throbbing in my jeans. Easy boy. She's not that kind of girl, and she's much better off without you.

Chapter Five: Dani

At lunchtime, I prepare to go to the cafeteria when Hazel says, "I've got to go. Mom is picking me up early today."

"Oh, right. I forgot. You're going to Lake Tahoe for the weekend."

"That's right." She beams, rubbing her palms together in excitement. "And the week after Valentine's Day, we'll go to London. Mom is at the principal right now, trying to convince him to give me two weeks off, so we can make a tour."

"I'll be surprised if he doesn't agree. Your mom can talk anyone into anything." I know it's selfish, but I'm jealous of Hazel. She and her parents do something together every other weekend. Sometimes they take me with them, but it's embarrassing to intrude on their family time too often. Their family time feels real, not a wisp of resemblance to the weekly Thursday night dinners at my house. They laugh together, and Hazel's parents get involved in every way in her life. I crash at her place often. The weekends I don't spend with Hazel, I try to spend with James. Nothing like my brother to ensure my belly hurts from too much laughing. The time with him is almost enough to fill me with energy for a week of being ignored and being on my own in my parents' enormous mansion.

Almost.

***

I say goodbye to Hazel and her mom, then buy myself lunch and go up to the roof, as usual, only to find it occupied. Damon is lying on his back, his eyes closed as he soaks in the sunlight. Next to him is a half-eaten sandwich.

"What are you doing here?" I ask loudly.

"Avoiding people." He pushes himself up in a sitting position, and I'm distracted by the wind blowing through his hair. It dislodges a few dark tresses, and they stray around wildly. "What are you doing here?"

"This is where Hazel and I eat lunch. Same reason as you."

"Isn't the roof off-bounds, at least for nerds with a teacher-defending streak like you?" His comments should rub me the wrong way, but he's smiling—not smirking— as he says it, and there is no malice in his voice. It flatters me. He takes a bite of his sandwich and grimaces in disgust.

"Oh, but nerds like me know where the good food is in the cafeteria." I sit next to him and hold out my burger, beckoning him to take a bite.

"This is good," he says incredulously. "How did I end up with this crap?"

"It's your fault. Why did you go to the sandwich and salads corner?"

"Because there was no line there."

I grin. "That should've been a straightforward hint that the food there sucks."

"They charge a shitload of fees. Shouldn't all the food be good?"

"Well, technically, that," I point to his sandwich, "is the best food. It's in the healthy corner."

He snorts. "Figures. World's weirdest paradox. Everything that's healthy tastes like crap."

"They had a decent tuna salad yesterday."

"You eat tuna salad? And I thought you were okay."

"It wasn't too bad. More burger?"

"Aren't you going to be hungry later on? It's not that big," he says. I assure him it's all right, and we share my burger in silence. I become aware of his proximity, and I remember how it felt to have his arms around me, to breathe in his breath. A flutter in my stomach alerts me that my thoughts are heading into dangerous territory. It probably meant nothing to him. Still, watching him eat and licking his lips fills me with more strange sensations...like heat and ache for something unknown.

"Where is your friend?" he asks. "The one you sit with in all the classes?"

"Her mom picked her up early today. They're traveling this weekend."

He twists a leather bracelet on his wrist. Like everything else he wears, it's black.

"Who are you mourning?" I ask. Damon pauses in the act of playing with the bracelet. The skin around his eyes tightens a notch. "Sorry, that's none of my business. You don't have to tell me. I shouldn't have asked."

"My mother."

"I'm sorry."

His eyes drift over the trees in the distance. "She died of a stroke. She had her first one four years ago and it left half her body paralyzed. She had her second one last month and died." His eyes are bright and shiny. I think he's withholding tears, which bewilders me. Not because he feels pain, that's natural. I just didn't expect him to express it in front of me.

"And you came here to live with your dad."

His posture changes in the fraction of a second. "Yeah," he says through gritted teeth. Something tells me he knows how to deal with anger better than with pain. "First time I saw him was at Mom's funeral."

"What?"

He balls his palms to fists. "He knocked up Mom when she was sixteen, and then took off. Mom never heard from him again. Still can't believe he had the nerve to show up at her funeral."

"The bright side to this is that you didn't get sent to a group home. You're not eighteen yet. Do you have any other family?"

"Grandparents. My mother's parents, but I never met them. They didn't want anything to do with Mom after she had me."

"Oh." Really, oh; that's terrible. I make a mental note not to complain about my parents anymore. They might not be the most affectionate people, but they would never turn their back on me or James.

"You were right this morning," he says.

"About what?"

"That I'm frustrated and lash out at people."

"Does that make you feel better?"

"Not really. But this," he gestures with his fingers between the two of us, "does. You're easy to talk to." His pulls his gaze to me, and an involuntary sigh escapes my lips. There's something devastating about the intensity of his green eyes. It muddles my thoughts. "You put something in that burger?"

"A truth potion?" My voice is strangely high-pitched.

"You know if you ever tell anyone about this conversation, I will vehemently deny it?"

I grin. "Ah, you're careful not to ruin your bad boy image. Don't worry. I won't tell anyone. But I warn you, if you behave like an asshole again, I'll have no problem calling you out on it in front of people."

"Is this a threat?" He leans forward, and I'm suddenly too preoccupied with his lips to come up with an answer.

"You bet it is," I finally stammer.

"Fair enough. Someone should call me out."

"People do. Principal Charleston did this morning."

"Yeah...Older people do all the time. But if you call me out, I must be doing something wrong."

"Interesting yardstick you're using to measure how much of an asshole you are."

He studies me, stretching out lazily. "What brought this on?"

"What do you mean?"

"Yesterday, it seemed like you'd be happy if I disappeared."

I hesitate. "Do you know our fathers work together?"

"Your last name's Cohen, right? I heard it in class and thought it sounded familiar."

"Yeah."

"I didn't get the impression your parents like my father too much. They're smart."

"You're right, they don't like him. They said I should steer clear of you."

Damon breaks into guffaws, grabbing me by the shoulders and pulling me toward him so I land face-first in his chest. "And you decided to do the exact opposite?" His aftershave catches me unprepared, the mix of musk and the manly scent coming off his skin dizzying me. I'm trembling with the awareness of our closeness.

"Yeah."

He laughs the same heartfelt laugh for a full minute before calming enough to say, "I like you, Dani Cohen. Very much. You always say what you think, don't you?"

"My brother keeps telling me this."

"He's right."

"Where did you live before?" I ask.

"Rhode Island, but I don't want to talk about home. You do the talking while I busy myself finishing your burger."

"What do you want me to talk about?"

"What are you doing this weekend?"

"Oooh, I'm doing a movie marathon with my brother. He lives in a penthouse in San Jose and has a home theater."

"What are you watching?" he asks between bites.

"All movies based on comic books from the last twenty years."

"Doing your homework before the big superhero reboot comes in cinemas? Like anyone needed a new version."

"I know, right? But I'm a sucker for comic book-based movies, so I'll go see it."

"Me, too. We could go together." He throws the words casually, but my pulse starts jackhammering. Taking the very last bite of my burger, Damon lies on his back, resting his head on his palms. "Do you hang out with your brother often?"

"Yeah. We mostly watch movies, go shopping, or eat out. Sometimes, during the summer vacation, we go sailing. He's a bit of an adrenaline junkie, does skydiving and stuff, but doesn't take me with him for that."

"You'd like to skydive?" There is so much disbelief in his voice...it's almost insulting.

"No idea. How can I like something if I've never tried it? You can't discard anything as bad until you've tried it," I say. His eyes glint so darkly it sends a shiver down my spine. I like this—both the glint and the shiver.

"Careful, Dani; this type of thinking can get you into trouble."

"You know all about it, don't you?"

"Trust me, I do. I'm walking trouble. You should stay away from me. It's catchy." Something in his tone tells me this is the last thing he wants to say on this topic.

"How do you get along with your dad?"

Any trace of a smile melts from his beautiful face. "You mean when I don't want to punch him? I hate him. He hates me, too."

"I don't think that's true. Why would he have taken you in otherwise?"

"Remorse or something. I don't know. But it's clear he doesn't want me here. We avoid each other, and when we do end up in the same room, we fight. I feel like a prisoner in that fucking house. It's so big you could fit ten families inside, but it feels like a prison."

I don't say anything. I haven't been through what he has, but the feeling of being trapped is familiar.

"If you need to talk, you can call me." I poke him in the ribs playfully. "Since you have my number and all."

We walk together to the afternoon class, which garners us incredulous stares. Damon doesn't notice, but I do. James texts me that he'll take the bag of clothes I left at home and pick me up right after school to start our weekend together. That's a bonus few hours with him since the original plan was he'd pick me up from home tonight.

When classes are over, I tell Damon, "Promise me you won't get into trouble with your dad."

"I promise."

Chapter Six: Damon

The shouting begins the moment I set foot in the house. "Your behavior at school is unacceptable." George stands in the lobby of the monstrosity of glass and steel he calls home. It's as cold as ice, and cost him a fortune. Giving Mom the proper care would have cost him a fraction of that.

"Tell that to someone who cares; I've got to go." I throw the backpack on the floor, pushing it away with my foot.

"Where are you going?"

"That's none of your business." I make a point to stare anywhere except at him. I look like him, and I hate myself for it—what if I'm like him? What if the greatest things I'll achieve will be gambling my way through life and ruining other people? I take a step back, repelled by his presence. This man represents everything I hate.

"You live under my roof, Goddamn you." He does a poor imitation of a father figure, not that I can compare him to anyone. I never had someone to fill in that role, and I was happy with the way things were.

"Not by my choice. I'm happy to leave."

"You need to behave, boy." His face grows harder by the second, the veins in his temple thickening. It's almost comical. "I am just starting to build a reputation with my business partners, and you will not ruin it."

Squinting, I chortle. "So that's what this is about."

"The principal called me today and told me you were seen with the Cohen girl."

"What the fuck?" I force myself to breathe in and out and to keep my hands from throwing punches at him, which is something I've wanted to do since I first saw him. "You pay him to spy on me? That's low, even for you."

"Damon, you're a ticking bomb." Throwing his hands in the air, he looks a tad theatrical. Fake it till you make it holds true for wannabe parents, too. "He's watching you for his school's sake, not because I'm paying him. Stay away from that girl."

"Stay out of my business," I say through gritted teeth then trot past him, heading for the door.

"Where are you going? We're not done."

"I'm done," I throw the words over my shoulder before banging the door in his face, stepping out right in the blinding light. "Fuck." Is the sun always up in this craphole even in January? I miss home: the rain, the wind. I could always count on that to cool me off.

I cooled off when I was on the rooftop with her. I could lie to myself and say it was the breeze, but it was her presence. Her innocence made me think that maybe not all good things in this world have ended. Her laughter filled a void that felt unfillable and her curiosity about me...it almost convinced me that I'm more than a fuck-up without a future.

I like her.

In other words, I'm screwed.

Chapter Seven: Dani

On Monday, Damon comes to school with a black eye and a split lip. I watch with horror as he enters Trig, fifteen minutes after Mr. Smith started torturing us with the lesson. Damon proceeds to his seat, ignoring the teacher's reprimands. But there is more in Mr. Smith's tone than annoyance at Damon's late arrival. There is worry, and I worry, too.

"What do you think happened to him?" Hazel whispers, while pretending to solve the exercise Mr. Smith gave us. We both dislike Trig, which makes this class downright painful.

"I don't know." Secretly, I have a somber feeling I do know. I flip my smartphone between my fingers, tempted to text him, but I'm not bold enough. He hasn't texted me at all since Friday. Maybe it was just a one-time thing.

"Ask him," Hazel beckons as if reading my thoughts.

I glance at him, making a truce with myself: if he's playing with his phone, I'll text him. If not, I'll swallow my curiosity. To my astonishment, Damon is bent over a notebook, scribbling. I suspect he's doing crosswords or whatever, but when Mr. Smith asks, "Anyone have the answer?" Damon is the only one who says yes.

Mr. Smith reluctantly asks him to explain his solution on the whiteboard. Damon writes out the answer with a mix of carelessness and confidence. Anna and her friends watch him, whispering continuously. I have a hunch they're not gossiping about his Trig knowledge. None of them looks at him with worry, though. I guess the bruises just make him even more attractive. Whatever.

"He's hot and good at Trig?" Hazel says, groaning. "This should be illegal." As should showing up bruised at school. "I think we should resign from our jobs as Chief Nerd Officers."

"What?" I ask, confused.

"What's the point of being a nerd if I have to spend hours studying for Trig to get it, and then someone like him walks in and just knocks it out of the park?"

I swear that when he puts down the marker and swirls around, biting his lower lip, there is a collective sigh from Anna and her friends.

"That's a neat way to solve that exercise, Damon," Mr. Smith says, clearly impressed. "Were you in an Advanced Placement course in your previous school?"

"No, but I was in a math contest. Our teacher did some extra lessons with the participants."

"Well, your teacher did an excellent job." Mr. Smith eyes Damon's bruises like he wants to say something about them, but then dismisses the class. Hazel and I barely pack our bags when Anna is already at Damon's desk, trying to make conversation. There goes my chance to ask him about his weekend during this break.

"I bet she's asking him for tutoring in Trig," Hazel says.

"I think she can come up with more exciting activities, Hazel."

"Come to think of it, maybe we should ask for some tutoring." She nudges my shoulder. "You could ask him."

"Why me?" My neck grows warm. I told her about having lunch with him on Friday, though I didn't go into much detail.

"You know why. Go ahead; ask him."

I nod, but I want to ask him something else.

**

I don't get to talk with Damon all morning because during the breaks, Anna is hovering around him. At lunch, Hazel and I are among the last to arrive in the cafeteria. We stand in line for the unhealthy food—pepperoni pizza today.

"Lunch on the roof?" a deep voice asks right into my ear. My reaction is instantaneous and unsettling. Goose bumps dance on my neck and arms, and when I swirl around and meet his eyes, there is this weird jumble in my stomach again.

"Yes. I see you found the right line today," I say.

"I'm a fast learner," he declares proudly.

"So we've heard in Trig," Hazel interjects.

I can't help looking at his split lip and black eye, but I can't say anything with Hazel around. We get our food in silence, and then Hazel says, "I'll eat inside today. I need to finish my Physics homework."

"You finished it this morning before Trig," I say dumbfounded.

"I want to go over it again. I think I got one wrong."

"We'll stay inside, too—"

"Nonsense," Hazel says. "You two go up and soak in a bit of sun. I'll see you later."

Only when Damon and I are already on the roof does it occur to me that Hazel might have wanted to stay inside on purpose, so Damon and I could be alone.

"How was your movie marathon?"

"Great." I'm surprised and pleased he remembers my plans for the weekend. We eat in silence, and when he swallows the last bite and leans on his back, I finally pick up my courage and say, "You promised not to get into trouble with your dad."

"I didn't."

"This is how you look when you don't get in trouble with him?"

He narrows his eyes. "You think my father did this?"

"He didn't?"

"No, Dani. He didn't." He runs a hand through his dark hair, ruffling it. "Trust me, if he ever attempts to, he's a dead man."

"So, why are you looking this way? You did get into trouble with...someone."

"That's my problem," he says flatly.

I lower my eyes to the uneaten crust of my pizza slice. Damon's phone buzzes.

"Aren't you going to stop that thing?" I ask.

"No. That's Anna, asking if I want to buy her lunch."

He gave her his number. I feel a pang of something gripping me. With dread, I realize it might be jealousy. "Why don't you? Anna is beautiful."

"Not my type." He groans, winking at me. "I don't even know how she got my number."

I stare at him. "She's everyone's type."

"Do I look like everyone to you?"

"No," I tease. "You're special. Don't all bad boys think they're special to everyone?"

"I'm not interested in being special to everyone. I want to be special to someone. That'd be enough for me."

"That's a hell of a statement for a guy."

He laughs softly. It's a surprisingly melodic sound. "It's your fault. I don't usually wear my heart on my sleeve. You make me feel too comfortable around you. When you don't insult me."

Comfortable. What's that supposed to mean? That's the kind of word you use to describe fluffy pajamas you love wearing on lazy days, but wouldn't be caught dead wearing outside the house.

"Do you keep in touch with your friends back home?" I inquire.

"I didn't have too many close friends. Mom was one of my best friends."

"Oh," I say before I can stop myself. "It must have been rough, what with her illness and all..."

"It was challenging because she could hardly move on her own." He hesitates, his fingers twitching. His chest rises and falls in slow, uneven beats, as if breathing has suddenly become a chore. I study every line on his face; the way his brow furrows in what he'd like to pass off as concentration, when it is, in fact, an effort to withhold tears. "We managed. A neighbor helped us a lot, looked after her when I was at school and work."

"You worked?" The concept of work is foreign to me. I volunteer often, but I haven't worked one day of my life.

"Had to," he says in a clipped tone. "Mom's benefits barely covered our basic needs."

"And you also had time for math contests and such? That's impressive."

He shrugs. "School was important to Mom. I wanted her to be happy."

I lie on my back next to him, watching the clouds.

"What was she like? Tell me. What was her favorite food? Music?"

"She listened to eighties hits, mostly. She loved lasagna. After she got sick, she couldn't cook by herself. It took me about two years to get that damn lasagna right." His voice is a tad uneven. "No one's asked me about her. It's like everyone wants me to forget she existed."

"I suppose they think it would be easier for you."

"And you don't?"

"I don't know," I admit. "Does it hurt talking about her?"

"Not with you. I liked taking care of her. It was such an integral part of my life. And now that she's gone, I feel lost."

Many people feel lost at our age, but for very different reasons. He was forced to mature earlier, to take care of someone else, and now that she's gone, he doesn't know how to fight the loneliness. I wish I could show him he's not alone, but what can someone who only knows loneliness teach him about driving his away? He looks so desperately lonely that it hurts me. Out of the corner of my eyes, I see his lips curl upward in a smug smile. Before I can read too much into his smile, though, another thought takes hold of me: those are some beautiful lips.

"You're not all that bad for a rich girl," he says.

This snaps me out of my daydreaming. Or, well, lip-dreaming. "You say it like I should take it as a compliment."

"It is a compliment. You're a breath of fresh air." He shifts on his side, facing me.

"So are you. You're different from everyone I know."

"Is it because I'm devastatingly good-looking?" he says mischievously.

I roll my eyes at him. "It's because you are extremely modest. We should go back. You know, hanging around with me is going to ruin your reputation."

"What's that supposed to mean?"

"You didn't notice the way people looked at us last Friday? Or today in the cafeteria?"

"So what?" His eyes widen, and he grins. "You're ashamed people might see you with me?"

I gasp slightly. "That's not true."

"You're afraid they'll think we were secretly making out," he teases.

"They will not think that." Heat surges in my cheeks.

"Hazel seems to think exactly that."

I can't be blushing. I can't be blushing. Damon eyes one of my cheeks and then the other. His grin widens. Of course, I'm blushing.

"You'd like to make out with me? You just have to say it. I assure you I'm a perfectly good kisser." He leans into me, his eyes scanning me playfully. Does he know what he's doing to me with his dark green eyes and his annoyingly beautiful lips? He, who must have touched tens of other lips with his, and toyed with as many hearts? My heart beats so fast I legitimately fear I might faint. He's just joking, Dani.

"Not every female around wants to kiss you." How I muster the wits to say the next words, I'll never know. "You're not as good-looking as you think."

"But you admit I'm good-looking?"

"I didn't say that."

"You didn't deny it," he says.

"Please, go work your charm on someone else who is more experienced with these games. I'm not."

He pulls back. "What do you mean?"

"We have to go." I take my plate and jump to my feet. He catches up with me on the stairs, grabbing my arm.

"You've never been kissed?" he asks.

I debate lying for a second, but I've never been any good at it. "No, I haven't. Go ahead. Laugh."

He's not laughing. "Why?" he seems genuinely confused, and I almost laugh. He reminds me so much of James right now, who is always completely bewildered by the fact that no guy is into me.

"I don't think I'm anyone's type here at school," I explain.

"Figures. I knew most here are idiots; I didn't realize just how much."

The implication in his words fills me with warmth and relief: that there is something wrong with them. Not with me.

"So, no one was lucky enough to taste your lips," he says, and then does something that petrifies me. He runs his thumb over my upper lip, then my lower one. My thighs involuntarily press themselves together as heat billows between them. A whiff of breath rushes through my lips.

"We should go to class," I murmur.

"Sure." A smile plays on his lips all the way to the class. We attract stares, just as I predicted. This time, he does notice them. Leaning into me, Damon says, "You were right. They are looking at us, but I was right, too."

"What do you mean?"

"They're convinced we spent the entire break making out. And if you continue to blush so deliciously, I'll wish we had."

***

Tuesday, I give in and ask Damon for help with Trig. He agrees instantly, and we decide to study on the rooftop, which is slowly becoming our designated meeting place. Hazel was supposed to study with us, but she came up with an excuse at the last moment. I suspect she wants us to be alone.

When we take a break from the exercises, I listen to Damon rant about how awful California is for five minutes before I can't stand it anymore and interrupt him. "Why don't you focus on the fact that you are awesome at Trig?" I want to push him to see his strengths and play with them. It has an immediate effect on him; he straightens his shoulders as if a weight has been lifted. Unfortunately, this also makes the lines of his toned chest much more visible, which means I'll pay zero attention to Trig.

"Focusing on me is boring," he says with confidence. "Let's focus on you." He pushes the books away, propping himself on an elbow, his green eyes scanning me intensely. "Tell me about you."

I swallow hard, peeling my eyes away from his body. I'm not used to talking about myself, not even with Hazel or James; though for some reason, opening myself up in front of Damon seems less daunting. "I'm more of a listener."

"Do things differently for a change." Leaning in to me, he whips my breath away. "I've told you enough about me. I want to know more about you. I'm listening."

Under his watchful gaze, words tumble out of my mouth without effort. "I like ice cream and chocolate. Christmas is my favorite holiday. I want to try bungee jumping on my birthday."

"See? That wasn't so hard." He pushes himself up on his forearms. "What's your favorite color?"

"Why do you want to know that?" I ask suspiciously.

"So I can paint a mental picture of you in a bikini." It takes a few seconds for his words to sink in. When they do, there is nowhere to hide. I cover my arms, hoping I can hide the goose bumps on them, but I'm not fooling him. In fact, he relishes what he's doing to me, a grin cracking on his face. "Or maybe I want to buy you something in your favorite color. You'll never know if you don't tell me."

"I have two. White and red, but I don't wear red much. It feels like drawing attention to myself."

"So what?" His eyes widen all of a sudden.

"I don't feel comfortable when people look at me. I don't like being the center of attention."

"How about when I look at you?" He wiggles his eyebrows in an exaggerated move.

"I—well, I..." My words come out jumbled, so I decide it's best to shut my mouth. I now understand why the word 'crush' is so popular to describe these butterflies rumbling inside me. The feeling crushes everything in its way—including my ability to think. Let's hope it won't break my heart, too.

"I think you should put yourself in the center of attention," Damon says. "Look at me; I do it all the time."

Drumming my fingers on the tiles, I can't help snapping, "You're the center of attention because you're a jerk to everyone."

"Not to you." He wiggles his eyebrows again, fixing me with his eyes.

"You have to stop doing this."

"What?" His tone is a little too innocent.

"You know what." My throat goes dry as my eyes wander to his lips. "Let's get back to Trig."

***

One and a half weeks later, Damon texts me to meet him in front of his locker before going to the first class. He waits for me propped against the metal door, wearing a smug look and keeping his hands behind his back.

"What are you doing?" I ask. "The class started already."

"We're late anyway, another minute won't hurt. I want to give you a present."

"Oh." I readjust the strap of my backpack on my shoulder, looking down and trying to keep the excitement from showing. No use. It runs like a current from my toes all the way up to my ears, and I grin like an idiot. "Why did you get me a present?"

"Because it's Valentine's Day. What did you get me?"

"I—didn't..." Words fail me as I try to make sense of all this. Why should I have bought him a present? It's not like we're dating...Are we? Alarm flits in my mind until he grins.

"I'm kidding. I just bought it yesterday and didn't want to wait to give it to you."

"What is it?" I make a mental note to find a way to get back at him for fooling me. Though I won't deny, the thought of dating him, even if it was an illusion, was wonderful. On second thought, I should get back at him for not making the dream last longer. Or making it real.

"I'll only show it if you promise you'll use it."

"Pfff..." I try to play cool, though I'm dying to see what he got me. "No. You'll give it to me anyway because you'll look like an idiot carrying whatever that girly thing is."

"Fair point. Well, if you won't wear it willingly, I'll make you wear it." He moves his hand, revealing a bright red scarf. It's beautiful, made of smooth silk.

There are a thousand more appropriate reactions, but all I can come up with is, "Why?"

"Because sometimes it's good to push past something that makes you uncomfortable. Will you wear this?"

"Yeah, sure. It's gorgeous. Thanks."

He steps up to me, swinging the scarf over my head, letting it fall over my hair, electrifying it in the process. I raise my hand to smooth it, and meet Damon's. The split-second our fingers touch, the current of excitement from earlier turns into a full-on fire.

"Let me do it." His voice is breathy and uneven as he pats my hair, which only makes it worse, but I'm not about to complain. I hold my breath when he arranges the scarf around my neck, watching him run his tongue over his lower lip then nip at it with his teeth. I'm painfully aware of the heat in my cheeks, but hopefully my flush will go unnoticed next to the bright red fabric. "There you go. Happy Valentine's Day, Dani."

He throws one last look my way before opening the door to the classroom, and I'm a goner.

Chapter Eight: Dani

The next evening, I go out to dinner with James and Parker. My family's driver, Paul, takes me to the steak restaurant I go to with James every once in a while.

The two men await me inside the restaurant, already sitting at a table. They both smile when they see me. Given how busy they are, I'm beyond happy they made time to eat dinner with me.

"Hello, cousin," Parker says as I approach them, grinning from ear to ear. His thick British accent is music to my ears. "Long time, no see."

"She'll be all yours in the fall when she moves to England," James says.

"Can't wait," Parker and I say at the same time.

The waitress arrives and asks us what we want to drink. She sizes up both men, pushing her chest out and fluttering her eyelids. She's ridiculous, but I can't really blame her. James and Parker are both stunning. Each of them has a devastating effect on women. When they're next to each other? It's just too much awesomeness. Ridiculously flirty behavior is accepted.

After the waitress brings our drinks, Parker asks, "How are prom preparations going?"

I choke on my soda, eying him to see if he's pulling my leg or not. Nope, it's a serious question. But I suppose he thinks this subject is a hit with senior girls. Chuckling, I say, "I can't believe I'm having dinner with two men, and prom is brought up. It's still months away."

"Well, when we were in boarding school," Parker says, pointing to James and himself, "that was all girls talked about in senior year. Granted, a long time's passed since then, so maybe things have changed."

"We're not that old," James says. Turning to me, he adds, "You were thinking about not going at some point."

"I think I'll go." As I say the words, Damon's green eyes pop into my mind. What is wrong with me? "Hazel and I will go shopping for dresses in about a month or so."

"I can join you if you need a second opinion," James says. My brother must love me very much if he's willing to endure hours of shopping to spend time with me.

"You'll get bored to death," I tell him earnestly, though I secretly wish for him to join Hazel and me.

"I can tag along," Parker offers. "James and I can talk about business while you and your friend try out dresses."

I could hug both of them right now. "That sounds great."

"Now, why don't we order?" Parker asks. "I'm famished."

I don't even glance at the menu. "We recommend the house steak."

"Yeah, it's our favorite. We eat it every time," James adds.

"Nah," Parker says. "I only eat steak back home. Americans overcook the meat."

"Parker, this is a steak restaurant," I clarify.

"They must have other stuff, too." Parker inspects the menu with such concentration, you'd think it was a balance sheet.

James looks at him as if Parker grew a second head. "I really don't think a Brit can comment on food."

"Those are all clichés," Parker says, making a dismissive gesture with his hand. "Bad food—"

"Worse weather," I offer. The three of us burst out laughing. A warm feeling spreads through me. It lasts for the entire evening, while we sit through a main course and two desserts.

This is what family time should feel like.

Chapter Nine: Dani

If I could describe the rest of the week using one word only, it would be dazzling. I gravitate toward Damon because his presence has the inexplicable effect of sending me into a happy zone. We have an unspoken agreement to meet on the rooftop every day for lunch. He still ignores everyone, and snaps at teachers at least twice a day, which earned him another trip to the principal. But when it's just the two of us on the roof, he changes. He jokes and laughs...and flirts.

Or at least, I think he does. I've never been flirted with, so I can't be sure he's not just making fun of me. At any rate, I'm enjoying it. Damon is the only person, aside from James and Hazel, who sees me. Also, he is smart. A plus that seems unfair, as Hazel says, for someone blessed already with good looks.

"I can't believe you're so good at this stuff," I tell him the next Tuesday when we study Trig again. Hazel did join us this time, but she took off earlier because her parents are picking her up. They're starting their two-week trip today.

"It's not that hard."

"At what other subjects are you ridiculously good?"

"Physics and computer science."

I groan. "So, you're a numbers guy. Remind me to introduce you to my brother."

"I also like reading."

I look at him cautiously. "Now you're just making fun of me."

"I am not," he says indignantly. "Try me."

"What's your favorite book?"

"I, Robot."

I scoff. "That's not literature."

"Now, don't go all Dickens on me. I never said I liked fancy books. I just like reading," he says. I squirm, and he laughs. "You look like you're about to confess a deadly sin."

"How do you know?"

"You are so easy to read."

This sobers me up. Just how easy? Does he know I think of his lips more often than I should? That each time he flirts, my heart does a somersault?

"So, what do you have to confess?" His eyes bore into mine as if expecting some profound secret.

"Well, my absolute favorite series are Harry Potter and Lord of The Rings."

"I've never read them."

"What? Oh, that's a big minus point."

"You're giving me points? What for?"

"I...um..."

"What do I get plus points for? Being good-looking? Irresistible?" He eyes me intensely, inching closer to me. "I might not get points for my reading, but I can do other things very well." His raspy voice sends tendrils of heat low in my stomach. After a few seconds, he must decide he's tormented me enough because he pulls back. I breathe in deeply. "And you were judging my reading tastes?" We laugh together, stretching on the roof. It's such a liberating experience.

"I want to study English Literature," I explain. "These series are sort of pariahs for serious literature readers." At least they were for my interviewer at Oxford.

"You're incredibly sweet, my Dani."

My Dani. The words ripple through me. I know he probably didn't mean it in any significant way, but at the moment, it just gives me delicious chills.

"What is your favorite serious literature read?"

"A Midsummer Night's Dream," I say.

His face falls. "It was my mom's favorite, too. I used to read it to her very often."

"You read to her? That's nice."

"Yeah. She had trouble reading, so I did it for her. Reading was her way of escaping her reality, forgetting how incapacitated she was."

"Isn't that why we all love books, because they help you escape into a different world?" For brief moments, that magical feeling of being utterly buried in the pages of a book washes over me, then Damon's words snap me to reality.

"You have everything, Dani. What could you possibly want different?" His voice has a tinge to it that makes my stomach tighten. It's not accusing, but incredulous. I instantly feel guilty.

"You'll laugh at me."

"No, I won't," Damon assures me, his eyes wandering curiously over my face.

"I just wish I had a warmer family. All those things you did with your mom—reading, cooking—I never did that with my parents. When I was very young, my live-in babysitter used to read me bedtime stories. My parents always had...other things to do. I know it's not such a big deal. I mean, not compared to the problems you had to—"

I stop when Damon puts his hand over mine. "Sorry, I didn't mean to come off as judgmental."

"When I have my family, it'll be very different," I say with conviction.

"I'm sure it will."

Staring at our interlinked hands, I voice a deep fear. "But what if I won't know how to be different? I mean, aren't we supposed to learn from our parents how to be parents?"

"You will be exactly who you want to be, Dani. You are a very warm person. That's not the kind of thing you learn from others. Otherwise, I'm doomed to be a crappy father." Damon says the last words with a grin, but beneath it I detect unease. His fingers tic on the rooftop, and then we finally get on with our Trig exercises.

**

On Wednesday, we go into an hour-long debate about movies. He's a fan of old-school movies, but I vehemently defend the latest blockbusters. That night is the first time he calls me. We end our talk at four o'clock in the morning. On Thursday, we both show up at school with dark circles under our eyes. I nearly fall asleep in Trig, which makes Mr. Smith angry. He's used to my average performance in Trig, and never seemed upset by it— probably because I'm a stellar student at the other subjects. At lunch, between Trig exercises, Damon and I talk about music. Maybe it's his mom's influence, but his tastes smack of the eighties. Despite my best efforts, he refuses to tell me how he got his bruises. It's a whiff colder than the past few days, so we stay huddled together on the roof. He asks me if I can help him out in Biology, and I agree with the added request that he also let me introduce him to modern music.

"Pffft," he exclaims. "Only if you let me do something in exchange."

"What?"

"You've never been kissed before. How about we remedy that?" The proximity of his lips wipes away any thought. At the moment, the only thing I can concentrate on is how his teeth tug at his lower lip. "Dani?"

"I...um..." My voice trails as I try to make sense of what he just said, but his lips are distracting me. Is he joking? What kind of response is appropriate for this?

"You just tell me when you're ready."

His tone is so casual; he might have just asked me if I want a bite of his steak. I am ruined for the day.

***

On Thursday night, we spend hours on the phone again, so I'm a zombie in class on Friday. To top that, Mr. Smith catches me texting Damon instead of solving an exercise. I end up with detention—for the first time in my school career. Damon visits the principal's office again.

I buy lunch for both of us and go on the roof, waiting for Damon. He shows up ten minutes later, sporting a somber look and a hellish mood. He kicks a small twig that fell out of the oak towering over the roof. Every muscle in his body contorts with anger.

"I can't wait to be eighteen and get out of fucking California."

"Damon—"

"They know." He turns to me abruptly. "The teachers. I thought the principal would have the fucking decency to keep it to himself, but he told them. They know about Mom."

"That's not so bad," I say, thinking that now they'll understand why he acts out.

"They pity me, Dani. I don't want their pity."

"Oh."

He sits in front of me, his legs crossed, his shoulders hunched. He's buzzing with tension; I'm waiting for him to snap at any moment.

"Sorry about your detention."

"Oh, it was about time," I say cheerfully. "Hazel is very proud of me. She just texted me."

"Your parents?"

I snort. "Don't worry. Unless I drop out of school or something, they'll never take an interest in what I'm doing. They never do."

"James?"

That makes me pause. James does take an active interest in what I do. Yes, he occasionally mocks me for being such a good kid, but I know he doesn't mean it.

"I don't think they'll call him or anything. They never have before."

"They never had a reason before," he points out.

After we finish eating, he lies on his back, putting his head in my lap like it's the most natural thing to do. Instantly, warmth pools low in my abdomen and the spot between my thighs like someone lit up every single cell. I stay still like a statue, hoping my body's reaction to him is noticeable only to me.

"Dani, I want to ask you something and you to answer honestly."

"Okay."

"Why are you putting up with me?"

"I know what pain does to people," I say quietly. I've seen it in my brother. Pain and loss are hard to bear. I was too young to help my brother, but I can help Damon. "It can lead you to do self-destructive things."

He lifts himself up until he is at the same level with me, and so close I can count his eyelashes. "What if I'm already on that self-destructive path?"

"Maybe I can pull you back." I watch the almost-healed lip, and the still-black eye. He is on that path; I know it. "Would you let me?"

"You might be the only one I would, but I don't think I should. I might end up pulling you with me instead."

"I'll take my chances."

"You shouldn't. In fact, you should stay away from me."

"You've said this before."

"I'll keep repeating it. Maybe you'll eventually listen. To tell you a little secret, I hope you won't."

He runs his finger up my forearm once, setting my skin ablaze. He leans in a tad too close, so I inhale the smell of his skin and aftershave and lose my trail of thoughts.

"You're so beautiful when you blush," he says in a hoarse voice.

A slight shudder runs through me. No one's called me beautiful before.

"I'm tempted to do this again and again just to see the flush on your cheeks. And your neck." He looks at my neck with a dangerous glint in his eyes that undoes me. He could ask anything of me right now. Anything. I would give it to him. "Look at you," he murmurs, as if just for himself. His gaze wanders further down from my neck, and though he doesn't touch me at all, my skin burns. "Of course, you could just admit that you put up with me because I'm ridiculously good-looking, and I would stop teasing you."

I shove him away playfully. It's in moments like this that I don't know if he's flirting, or playing, or doing something else entirely. "Get over yourself, Damon."

Secretly, I fear I'm the one who won't be able to get over him.

Chapter Ten: Damon

On Monday, I show up at school with more bruises. Every single teacher assures me that if I need support, I can always come to them. They tell me they understand. Like hell. I tell all of them as much, occasionally adding a full-on swear, so they know I mean it.

Thursday, the principal asks me what I think of shrinks. I tell him it's my honest opinion that every teacher in this school, himself included, could use a visit to one. The old man loses it. He all but throws me out of his office, which gives me a brief sense of satisfaction, then guilt, because I promised Dani to behave.

Today, as I prepare to leave for school, I'm determined to keep my promise. Something about disappointing her makes me uneasy.

I'm almost at the front door when George says from behind, "I've spoken with Principal Charleston this week already."

"Oh, what a tragedy."

"I didn't bring you here to cause me trouble."

"What did you expect? An obedient and respectful son? Then you're more delusional than I thought. You ignored me and Mom for the past seventeen years."

"Look, boy, if I hadn't brought you here, you would be in a group home right now."

"I'd prefer that."

"Then walk out. Go on. Ignore your mother's last wish."

"You're a jerk." Mom's last wish was that my father should take me in. I should give him some credit for having shown up at all and taken responsibility for me. But then I remember how my mom had to work day and night in the most miserable jobs, which led to her having a stroke at the age of thirty. Thirty. My beautiful, kind mother was defeated so young. She was unable to move on her own, or read or write. Sometimes, she mixed up days, and sometimes, in the middle of a conversation, she would forget what we were talking about.

Near the end, she frequently forgot who I was, too.

The doctors said such powerful strokes sometimes lead to premature dementia. But my mother was young; I was sure that couldn't possibly apply to her. I kept hoping she would get better. The opposite happened. She became a shadow of herself, her condition deteriorating with every passing day. We couldn't afford to care properly for her, so her deterioration was even quicker. He never helped. No, credit is the last thing he deserves.

"Where are you disappearing every weekend, returning like that?" He points at my bruises. When I don't answer, he continues, "If you get into trouble, don't expect me to get you out of it."

"I don't. I've spent seventeen years getting myself out of trouble. I'm proficient at it."

"At the moment, you are only getting yourself into trouble. Principal Charleston also told me you spend a lot of time with the Cohen girl."

"That's right. I do."

"I told you to stay away from her."

"I never agreed."

"You will agree. My deal with her father is too important to let you fuck it up."

"Is that all you care about?"

"What exactly do you pretend? To piss me off?"

"My spending time with her has nothing to do with you."

"So, what, you have a crush on her? Look at yourself; for her own good, leave her alone. You'll just fuck up her life."

"Oh, yeah, like you fucked up Mom's life?"

"Exactly like that."

I curse loudly on my way out.

I curse all the way to school. Part of me is afraid I will fuck up her life. Sweet, innocent Dani... Whose presence is an inexplicable cure to my anger; a breath of air when I feel like I'm drowning. Her laughter makes me feel something I never thought possible after the funeral: relief. The ground has been shaking beneath my feet since Mom died, and I only regained balance when I met Dani. She makes me face my pain and fight it instead of masking it with anger. This girl can undo me with just a look from behind her large, round eyes. She bites her lip so innocently, not knowing what it does to me. Seeing her blush makes me hard. Thank fuck she can't tell, but I've seen how she looks at me.

I'm already treading on a fine line, and if I keep this close to her, I will snap and kiss her. In fact, I'll do much more than kiss her. Damn it. I wasn't a catch before, and I sure as hell am not now when I've turned into the literal dark version of myself. I have no future and no aspirations except to break out of this prison and never come back. There is nothing I can bring Dani except trouble. I've dealt with that my whole life. I know how to live with it. She's grown up in a glass ball, and I won't be the one to break it.

Of course, for that I'd have to stay away, and I can't.

Chapter Eleven: Dani

Damon avoids meeting my eye the entire morning. I corner him after Biology, once everyone has left the laboratory, and it's just the two of us left.

"You should avoid me today," he says when he sees me approaching.

"Friends don't avoid each other in bad times. Something happened today to make you extra moody?"

"I had a fight with George," he offers as an explanation. "We do a good job of avoiding each other usually." He watches me intently, and I see his resolve to avoid me today weaken with every passing second. "Let's grab lunch," he says eventually.

"After dissecting a frog?" I say skeptically. "No lunch for me today."

He grins. In a fraction of a second, he's behind me, slinging his arms around my waist. He pulls me so close to him I can feel the rippled muscles of his stomach against my back. My knees take on the consistency of rubber.

"I can skip lunch. Let's do something else," he says in my ear.

"Like what?" I hold my breath, waiting for his answer. When none comes, I begin to panic. Then he lowers his hands, lacing his fingers with mine.

"This feels good," he says, burying his head in my neck. "Do you want to be friends, Dani?"

"Aren't we already? Don't you want to be friends?"

"I do want to, but you shouldn't be friends with someone like me. I'm no good for you. You've known me for a few weeks, and you've already done something you've never done: got detention."

"There is a first time for everything," I say.

"What are you doing to me?" he asks in a whisper.

"What do you mean?" I ask, puzzled, checking whether I've stepped on him. "I'm not doing anything."

"You have no idea," he says, raising our interlaced hands to my waist and squeezing me tighter to him. "I can't stand being here right now."

"Then let's go."

"You want to skip school?" There is a mix of humor and sadness in his voice.

"We might be able to return before lunch is over. If not, Trig is right after lunch. I'll be glad to skip it."

"Where do you want to go?"

"I know what you need to let off steam."

I lead him to the stone pathway across from the main building. We walk about ten minutes before we come to a halt in front of a one-story hall where the Olympic basin is.

"We are skipping school on school premises?" he raises an eyebrow. "Why is no one around?"

"Because access to the basin is restricted to those training for swimming competitions."

"So, we'll be trespassing?"

"I have the key," I say.

"How come?"

"My detention is to prepare this place for the girls to be able to start their training next week. We'll only be half-trespassing."

"Is there no one inside?"

"Nope, trust me." When he doesn't look convinced, I add, "You know, for someone who shows up bruised every Monday, I thought you'd be more adventurous."

"I just don't want you to get into more trouble, that's all."

"I won't."

I unlock the door with sure hands. Inside, we pass the supplies room, and then we arrive at the pool. It was filled with water yesterday.

"You should swim. Swimming always helps me let off steam," I say.

His hands in his pockets, his lip curls into a smile, as if he's laughing at a private joke.

"Do they have bathing suits in the supplies room?"

"Oh." I slap my forehead. "No. There are towels and thirty-five different types of equipment for training. But no bathing suits. Well, this is a fail. We might as well go get some lunch then."

"No way. I'll swim, but under one condition. You swim with me, too, and we'll be skinny-dipping."

I pad back, my throat suddenly dry. "What?"

"You heard me." A smile plays on his lips as he throws his jacket on the floor and starts unbuttoning his shirt.

"I've ne-never done this before," I stammer, looking away.

"Weren't you just saying earlier there's a first time for everything? I won't look when you undress. The water will cover you in the basin."

I raise an eyebrow. "The water is transparent."

"Lucky me." He takes off his shirt, and in a fraction of a second, heat pools low in my abdomen. I also register a tattoo running all along his right arm. I bite my lip, turning away, afraid he might tell how much I'm burning for him.

Oh, God, if I react like this just by seeing him without a shirt...Just hearing him undo his belt and unzip his jeans makes the heat spread inside me. When a soft thump resounds, I'm almost swaying. Did he just drop his boxers?

"You can look, you know," Damon says. "I give you permission."

Despite myself, I do peek at him just as he's entering the water. His back and butt greet me. I gulp. He must work out a lot. Every muscle looks sculpted. I wonder how it would feel to touch them. Abruptly, he swirls around, and I'm rooted to my spot. I take one glance down at his shaft and hyperventilate.

He laughs. "So you are looking. You are a bad girl, Dani. You like what you see?" he asks cockily.

"You're not bad," I mumble.

He frowns as he lowers himself into the water, and I sigh with relief as more and more of his body sinks in until only his shoulders are visible. "Compared to who?"

"What?"

"You said I'm not bad. Compared to who? Who have you seen naked?"

"No one. Turn around, so I can take off my clothes." He starts swimming and I hurry to undress and get in the water. It's freezing. Trying very hard not to think of how Damon and I are both naked, I swim for fifteen minutes, then stop, out of breath.

"You're good," Damon calls. I startle, covering my boobs and lower lady parts. "Any chance I'll get permission to look at you?"

"No," I say in panic. I turn to swim again, but Damon grabs my arm. Warmth seizes me low in my body. "I can't touch the bottom; I need my arms to keep myself afloat."

"I'll keep you afloat." He turns me around, sliding one hand along my thigh, pulling it up around his waist, all the while staring intensely at me as if waiting for me to pull back or say no. He draws in a sharp breath as I hitch my other leg around his waist, and then I feel his hands on my ass. My. Ass.

"You have such a sweet little ass." His voice comes out in a growl. I cover my breasts with one hand, but I know it's too late; he saw them already. He moves his hands to my back.

"I don't remember giving you permission to look at me." I'm aware that despite my embarrassment, I'm not doing anything to move away.

"I'm not asking for permission anymore. I'll ask for forgiveness later. I suggest you don't move lower, though. Or you'll see just how excited I am about this."

"What do you mean? Oh," I say, squirming in shame as I realize. "I thought...um...isn't cold water supposed to be an antidote to...um...erections?"

"Cold water stands no chance against a hot, naked girl in my arms."

"I'm not hot," I say before I can stop myself. He blinks. "Well, I'm not. I have no boobs or hips." I bite my tongue. Why did I just tell him this? Nothing screams turn-off like a girl with insecurities. I remember reading this in one of Mom's magazines.

"I'll call you out on that." His hands slide from my back to my hips. "You have beautiful hips. And breasts," he says. I flush, wondering whether he would touch my breasts, too, if I weren't covering them. "I took a good look at them. And if you doubt me, you only have to slide a little lower. You are beautiful, Dani. Don't you dare think anything less of yourself."

I nod then run my hand over his tattooed arm. I don't understand the symbols, but they look pretty.

"I like your tattoo. What does it mean?"

"It's made of symbols for strength in several cultures."

We're very close. So close I can gauge my reflection in the drops of water on his cheeks.

"You're cold. Let's get out," he says.

Getting out makes me feel even colder. I dry myself with towels then get dressed, my teeth clattering. Damon, already fully dressed, also looks cold. I sit on a dry towel on the ground, rubbing my arms to warm myself up.

"You'll be warm in a minute," he says, sitting just behind me, wrapping me tightly in his arms. Maybe because we were naked earlier, this feels very intimate.

"You feeling better?" I ask.

"Yes. Much better. Thank you for coming here with me today."

"You seemed to need it desperately."

"It's like since I moved here, I can't breathe. Except when I'm with you."

I melt in his arms, and he buries his face in my neck. First, I feel his breath at the base of my neck, and then his lips. He moves them gently on my skin. The tension building inside me is anything but gentle. It makes me want to dig my fingers into the ground...or his skin, pulling his lips even closer to me.

"Do you like this?" he murmurs.

"Yes," I whisper.

"So do I."

I stay in his arms as he continues to plant little kisses on my neck. Shuddering, I try not to acknowledge the heat between my legs, but I fail. It gets so unbearable, I don't know what to do with myself. Finally, he unhitches his lips, and I can think straight again.

My body doesn't recover, though; the slight tremors continue, and he's trembling, too.

"I lied to you earlier, Dani."

"About what?"

"I don't want to be your friend. I can't be."

"Oh." I duck my chin, disappointment washing through me.

"If I were your friend, I wouldn't fantasize about your lips, kissing you and doing a whole lot of other non-friendly things," he says. My breath catches, my body liquefying in his arms. "Do you agree?" Damon asks. I lick my lips, thinking hard of what would be an appropriate reaction. When nothing comes to mind, I give a quick nod. His fingers trail up under my chin, caressing me, and then slowly turning my head to him. He moves a notch further to my side until we can look at each other.

"First time for everything, right?" I ask, swallowing hard.

A rueful smile plays on Damon's lips. "Right," he answers. I close my eyes, every nerve in my body simmering with anticipation. His lips settle onto mine, warm and soft and full. Ever so slowly, his tongue pushes my lips open, sliding inside my mouth. When our tongues touch, my veins fill with liquid fire, burning with an excruciating intensity. Damon coaxes my tongue with his—an invitation to a dance that is unknown to me, but one I am eager to discover and learn. I barely move my tongue in the beginning, afraid I might push his out involuntarily. Eventually, I pick up Damon's rhythm, allowing him to guide me. He cradles the back of my head with one hand, making me whimper with emotion as he deepens the kiss. It's so wonderfully delicious; I forget to breathe. When we break off, we are both gasping for air.

"Dani," he whispers hoarsely. I tug with both hands at his jacket, beckoning him to kiss me again. His tongue trespasses my mouth again without hesitation. Desperation grips both of us. I feel it in the way his hand shoots up, entangling in my hair. I feel it in the way my legs yearn to hitch around his waist again, like in the water. The unspoken need crackles between us and Damon lifts me off the floor, pulling me into his lap. When we stop the kiss this time around, we laugh, our foreheads pressed together.

"I've been dying to do this since we were in the water. You taste even better than I imagined," he says.

"Why didn't you kiss me in the water?"

"We were both naked. It was too dangerous."

"And this is safe?" I smile, pointing to our telling position.

"This is perfect." He pushes a strand of hair behind my ear then wraps his arms tightly around me. "You're cold," he adds, taking off his jacket and putting it around my shoulders. Something about his gesture tugs at my heartstrings. A conflicted look grips his features.

"What's wrong?"

"Dani, I don't want to make any false promises. I'm no good for you." The timing of his confession isn't lost on me. Right after our first kiss. I take the cue all right: I should have no false hopes, harbor no romantic dreams.

"I disagree," I say in a trembling voice, fixing my eyes on the top button of his shirt.

"I don't have anything to offer to you, any set future. Any future at all, actually. I assume you have big plans, and I don't want to stand in your way. You'll go to college. I don't plan to. The minute we graduate, I'll go as far from California as possible." I remain quiet, feeling my eyes burn, praying I won't tear up. "I don't want to hurt you."

"You won't."

Cupping my cheeks with both hands, he utters words that fill me with hope like nothing else could. "I'll do my best. You mean more to me than anything else in my life right now."

Chapter Twelve: Dani

I spend Friday afternoon daydreaming and texting Hazel every detail about the kiss. Normally, I would have waited until Saturday morning to tell her about it, during our weekly yoga class, but since she won't be back from her trip until Monday, texting will have to do. She'd kill me if I kept this to myself for so long.

On Saturday, I end up doing two yoga classes and only arrive home mid-afternoon. Of course, no one is home except the cook. She heats me up food, and I eat a very early dinner in the kitchen with her. She tells me my parents are in San Francisco, attending a charity gala. They didn't mention it to me at all, but I've long since given up trying to keep up with their social commitments. I decide to read after dinner, but find myself daydreaming about Damon again. I run my fingers over my lips, remembering how it felt when he kissed me. It was so surreal; I'm almost afraid I imagined it. He makes me pulse with life. When he looks at me, it's like he can see right through me. The fact that I haven't heard from him since yesterday is starting to worry me. I drag myself to the wall of books in my bedroom, trying to decide what to read. My phone buzzes with an incoming message. My stomach jolts. The sender: Damon.

"What are you doing?"

"Reading," I text back fast.

One second later: "Any plans for tonight?"

My stomach jolts stronger than before. "Other than more reading? No."

"Want to go out?"

I read the words over and over again, excitement dusting all over my skin. "Is it a date?" I want to type more, but I see the little dots indicating he is writing, as well. I wait, my heart hammering.

"You'll be the judge of that."

My stomach sinks. "Is this about the fact that you're not good for me?"

"It's exactly about that."

"I have no reason to believe you."

"I'll give you one."

After a long pause, the little dots indicating he's writing appear again. "Can I pick you up at eight?"

"Yes. What's the dress code?"

"Casual."

***

I stare at my closet for about thirty minutes, making a mental inventory of everything I own before I accept that I have no appropriate item for tonight. I have jeans, hoodies, t-shirts with my favorite bands, but I have nothing to wear on a date. God...everything about Damon is too much. I drag my hands down my face. I like being near him too much, laughing and talking to him. I like the way his green eyes bore into mine, making my skin tingle with heat. If he were to disappear from the face of the earth tomorrow, I'd be devastated. It's a strong word, but it feels like the right one. That's when I realize how much trouble I'm in.

What's a girl to do when her closet fails her? The answer for most girls my age would probably be shopping. But since it was my nerdtastic taste in clothes that led to my poorly stocked closet in the first place, that's not a smart move.

I have a much simpler solution: breaking into Mom's closet. I've only been in it a few times before, but it's the size of my bedroom. I'll find something appropriate. Thankfully, Mom doesn't like to own up to her age, so most of her clothes look young. I hear my parents' car pull in and then a screaming match blowing up downstairs. When I was young, I used to play a movie at maximum volume when they started fighting, but now I can block their voices out all by myself. I'll just have to be extra careful when I leave so they don't see me.

I end up with a nude-colored dress with straps. It's not extremely short, but it's tight. The exaggerated cleavage makes me blush. I feel naked in it, so it must be right for a date. I put on some peep-toe sandals and a light jacket and sneak out. Not the easiest task, because both Mom and Dad are downstairs. I told them I'd go over to Hazel's tonight, which is a risky move since she isn't in the country. If they see my clothes, I'm in trouble. Mom pushes me to dress differently, but I have a hunch she won't appreciate my stolen outfit. Once I get past the front door, my muscles loosen a notch. I only allow myself to take a deep breath after passing our humongous garden and the front gate. The relaxing moment only lasts a few seconds as the realization that I'll be meeting Damon in about two minutes kicks in. I managed to stave off the nerves while I was preparing, but now as I approach our meeting place, all the jitters come back with a vengeance. When I reach the junction where Damon is supposed to meet me, he's not here.

This doesn't help the jitters in the slightest. I pace on the pavement, chewing the inside of my cheek, rubbing my sweaty palms on my flimsy dress. Maybe he's changed his mind. A motorcycle roars from the distance, approaching with a mind-bending speed. I shake my head. I'll never get their appeal. For me, they are nothing more than death on two wheels.

When the motorcycle stops in front of me, I am speechless.

When Damon descends from it, I catch my breath. Removing his helmet, he just stares at me, his lips parted, his bright green eyes wider than I've ever seen them as they travel over my body.

"You have a motorcycle?" I ask at the same time he exclaims, "What are you wearing?"

I become ten times more self-conscious than I already was, trying to cover myself up. "You don't like it?" I murmur, looking away.

"It's… Well, you…I didn't think you owned something like that."

"I could say the same about you," I say, gesturing at the motorcycle.

"Really, is it that surprising? I have a bad attitude, tattoos, and hate everyone in California except you. Is a bike that much of a surprise?"

I grin. "I guess not."

"But nothing about your Linkin Park t-shirts led me to believe you might own something that shows your boobs and ass at the same time. You usually hide both."

My cheeks are on fire. "It's not my dress," I mumble. "It's Mom's." She looks better in it.

"Dani, don't misinterpret what I'm about to say, okay?" Damon takes a few steps, stopping in front of me. He puts his hands on my shoulders.

"You look stunning. But you can't come with me dressed like this."

"Why not?" I challenge. "It's...casual."

"Jeans are casual. This is hot. I would never object to that, but where we're going tonight...it's not a good idea. And you'll freeze on the bike. Go change. I'll wait for you here."

"I can't go back. My parents will see me."

A smile crosses his lips. "You snuck out? They don't know you're out?"

"They think I'm at Hazel's. I can't make it inside without them seeing me."

"Dani..." His eyes are pleading.

"We should go. We'll be late."

He frowns then unzips his black leather jacket.

"What are you doing?" I ask suspiciously.

"Making sure you won't get sick." He holds his jacket, motioning for me to put it on.

"But then you'll get sick."

"No, I won't. Come on, no argument."

Obediently, I let him put the jacket on me and zip it up. He then proceeds to put the second helmet he has with him on my head. I feel like a small child, but I relish being taken care of. He shows me how to mount the bike. He sits first, and then I do, right behind him.

"Hold on to me tight, okay?"

I sling my arms around him, my fingers resting on his chest. I can feel his rippled muscles under my fingers. Moving closer to him, my thighs come to rest next to his. My dress slides up my thighs, revealing bare skin. Damon's hands, which were hovering a few inches in the air, probably preparing to make sure my thighs are sitting right, freeze in mid-air.

I quickly readjust my dress, but there seems to be a sudden something looming in the air. It fills the few inches of space between my chest and Damon's back. It makes the skin on my thighs tingle.

I bury myself in Damon's jacket. It smells of aftershave and him. The smell invades all my senses, luring me toward unchartered sensations. The tingle on my thighs transforms to heat. As Damon revs the engine and I hold tighter to him, I find the courage to say something I never would have if we were face to face. "So I look stunning, huh?"

He chuckles. "Oh, you do. That's not good, seeing where we're going, but I'll take care of you."

I keep my eyes shut the entire time we're on the road. I'm freezing, but smiling. I still think the bike is a death machine on two wheels, but I find a redeeming point: I get to be closer to Damon than I ever hoped. As I cling to him for dear life, I tune out the sound of the wheels speeding and the wind blowing through my flimsy dress, pondering something he said earlier. I hate everyone in California except you. This fills me with both elation and sadness. I resolve to find a way for him to feel happier here. Living in hate is awful. Hating others eventually leads to one hating life itself. Look at my parents. Of course, my parents only hate each other, but they do so with a passion that has turned them both to stone.

When the bike stops, I finally open my eyes. Damon helps me off, and I take in our surroundings. I've never been here before. There are only a few large buildings that resemble warehouses. The first rows of houses are visible in the distance...about ten miles away. Unease overwhelms me. I take off my helmet and Damon's jacket and hand them both to him. I realize he's watching me. Perhaps he's done so for a while. A slight frown crosses his features.

"Why have we come here, Damon?"

"So I can show you why you should stay away from me." He runs a hand through his hair, shaking his head. "That was my intention, but now I think it was a horrible idea to bring you here. You know what," he continues, preparing to put his jacket on me again, "I'll drive you to a cafe in the neighborhood over there. It looks safe. I'll pick you up after it's over."

I take a step back. "No. I'm not a chicken."

"It's not about that, Dani. It's about the—"

I never find out what it is about. A man looking a few years older than Damon interrupts us. He has light hair that falls to his shoulders and tired, blue eyes. He must have come from behind the nearest warehouse.

"Damon, it's good you got here early. Everyone is already—" The man stops dead in his steps when he sees me, his eyebrows furrowing.

"She's with me, Alex." Damon's tone startles me. It's strong. Authoritative. I've never heard him speak like this. Even though they're the same height, and even have a similar build, the man takes a giant step back.

"You'd better hurry inside. The crowd is restless already."

The crowd?

Damon looks at me, and before he can bring up taking me somewhere else again, I say, "Let's go."

He takes my hand, and I feel oddly secure as I walk beside him, even though this place creeps me out. As we walk by a few warehouses, I can't help thinking Damon was right. My dress, my shoes...they don't belong here. They make me feel out of place and vulnerable. We finally come to a stop in front of one of the warehouses.

It looks like all the others, but there is one notable difference: while the others were silent, obviously empty, it's clear this one isn't. The crowd Alex was talking about must be inside here. We go around the warehouse. In front of the entrance, I see two dozen or so bikes and as many cars. Damon squeezes my hand gently as Alex opens the door to the warehouse.

A few people whistle as we go in, while others chant, "Finally." It's obvious the welcome is for Damon, but he doesn't acknowledge them. I look around wildly, trying to make sense of what I'm seeing. In the center of the warehouse is an empty circle with rows of people huddled, waiting for something. Once I see the guy pacing inside the otherwise-empty circle, things get more confusing. When the crowd parts at the sight of Damon and someone from the crowd yells, "I've bet on you, Damon. You'd better win this one," I finally get it.

"You're a fighter," I whisper. Of course. That explains the bruises. Damon lets go of my hand, turning to me. His eyes have lost their usual sparkle. He assesses my outfit again.

"Alex," he calls. "Keep an eye on her."

"I will. But that doesn't mean others will keep their hands off her. Especially dressed like this. No offense, but they might mistake her for a hooker."

Damon curses. "Just stay put here; nothing will happen to you."

"Why are you doing this?" I ask.

"I'll explain it to you later. Just—damn it, I shouldn't have brought you here," he says through gritted teeth. To our right, a group of three hooligans stare at me hungrily. They definitely think I'm a hooker.

Damon shoots daggers at them with his eyes. He puts one hand on my waist, still watching them. He seems to consider something—possibly punching them. Then he turns to face me. With a jolt, he pulls me toward him until we are so close, so impossibly close that I feel his warm breath against my lips. I look at him, a question hanging on my lips. He answers it with a kiss. The moment his lips touch mine, something ignites inside me. Warm and rough, his lips are like magnets—they pull me in with a devastating force. Everything else fades into meaninglessness. The sounds, the people...

When we break apart, my knees sway. Luckily, Damon's arm is still around my waist. The moment our gazes lock, I become aware of the voices around us, beckoning him to start the fight. Damon drops his jacket and the two helmets on a nearby table.

I'm still floating somewhere above everything while Damon walks backward toward the ring. Just before he turns around, he mouths something that instantly snaps me from the clouds. One word. Sorry. I watch him step inside the ring while the question haunts me: sorry for what? Kissing me? The question drowns in fear when the fight starts. Punches fly in both directions.

"Don't worry," Alex says. "Damon's a pro."

"He's got bruises all the time," I counter.

"Of course. It's part of the job."

"How long has he been doing this?"

"Who knows? He joined us a few weeks ago and fights like he's been at it for a few years. He's the best there is right now. All the other fighters hate him." He beams.

"Why are you so cheerful about it?"

"Means he and I can make some good money. Tonight's match will turn the tide, so to speak."

"What do you mean?"

"Gabe," he motions to the guy Damon's fighting, "used to be the best before Damon arrived. It looks like Damon will beat him tonight. That'll mean a lot of money, but also trouble. Gabe isn't used to losing. He's the leader, and owes a lot of dangerous people money. If he starts losing matches, he'll have nothing to pay them back with."

He directs his attention to the fight next. I can tell he'd like to go closer to watch, but he stays put, throwing a glance in my direction every now and again, keeping an eye on me, the way Damon asked him to. He needn't bother. The same guys who looked at me with what were clearly indecent thoughts in the beginning, now look at me like I have a disease. I realize the kiss was Damon's way of letting everyone know I am out of bounds. And he was sorry for the kiss. Well, I'm not. It made me blissfully happy, even if just for a moment.

As the fight gets more violent, I can't help moving forward. The punches grow more vicious, thrown with one purpose: win. Damon's good; even I can tell that. Still, he gets hit, and every time that happens my stomach churns violently. At least he manages to block most of the punches Gabe aims at his face. I turn around when I'm sure the fight is only minutes away from being over, unable to watch anymore. When the crowd erupts in cheers, congratulating Damon, I breathe with relief.

"Well done, Damon," Alex calls loudly.

"Shouldn't we go to him?" I ask.

"No, it's best to stay out of the ring, even after the fight is over." Alex remains by my side as the crowd moves. One moment, I see Damon washing himself at a sink at the back of the warehouse, but the next moment, I lose him. I bite my nails, only stopping when he appears in front of me.

"Dani, are you all right?" he asks.

"Yeah. You—?"

"I'm okay. I'll just have a black eye." He smiles tightly. "Let's go. Alex, I'll call you tomorrow."

The hall is still buzzing with people when Damon puts an arm around my waist, beckoning me toward the exit.

"Damon," a strong voice resounds in the hall. The buzz turns to silence so fast it's scary. Though I never heard his voice before, I know it's Gabe who spoke. "I want a rematch."

Damon and I turn in unison. A livid Gabe stands at the edge of the ring. People step apart, forming a corridor between us and Gabe.

"Certainly," Damon says in a measured tone. "Alex can schedule it."

Gabe smirks, but his eyes grow colder with fury. "Make sure you don't bring your beautiful friend. It might turn ugly for you. Wouldn't want her to witness it or...get caught in between." Damon's arm grows rigid around my waist. For the first time tonight, I feel a real pang of fear. Damon opens his mouth, and I sense he won't reply so calmly this time. Alex must sense it, too, because he steps in.

"I'll schedule the match. Let's go."

Damon grabs the jacket and helmets from the table. People still congratulate him on the way out, but much quieter than before. They are afraid of Gabe.

The second we're out the door, I ask, "Why did you agree to a rematch?"

Damon looks at me in surprise. "You can't deny an opponent that."

There is a lot of commotion outside, as people rev their bikes and cars.

"I don't like it," I say.

"Neither do I," Alex says. "Gabe won't fight fair next time."

"I'll deal with that when it comes to it," Damon replies in a final tone. "Alex, call me when you've scheduled it."

Chapter Thirteen: Dani

We walk in silence past the warehouses until we reach Damon's bike. As he puts his jacket around me and I slip into the smooth leather carrying his scent, I remember how his lips felt on mine and shudder. "Where are we going now?"

"Depends." He doesn't meet my eyes.

"On what?"

"On whether, after everything you've seen tonight, you want to stay as far away from me as possible or go on a date."

Suddenly, I'm dizzy. I inhale deeply, his scent overwhelming me. It doesn't help the dizziness. "Why did you say you were sorry after you kissed me?"

His lips inch upward in a smile. "Because bringing you here was a lousy idea. I didn't anticipate you'd dress up like this, but I knew if those idiots thought you were mine, they'd leave you alone."

Mine.

Shivers run through me at the word. Coming from his lips, it sounds just right.

"You didn't answer, Dani. About the date." He looks wearily at me as if there might be a real chance I would say no.

"Why wouldn't I want one? Because of this?" I point around to the warehouses. "It's not what I expected, I admit. But you have your reasons.

You can explain them to me if you want to," I grin, "on our date."

"I can think of better things to do on our first date."

"Okay," I say, almost out of breath.

"Where do you want to go?"

"The beach. I know it's dark, but—"

"The beach it is. Do you have one in mind?"

"Yes."

I give him directions, and we settle on the bike again. This time, I cling to him even tighter. Part of me fears that none of this is real. I'd like to pinch myself to see if I wake up, but once the death machine starts speeding, that's impossible. The light evening breeze turns into a cold wind during our ride, but funnily, I don't feel as cold as I did the first time. Warmth bubbles up inside me, fueled by the memory of his lips, and that one word: Mine.

***

When we arrive at our destination, we leave the bike in a small parking lot then proceed to the beach. There are a few light stations along the length of the sidewalk adjacent to the beach, giving a faint glow. I passed this beach a few times when James drove me from home to his apartment, and I always wanted to come here. Taking off my shoes, I relish the familiar feel of sand beneath my toes and discover I'm shivering. When Damon takes my hand, interlacing his fingers with mine, he notices, too.

"You're cold."

"Not at all," I lie. I don't want to leave. We make our way to the shore, and the light from the streetlamps barely reaches us as we sit on the sand.

"Do I make you nervous?"

I'm grateful for the darkness. "Yes," I admit in a small voice.

He takes me in his arms from behind, so I sit with my back to him, facing the sea.

"What kind of nervous?" he whispers playfully in my ear. "The good kind, or the bad kind?"

"Definitely the good kind." I fidget in my spot, sweat dotting my palms. What if he doesn't like this place? I bet he had something more fun in mind when he thought of a date. I should have let him choose the spot. "Do you like it here? We can go somewhere more fun if you want, where there are people—"

"This is perfect," he interrupts. "If there were more people around, I'd have to share you, or at least your attention. I'm greedy. I want you all to myself."

"Oh."

I freeze when I feel his lips tugging at my earlobe, then trailing along my cheek.

"Dani?"

"Yes."

"Are you still sure about this? I can take you home if you want. We can pretend this night never happened. It won't change anything, I swear."

"Why do you keep asking that?"

"Because I keep thinking you'll finally come to your senses and realize you should be going on a date with someone more like yourself. Someone who's grown up in a mansion, plays lacrosse in their free time, and has an Ivy League spot waiting for them, and later a brilliant career. He should've had the privilege of having your first kiss. I hate him already."

"I already gave my first kiss to you." I pull his arms tighter around me. I don't have an Ivy League spot waiting for me, but Oxford. This doesn't seem the right time to bring that up.

In fact, in this very moment, the idea of attending college across the ocean doesn't fill me with the usual elation.

"Tell me about the fighting. Why are you doing it? How did it start?"

"After Mom got sick, she couldn't work anymore. Her benefits were a joke. I had to get a job. She wouldn't let me drop out of school, so I could only work a few hours after school and on weekends. I tried different jobs, but they paid almost nothing. Then someone approached me about fighting. When I realized I could make more money working less, I didn't look back. I never told her."

"What did she say about your bruises?"

"She thought I was getting into fights at school." His voice trembles slightly. "And toward the end, she was too far gone to notice."

"I'm sorry." I wedge myself closer into his arms, and he rests his head in the crook of my neck. "You don't have to keep doing it now, though."

"Yes, I do," he says forcefully. "I don't need that prick's money."

I let the subject drop, and we remain in silence for long moments.

"Damon, is this how first dates are supposed to be?" I ask, worried he wants something more exciting.

"Not at all. First dates are showtime, where people pretend to be something they aren't to impress someone who is acting just as fake. This—...you and me—...it's different." He shifts until he's next to me, and then kisses me gently until I melt in his arms and moan against his lips.

"I didn't know kissing could be like this."

After a pause, he whispers back, "Neither did I."

"You've kissed a lot of girls, haven't you?"

"None like you." I shiver in his arms as a cold breeze reaches me. "Are you cold? Don't lie."

"No," I lie, but then I sneeze.

"Okay, that's it, I'm taking you home."

***

"This tops all the firsts we've had until now. Breaking in my house, in my room." I decided it was too risky to use the entrance, in case my parents are still downstairs. My bedroom is on the second floor, but climbing there isn't too cumbersome. There is a massive oak tree right in front of my room with a tree house in it. We have no business with the tree house, but the ladder leading to it comes in handy. Luckily, I left the window open. Reaching inside, I turn on the lamp on my desk in front of the window with shaky hands. I've never had a boy in my room.

As we both climb inside and down my desk, Damon asks, "A lot of firsts with me, huh?"

"I hope to have a lot more." I swallow hard, glancing at him in the dimly lit room. We're both still leaning on the desk. "You made all the firsts extraordinary."

"That's what you deserve."

"Thank you for climbing here with me. You didn't have to."

"I wasn't sure you could climb that ladder on your own. You don't seem very sporty."

"Hey, I do yoga."

"That's...not a sport."

"Stay here tonight." I take a deep breath. "I mean, um...just to sleep."

"I know what you meant," he says reassuringly. "I don't think it's a good idea. What if your parents walk in?"

"My parents never come to my room. Their rooms are each in opposite wings of the house. Mine is right in the middle."

Damon frowns. "They sleep in different rooms?"

"They don't get along." I sneeze.

"Aha, you're getting a cold. I knew it."

"I'll make myself some tea," I say, pointing to the table underneath the book shelves. I have a water boiler and a broad selection of tea.

"Why do you have all this in your room?"

"I do all my homework and reading here, and I drink lots of tea. The kitchen is too far, and I feel bad asking our cook to bring me tea."

"Do you have some rubbing alcohol and cotton pads?" Damon asks, pointing to his lip.

"Sure." I bring a bottle and some pads quickly. "Do you also need ice? So you don't get so many bruises?"

"Nah, it's fine." He pours alcohol on a pad then brings it to his lip.

I break out into sneeze after sneeze. To my embarrassment, it goes on for about a minute.

"Go take a hot shower," Damon says. "It'll help with the cold."

"Will you be here when I return?"

He smiles my favorite smile, heartfelt and relaxed. His dimples are showing. "You can bet on that."

"Make yourself comfortable. I'll be quick."

My bathroom is adjacent to my room. I'm a nervous wreck the entire time I shower. The muscles in my thighs twitch and an empty feeling settles in my stomach. By the time I finish the shower, the twitch has turned into downright trembles. I can barely believe Damon is in my room.

And I can't believe that every single pajama set I own consists of shorts and a simple cotton t-shirt. I don't have anything of silk or lace or any sexy fabric.

When I get to my room, Damon is sitting on my side of the bed, holding a cup. His eyes find mine, and I bite my lip as his gaze dips down my body. I don't think he minds my pajamas. I try to remember that he saw me naked, and this is nothing in comparison.

"Get in the bed, come on," he says eventually, and I detect a delicious tingle of tension in his voice. He pats the sheets twice, and I climb in silently. "I made you tea."

He thrusts the cup he was holding in my hands, and I melt. I usually make tea for myself when I'm sick, or the cook or maid does it. Mom avoids me like the plague whenever I get a cold because she has a fragile immune system and gets sick quickly. I'm not sure Dad ever knows when I'm sick. Damon isn't avoiding me, and having him next to me fills me with warmth. It also fills me with something else I can't identify, but I desperately want more of this feeling.

While I drink tea, Damon stands up and paces around my room, stopping in front of the bookshelves. "You have an impressive collection here."

"I'm very proud of it."

The second I put the empty cup on the nightstand, Damon returns to my bed. He watches me carefully. Concern and tenderness war with desire in his green eyes. Putting one knee on the bed, he leans over me, cupping my face in his hands.

A smile blooms on his face. "Would you mind sleeping next to an almost-naked man, Dani?"

"D-define almost nak-ked," I manage to stutter.

"I'll lose my jeans and stay in my boxers." After a small pause, he adds, "I'll keep the t-shirt."

"Lose the shirt, too," I say mischievously then hide under my cover, drawing it up to my chin.

"I don't mind if you look, you know," he says with a grin.

"I think we already established that."

"This is the second strip you get from me in two days. That's quite an achievement, Dani Cohen."

"I didn't look the first time, so that doesn't count." My bold and flirty words surprise me.

"Ah, you took a good peek while we were in the water."

"No more than you."

He laughs. "I didn't take a peek. I took an eyeful, especially when you got dressed."

I gasp, feigning indignation. "So there I was, trying to help you, and you were spying on me. You're an opportunist, did you know that?"

"Only when the opportunity is worth it." He grabs the hem of his shirt with his hands. "Ready?"

I nod, a little spasm shaking me. When he reveals his torso, I let my eyes drink him in. The supple muscles of his abs. . .The defined lines starting from his sides, shaped in a V that goes downward, disappearing into his pants. I linger on those as he removes his jeans, petrified to look further down, even though he's wearing boxers.

"You can breathe now, you know," Damon says, and I realize I've been holding my breath. I let it out with a laugh. And just like that, he puts me at ease. I still feel my cheeks heat when I glance at the bulge in his tight boxers.

"Aren't you hurting from the fight?" I ask.

"Just a little sore. I've been doing this for a long time. I got used to the pain. I almost don't feel it anymore."

"I can take care of you."

"I'm fine, really."

I lie on one side, resting on my elbow when he slides under the covers with me. He kisses me slowly, his hands entangled in my hair. Then, without notice, he flips me on my back completely, interlacing his fingers with mine, spreading my thighs apart with his knee. I become hyper-aware of everything touching me: the silky sheets underneath me, the rough skin of his fingertips. When he kisses me anew, heat gathers almost instantly between my thighs.

"Dani," he grits, his raspy voice intensifying my shivers. "I love your smell. Can I kiss you here?" His lips feather gently over my collarbone. He moves the blanket, and I suck in a lungful of air as a chill reaches my dripping wet panties.

"Yes." My voice comes out in a whisper, breathy and needy. His next touch sets me on fire. Damon traces the shape of my collarbone with his lips and tongue. I immediately feel every inch where our bodies touch: his knee between my thighs, pinning me against the mattress; his hands laced with mine. My hips arch involuntarily, meeting his. His right hand lands on my hip, sliding slightly under my t-shirt. I wince and he removes it, leaving me feeling cold and empty.

"You can keep your hand there." I'm taken aback by the protest in my voice. I don't recognize the stranger who says the next words. They're barely a whisper, but they come out of my mouth. "You can move it further up, if you want to." It must be the heat between my thighs that turns me into a stranger.

Damon pauses, inching away from me. "Don't tempt me like this, Dani." Caressing my cheek, he says. "I'm here to take care of you tonight and kiss you, nothing more."

"I thought guys always want more." I bite my tongue. Why the hell did I just say this to him? I'm grateful he isn't pushing me, after all. A foreign need awoke in me tonight, it's true, but I know I'm not ready for this.

He looks amused. "I didn't say I don't want more. There will be plenty of time for more. I don't want to rush you, even though I'd love to kiss every inch of your skin. I would start here..." He trails his finger down my collar bone, and then to my right breast. I bite my lip, not breaking eye contact. As he trails his finger down to my knees, I wish he would kiss me. I'm not sure if that would bring relief or more torture, but he doesn't do it. "Then I would kiss you here." Now he drags his fingers from my knee up and up on my inner thigh. When he gets to the point where his fingers touch the edge of my very short shorts, a violent quiver shakes me. We both suck in our breaths.

"Damon." I fist his smooth hair in my fingers. The void between my thighs fills with more heat.

"I will make love to you soon enough, Dani. And it will feel so good." There is so much delicious promise in his voice. "But not tonight, not here. I want you to be ready for more." His lips nip tenderly at my neck and shoulders. I revel in the feeling, losing myself. His tongue darts into my mouth again, plunging with ferocity; it makes me think how that elusive 'more' would feel.

Our hips touch, the friction between us inciting a feeling like I'm blooming from the inside—or possibly combusting. The air between and all around us seems to consist of sparks. I feel them shimmering on my skin. I'm convinced I could extend my hand and catch the sparks. As if feeling where I need his touch the most, Damon tugs my shorts upward ever so slightly.

I regret wearing panties underneath my shorts. A whimper escapes my lips. The shimmers that were floating on my skin are now bouncing on my nerve endings, threatening to burn. As his fingers trail near my tender spot, the realization that my panties are soaked hits me. God, he knows what he's doing. His fingers hum just at the edge of my panties, but he feels how powerful my body's reaction to him is. I know because a deep groan reverberates from his chest and a spasm rakes him hard, completely undoing both of us. He cradles my face with his hands, kissing me deeply, urgently. His breathing pattern changes to frantic. My pulse slams and reverberates through me, making it impossible for me to think straight. Just when I think his resolve will crumble, Damon breaks off his kiss.

"Whoa."

"Yeah," I say.

"Dani, you are burning my control in a way I didn't think possible."

"Funny, I can say the same."

"Okay." He leans on his back, next to me. "No more kissing tonight or I will not be responsible for my actions."

I giggle.

"What?"

"Nothing. I can't believe you're here, in my room. Well, I can't believe that this—us—is real."

He turns to one side, frowning. "Why not?"

"I suppose it's because I spent so much time imagining what it would be like to have a boyfriend, constructing scenarios and...Don't mock me," I punch him lightly when he starts chuckling. "Girls do that."

"How's the reality compared to your little scenarios?"

"I didn't think it could feel this good and intense," I say truthfully.

"It usually isn't."

"Has it been like this before for you? With other girls?"

"Let's not talk about other girls," he says gently. "I have nothing to hide; I just don't think it's good pillow talk."

"You're right."

"And for the record, no. I have never felt this way."

I nod then blurt out the most inappropriate of questions. "You've made love to a lot of girls, haven't you?"

His gaze bores into mine for a long time before he answers. "No. I've been with a lot of girls, but I will only make love to you."

Chapter Fourteen: Dani

In the morning, I know he left without opening my eyes. The bed is cold, but it still keeps a whiff of his smell. I smile in my pillow, refusing to open my eyes. If last night was a dream, it was the best ever. When my eyes finally flutter open, my smile turns into a grin. My room is as large and peculiar as ever, but it suddenly seems less cold and empty. His mere presence here last night filled it with his warmth. The cup next to my bed reminds me of his gentleness. My tender lips remind me of his barely restrained passion. I see a note next to the cup and pick it up, the tips of my fingers prickling.

Thought it would be best to leave before everyone wakes up. You will have to tell me what you dreamt. You had the most adorable smile when I left you.

My stomach fills with butterflies as I read his note again and again.

"Dani!" My mother's distant voice reaches me through the closed door. It comes through the interphone on the corridor. She's up early for a Sunday. "Come to the living room."

I dress quickly and go downstairs, curious. Maybe it's last night's bliss, but I'm hoping Mom wants something she never has: to do something together today, like shopping or going to a spa together. Neither things are among my favorite activities, but Mom loves them.

I wonder if I could tell her about Damon and ask her for advice about dating and boys in general. Hazel's mom is always willing to give both of us advice on anything. I hold onto the hope that Mom can be like her today. I need her to be that mom today, whom I can tell a boy slept in my room and held me in his arms until I fell asleep. The mom who tells me what part is right, what part is not, and what my next steps should be. I'm self-sufficient in every challenge, but this is foreign territory, and I can't find the guidance I need alone. I need my mom.

When I enter the living room, I know something is wrong. Both my parents are inside, sitting on the couch. They're not fighting, screaming, or otherwise hissing swear words at each other. They're talking in a more civilized manner than I've ever seen them. They stop when they notice me.

"Take a seat, Dani," my father says, pointing to the chair next to the couch. After I do, he continues in an aggravated tone. "It was brought to our attention that you have been behaving in an unacceptable way lately." I let out a sigh. The school must have called them after all. "Your teachers are dissatisfied with you. You even got detention."

"One teacher is dissatisfied with me, and I sucked at his subject forever." I often get B's in Trig, only rarely managing to scrape an A. Two weeks ago, I got a C—my first C ever—but it's not the end of the world. "As to the detention, I got one in twelve years of school. I'd say it's about time, isn't it?" I study my parents' faces, trying to understand their sudden interest. Is it just because my school record isn't impeccable for once? Since when do they care what I do?

"We were also told you are spending an inordinate amount of time with Damon Cooper," Dad says.

"Ah," I say, half-relieved to finally understand where all this came from, and half-annoyed. "So that's what this is about. Damon."

"We specifically told you to stay away from that boy." Mom speaks now, her words clipped and almost whispered.

"You gave me ridiculous reasons for it. You don't like his dad. So what?"

"He used to go to a public school in one of the worst areas in Rhode Island. He acts like a hooligan. He probably is one." Mom shakes her head.

Now I am very annoyed. "You don't even know him, Mom." I have to look away from both of them as I feel tears forming, stinging my eyes.

"You shouldn't be around people like him, Dani." Mom's tone is gentler. "He has a bad influence on you. It'll just get worse."

"The low grades, the detention..." Dad says.

"I got one C; it's hardly the end of the world. I have A's in every other subject."

"This isn't you, Dani," Dad adds. "We know you."

Anger surges in my throat. I ball my hands into fists, trying to keep my voice calm. "Really? Let's do a small test. Mom: at what age did I get my period? When did I get braces, and when did I have them taken out?" I watch my mother, giving her a few seconds to think. She comes up with nothing more than a bewildered expression. I expected it, but it still hurts. She was never talkative with me, or willing to display any affection, but a small part of me hoped she was a silent observant. That she at least knew what was going on in my life.

Her blank face shatters those last fragments of hope. "What is my favorite meal? What is my favorite book?" I ask. Mom purses her lips. "You know nothing about me. You never wanted to know anything about me." I turn to Dad. "Do you even know what grade I'm in?"

"Don't be ridiculous. Of course I do."

"When was the last time you were at a school celebration? Never, that's when." Tears start rolling down my cheek. I don't bother to wipe them away.

"Dani, be reasonable. I work very hard, and your mother has her commitments. There was simply never enough time—"

"For me. You always found time for your weekly bridge game and gatherings with friends. You might not have paid attention to me, Dad, but I have to you. Up until I was sixteen, I still hoped you'd change and talk to me longer than to say good morning or good night. I believed the weekend would come when you'd want to spend time with me."

My parents look stunned. Underneath the layers of surprise, I also detect hurt. It pains me, but I've kept quiet long enough. If they think their behavior was right, it's high time I let them know it was not.

"Mom, you do nothing all day except meet up with other rich and bored housewives, or go shopping. You are so bored you redecorate the house once a year. And still, among all this sea of boredom, you never take a few minutes a day to talk to me, other than to remind me of my pitiful sense of fashion. You two either shout at each other or ignore each other. That is when you don't have to put up a good show for friends or business partners. Somewhere in this war between you, I was caught in the middle. Maybe you both grew so cold-hearted you never knew how to give me anything more than silence.

Fine, I respect that, but don't pretend you know me. I simply want to have someone who cares about me. Damon does."

"We might not have been the best parents, Dani," my father interjects, "but we are your parents, and you need us."

I laugh sadly. "No, Dad, I don't. You know when I needed you? When I was seven years old and our dog bit me during one of your garden parties. You instructed our driver to take me to the hospital because you were too busy entertaining your guests. I was scared and hurting, and I wanted my parents, not a stranger. I needed you when I was fifteen and I got appendicitis before Christmas. Neither of you were home and the staff had the day free. I took myself to the hospital in a cab. Then I had a hard time convincing the hospital to perform the fricking surgery. You see, they needed the approval of an adult who was in charge of me." My eyes burn, tears rolling down in streams. "Oh, how I needed both of you then. Do you remember what you said when I called you and asked one of you to return to stay with me?"

Of course, they don't.

"You said it's an easy surgery, and you must remain skiing with your business partner. You wanted to strike a deal with him by the end of the trip. James flew over here all the way from motherfucking Australia to be with me. You taught me how not to need you, and like the excellent student I've always been, I learned the lesson."

I look away, the sight of them too much to bear. I can't believe I imagined today would be the day Mom would finally act like a mother: kind and caring. What an idiot I am. Delusional, really.

"Why didn't you send me off to boarding school like you did with James?" I ask. "You had no problems shipping him away when he was a kid. Why didn't you do the same with me?"

My mother looks as if I've slapped her. "I wanted to be near you. Sending James off was a mistake. Children should grow up next to their parents," she says. I read the meaning of her words. I can tell I'm right by the resentful look she gives my father.

Dad always had his work. Mom was desperately alone after she gave up her career for him. When James was born, that loneliness was curbed. Then Dad insisted on sending him to boarding school. She refused to let Dad send me away. I imagine she thought of me as a pet of some sort...or a doll. She wanted me next to her, but had no idea how to be a parent.

"From now on," my father says in a business-like tone, "you will be watched." Ah, here it is. I've heard of his controlling nature, but never experienced it first-hand, perhaps because I've never done anything out of the ordinary. I've always blended in with the decor. I was the invisible daughter. "Paul will drive you to school and back, as always, but he will remain on your school premises at all times."

I want to point out that Damon goes to the same school, so that won't do anything, but I refrain myself.

"If you go to Heather's—"

"Hazel," I correct him.

"Paul will also drive you there and wait for you."

"What exactly do you think you'll accomplish by doing this, Dad?"

His features harden. "You deserve more than him."

I swallow my next words. He listens to me. He took care of me last night. Even made me a goddamn tea. When was the last time either of you did anything like that?

"He's just a thug who fights for money," he continues.

I freeze. So they know that, but they don't know I was with him yesterday at the fight, or that he spent the night here. If they knew, this conversation would be much uglier.

"Father, you do know I'll gain possession of my trust fund in a few months, when I turn eighteen, right?" My throat constricts. My clueless parents; they are more toxic to me than I ever thought. "After I graduate and move to England, you'll be lucky if you get a call once a year for Christmas from me."

Neither of them replies, so I leave the room, fighting tears. I just have to bear this until I turn eighteen. The trust fund was set up by my grandfather and will give me complete freedom. My parents might try to control my every move until I turn eighteen, but ultimately, there is nothing they can do to cut my wings.

***

Back in my room, I pace around until I calm down, and then call the only person in my family I can count on: James. He picks up right away, as usual.

"Hey," he says, his voice muffled.

"Ooops, you were asleep. Sorry. I can call you later at a better time—"

"There is no bad time for my little sister to call."

Warmth fills me and I climb on my bed, pulling my knees to my chest.

"What do you want to talk about?" James asks.

I gulp, realizing I haven't properly thought this through. James does encourage me to go out with boys, but there hasn't been one in my life until now.

"Err...so you know that new guy at school I told you about..." My voice fades as I try to come up with a good way to break the ice on this topic.

"Dani!" His voice is strong, the sleepiness from before completely gone. "Did you have sex?"

I groan. Leave it to my brother to break the ice with a hammer. Thor's hammer.

"No, James. You know me."

"Well, just checking. Hormones beat neurons most of the time."

"Thanks for the vote of confidence," I tell him.

"Sorry. I'm listening. What did you want to talk about?"

I fiddle with a pillow for a few seconds before I find the courage to utter the next words. "I...well, he spent the night here yesterday. But don't tell Mom and Dad."

"Define spent the night," James says. I swear he speaks through gritted teeth.

"We didn't do anything except kiss, James. I thought we covered that."

"No, we covered sex. That's fourth base. There are still two and three—"

"Okay, okay," I say hastily. "I don't need the talk. We only kissed."

James speaks after a few seconds. "I can't believe my little sister is going out with someone. I'm happy for you, and also extremely freaked out."

"You're my brother. Of course you are."

"What do you need?"

"The thing is," I say, "he's more...experienced, and I think he might want more soon. I'm not sure how soon is too soon, or how to handle this," I finish lamely.

James is silent for so long; I fear he might not enlighten me at all. But he does. "You will feel when it's right. I'm not talking about those times when you're both hot and bothered. Sex always seems like a good idea right then. I'm talking about moments when you're talking, or you're not even next to each other, but you think about him. If you're ready for more, you'll know it. If he's the right guy, he'll understand."

My shoulders slump in disappointment. "Yeah, that's what all the magazines for teenagers say. But does it really work this way? Won't he get bored or anything?"

"No, he won't. Unless he's a jerk and all he wants is sex. In that case, you'd better stay away from him."

"Damon is nothing like that," I assure James.

"Is he pressuring you?"

"Not at all. I just want to know...how these things work."

"Listen, Dani, this isn't an exact science. Just take your time, and enjoy each other. It'll work out."

"Okay."

"Do you want ice cream?" he asks out of the blue.

"Err...I don't believe I've ever answered that question with a no."

"I can buy some and bring it home. We could eat it in the greenhouse—just you and me."

"You don't have to do this," I say gently. "You'll waste a lot of time with a trip here."

"Nonsense. I'll come by in about three hours with ice cream. We can talk about whatever you want."

I love my brother to pieces. "Thank you, James."

Chapter Fifteen: Dani

I'm giddy on my way to school the next day. When we arrive, Paul throws me an apologetic look as he parks the car. Usually, he drives away immediately after dropping me off.

"I'm sorry, Dani. I have orders to—"

"I know," I say, unable to help my grin. "I hope you brought a lot of newspapers to read, or you'll get bored out of your mind."

Paul looks dumbfounded at my cheerfulness. The reason for my nerve endings being on edge is inside the school. I couldn't care less if they confine me within it. Damon awaits me by his locker and I walk right into his arms, not caring about the stares we attract.

"I've missed you," he whispers in my ear, sending tendrils of heat down my spine, lighting up my already delicate nerves.

"I missed you, too," I confess. His fingers trace my cheek, down to my jaw. He gently pulls me to him. When our lips touch, I turn to mush in his arms. Everything around us fades, and there is nothing else except his warm lips and the sweet way in which they mold to mine. The fierce impulses it sends through me weaken my knees.

We don't stop until we hear a loud and forced cough. Principal Charleston is standing right in front of us. I blush furiously.

"This behavior is not acceptable," he says. I wish I could dig a hole in the floor and disappear into it.

Damon doesn't let go of my hand, not even under the principal's stern look. Mischief dances in Damon's green eyes, and I suddenly don't feel as ashamed. His kisses are worth a few words of reprimand.

We don't talk during classes, and during the breaks, we busy ourselves with kisses. I save telling him about my parents for lunch. We eat in the cafeteria because the weather is too chilly to sit on the roof. Sitting on the same side of a corner table, we're sheltered from people's view, but I can't ignore everyone's stares when we get our food. Some of them hold so much incredulity they are downright offending.

Hazel sits at the opposite end of the table, listening to music in her headphones. She frowns at her spaghetti. I know she feels like a third wheel, and I'm trying to find a way for her not to feel like that. We refrain from kissing in front of her, though I wish we could. There is an insatiable craving inside of me for him. It consumes me permanently, but roars louder and more demanding when he is nearby.

"My parents know about us and also that you're a fighter," I tell him. "They don't know you spent the night at our house or that I went with you to a fight," I add quickly at his stricken expression.

"You had a fight with them?" he asks worriedly.

"Yes. And I...um...I think I handled that all right," I say proudly. My parents went back to ignoring me and each other after our talk, so it's not likely it had much of an impact on them, but I'm glad I told them everything I did. It was liberating.

"What happened? Tell me," Damon beckons.

"They forbid me to be with you. And our driver is now permanently following me."

"They've got someone watching you?" A vein pulses in his temple. "What the hell?" I grin at his indignation. I try to remember that, for ordinary people, this kind of behavior is outrageous. I grew up hearing about Dad having Mom, and then James, watched. I was never interesting enough to be watched until now. Maybe it's sick of me to think like this, but any attention is better than none at all. And this is the only kind of attention my father knows how to give. "Why aren't you more upset about this?"

I ponder explaining it to him, but I don't think he'll understand, so I just wave my hand. "We're together at school every day. And if we want to do something outside of school...well...sneaking out is more fun."

I thought this might lighten up the mood, but it seems to have the opposite effect on him. His brow furrows, and he purses his lips.

"I'm a bad influence, Dani."

I nudge him playfully with my elbow. "I think I needed just that."

"We both do," Hazel adds, making us both jump. "Go ahead, be as bad an influence on her as you can. Maybe I'll catch some of it, too. It'd be a shame to graduate high school with the good girl stamp on our foreheads. Every girl worth her salt must break some rules. The best rules are broken with bad boys."

"Who shared that piece of wisdom with you?" Damon huffs, scrutinizing her.

"My mother," Hazel says.

I grin as Damon frowns in confusion. You have to know Hazel's mom to fathom the mere idea that a mother could say this. The wild stories Hazel's mom recounts from her youth are nothing short of legendary.

"On that note," Hazel adds, "I'm leaving. Mom also says being a third wheel should be fined."

Damon grins. "I like your mom, Hazel."

"You would love her mom," I say as Hazel leaves.

Damon turns serious again. "How long is this tailing going to last?"

"Probably until I turn eighteen, which is one month after graduation."

"They'll just stop afterward?"

"No." A pit forms in my stomach as I realize I never told him of my plans to study in England. As a matter of fact, I haven't even thought about what that means for us. Oxford and Damon were in different worlds until recently. "But I'm going to Oxford to college. I'll be out of their reach."

"Oxford," Damon repeats. His voice doesn't hold the shock I expected. Quite the contrary. It even sounds optimistic as he says, "That's far away from here. I can come to England, if you want me to."

"Are you serious?"

"Of course I am. Dani, I've wanted to leave this damn place ever since I came here. For you, I'd stay here after graduation, but if we can both leave, that's perfect. I can find work anywhere."

"Fighting?"

"There is an audience for that kind of entertainment everywhere."

"Wouldn't you like to do something else?"

His excitement morphs into a sad smile within a split-second. "That's not good enough for you?"

"Is it good enough for you?" I bite my lip, realizing I sound like my parents. "You're smart, Damon, and doing well at school, despite trying your best to do badly."

"School was always important to Mom."

"I bet she wanted you to attend college."

"She did. I promised her I would apply to college, but I never did. There wasn't even a community college near where we lived, and I didn't want to move away from her. If it's important to you, I can apply to college. You're the only person besides Mom who can motivate me for that."

"What would you like to do?" I ask.

"Something math-related."

"Said no one ever." I laugh. "You're a whiz, like my brother. You two would get along well."

"You think he'd like me?" Damon asks doubtfully.

I nod, though I'm not so sure. James is a tad overprotective.

After a pause, Damon asks, "What if your parents stop you from going to England?"

"They can't." I take a deep breath. "My grandfather set up a trust fund for me. I'll receive it once I turn eighteen, and be free. Once that day arrives, it'll be just you and me."

***

Paul doesn't tire. He stays at school every day, keeping an eye on me. The first two weeks, he even sits in the cafeteria at lunch. The third week, he comes inside to pick up a sandwich, and then heads back outside. Still, we had no opportunity for a date. February morphed into March, and the only pseudo-dates we had were on the school premises.

"I like Paul," Damon says as we watch Paul exit the cafeteria.

"He's clearly on our side."

Hazel nods in agreement then goes back to reading her Biology textbook. Damon and I exchange glances. We've been dying to be on our own for days, but between Paul, Hazel, and the teachers, we don't get the chance.

"Honey, you have to come to my place tonight. My parents are gone." The three of us try to hide our grin as we peek at Anna and her new boyfriend. They are two tables away from us, but it's impossible not to hear Anna's high-pitched voice. "What do you say, honey?" I cringe inwardly at the word honey. By the look of excitement on the guy's face, he's game.

"If you ever call me 'honey', I will pretend I don't know you," Damon says, shaking his head.

"Glad we're on the same page. Same goes for 'baby'." I take a sip of my soda.

"Of course I wouldn't call you that. You're my precious."

I snort soda, just as Hazel bursts out laughing. Damon stares at us.

"See, that's why you have to watch Lord of the Rings," I say. "You'd never call me my precious."

"Explain," he demands.

I look at Hazel for help; she's better at summarizing. "Well," she begins, "there was this Gollum guy..."

"Was he good-looking?" Damon asks. This brings another round of laughter.

"Of course that's the only thing you'd be interested in." Hazel grins.

"Damon and Gollum. That's a fair fight." I roll my eyes just as he pulls me in an embrace. I catch a whiff of his aftershave, and a shot of adrenaline and warmth courses right through my body.

"Okay, Hazel, so this trio thing is fun, but I'd like some time alone with my girl," Damon says.

My jaw drops, but Hazel continues to grin. "I'll make myself invisible right away." Packing her books, she slings her backpack over her shoulder, leaving the table. As she passes Anna's table, a knot of unease tightens in my chest. I'm jealous of Anna and her freedom. I wish I could invite Damon over whenever I want to. Surely he must expect it.

Chapter Sixteen: Damon

I've done my fair share of sneaking around in my seventeen years, but trying to be alone with Dani is a challenge. I need her, and I want to be with her as much as possible. I don't know how long our time together will last. George has been quiet lately, and that can't be a good sign.

One day, between classes, we sneak inside an empty classroom. The second we're inside, I flatten her against the wall, putting one of my hands at the back of her neck, the other one encircling her waist as my tongue plunges inside her mouth. I pull back only when we're both breathless.

"Damon," she murmurs as I suckle down her collarbone, my hands roaming on her hips. I can barely refrain myself from slipping them under her shirt to feel her sweet skin.

"What are you doing to me?" I hear footsteps in the distance, the sound bringing me back to reality.

"We should go," Dani says.

"We should," I agree, "but I don't want us to go." I lean into her again. My need to taste her grows urgent, so I tug with my teeth at her lower lip then outline her lips with the tip of my tongue. The light brush completely ravages both of us. She starts shuddering in my arms, her hips bucking forward.

"I didn't know this would feel...like this. The more I get, the more I want." She looks at me for guidance, a sign that this is how it's supposed to be.

"Same for me." I claim her mouth with ferocity, my nails digging into her waist. "Dani, fuck, we have to stop."

"That's what I've been saying." She chuckles, but I don't think she actually expected me to stop, because a disappointed surprise grips her when I back away.

We wait a few seconds, listening to any sound that there's anyone outside the classroom. It's dead silent. The break ended about five minutes ago. Confident that everyone must be in class, we step outside. We almost bump into Mr. Bowman, deep lines denting his forehead, his arms crossed over his chest.

"Don't you have somewhere to be?" he asks in an irritated tone.

I don't miss a beat. "Ah, we do, the same place as you: your boring-ass class. This is more fun. I think you agree since you'd rather spy on us than teach. When did voyeurism become an approved hobby for a teacher? If you're hoping to improve your skills, I'd love to give you tips sometime. Bring your notepad; I'm sure you'll need to take copious notes."

Chapter Seventeen: Dani

"I don't get the logic. We're being given detention because we've been busted kissing, but the punishment is putting us together in an empty room? Which genius came up with that?" Damon asks.

We got detention after our stunt yesterday, of course. When I got home, my parents lectured me for an hour. My father was a bit too calm; I'm afraid he's plotting something. He has instructed Paul to trail behind me during every single break and lunch. I have this horrible sense of foreboding that more is to come. At any rate, this is the first I've been alone with Damon today. We're in one of the school's study room. It has three long rows of tables and one leather couch, on which we're both sprawled lazily.

"The teacher's room is next door, Damon. A teacher passes by every ten minutes, and that's a glass window. They can see what's going on inside."

"And that would stop us because...?"

"We don't want to get into even more trouble?" I suggest, unable to contain the sarcasm.

"I'd say we're being rewarded. If it weren't for this detention, I wouldn't get to be alone with you at all today," he says. My heart constricts and I fidget in my spot uncomfortably. How long before Damon realizes I'm too much trouble and moves on? There is no shortage of girls who'd love to fall into his lap.

They'd have no problems meeting with him after school, going on dates, or even spending the night with him.

"Let's not get into more trouble," I say. I don't know how to explain my suspicion that my father is preparing a nasty surprise for us without appearing paranoid or scaring him off. At that precise moment, the music teacher glances into the room, her eyes lingering on us for a few seconds.

I sigh. "I can use this time to prepare my speech for Rhetoric & Public Speaking class."

"That's not until Thursday," Damon points out.

"Yeah, I know, but I'm a mess when I have to speak in front of the class. I have to rehearse the speech like tens of times, so I don't look like a complete idiot."

Damon scans me. "It's true; you tend to lose yourself a bit when you have to speak in front of the class."

"You noticed, huh?"

"Kind of hard to miss it. What makes you so nervous?"

"I don't know. I'm self-conscious that I'll say something stupid or that my body language is awkward, and everyone will laugh at me."

"Ah, this is where not giving a damn about what everyone else thinks about you comes in handy." He smirks, clearly referring to himself. "Why don't you practice in front of me?"

My eyes widen at the horrifying proposal, and I try to put him in the spotlight again. "I've seen you; you're good at it, no need to brag. You can pull an entire speech out of your ass, can't you? You're just like James. Parker tells me he would show up to class in high school without homework or any idea what was going on, but he was so overconfident the teachers believed he knew the lesson backward."

"Who's Parker?"

"My cousin. He and James went to school together. Parker lives in—"

Damon holds up a hand with a tsk-tsk. "You're trying to distract me from the fact that I asked you to rehearse in front of me."

"That's not gonna happen, Damon. I'll read it until I memorize it while we're here, and when I'm home, I'll rehearse it in front of the mirror."

"You're not going to get over your fear of public speaking if you only practice alone."

"Well, that's my way of confronting my fear."

"That's running away from it, not confronting it," he says.

I ponder his words. In the recesses of my mind, I realize he's right, but I'm still not about to make a fool of myself in front of him.

"You're going to rehearse this now. Go over there and start talking." He watches me with a determined glare.

"Well, you're bossy."

"Oh, you have no idea how bossy I can be." There's a sizzling energy in his voice that sends ripples through me. "Come on."

I pick up the tablet with my essay and go to the front of the room. My palms clam with sweat the second I start reading from my tablet, and I pull at the silver bracelet on my left wrist. I keep my gaze on the tablet, only raising it occasionally to eye the door and even the window, wondering if I can make an escape.

I don't look at Damon at all until he interrupts me, saying, "You can't ignore the audience, Dani. I know you already know that speech by heart; you don't have to glue your eyes to your tablet. Look at me."

I draw a deep breath, raising my eyes ever so slightly. I pull at the bracelet on my wrist harder, wincing when the silver cuts into my skin.

"You're doing great. Go on," he beckons.

Encouraged by his words, I start speaking again, making frequent eye contact. I expect him to start smirking at some point, or laugh at my ideas, but he doesn't. My stomach loosens, as do the muscles in my limbs. I'm smiling by the time I finish.

"Now, that wasn't so bad." Damon grins.

"It was much better than usual. But it's just you and me here. As soon as there are more people, my tongue will turn to stone, and I'll get all sweaty."

"So pretend it's just you and me."

"It's not that easy."

"You're right." He sinks further down the couch, his grin growing even wider. "We have to make you think you're alone with me."

"How do we do that?"

"I know! Give me your panties."

I do a double-take, heat creeping up my face. "No, I won't."

"I can be persuasive."

"I'm not walking like that in front of the class."

Damon strides to me with such determination, I'm convinced he'll strip me naked. But when he reaches me, he merely pushes a strand of my hair behind my ear.

"Okay, but you'll wear the red scarf I gave you. And get that bracelet off; you'll cut yourself."

"That's a fair deal," I murmur, watching him remove the bracelet.

"You have a way with words."

"Yeah, written words. Speaking them is the tricky part. Thanks for doing this. I needed it. You can read my mind."

He traces a circle on my wrist with his finger, making my heart swoop. He looks intently at my hand, his brow furrowed as if he's trying to figure out what to say next. "I can't. But just like you can feel when I need a swim to cool off...I can tell what you need, Dani." My insides turn to jelly. "Right now, you need more confidence." He's right, of course. I mean, I know my strengths, but sometimes I do feel like I'm my worst enemy when it comes to championing myself.

"You are a smart, beautiful woman," he says.

"I'm not a woman yet." Swallowing hard, I fidget with my hands. Damon's eye glint and the intensity of his stare spears me, fire traveling through my veins.

"I'll enjoy making you one. And you'll like it so much, you'll become addicted to it."

***

To my intense surprise, the Rhetoric & Public Speaking class on Thursday goes well. When my turn comes, I rearrange the red scarf around my neck, and then find Damon's face in the crowd and focus on him. Then, slowly, I start looking at other people, too, and I still don't panic. Since it's the last class, everyone skids out after it's over. Damon and I stay behind, desperate for a few moments alone.

"What would you say if I asked you on our second date?" Damon asks.

"Mmmm...Where, on the school roof? Or the cafeteria? With Paul chaperoning us?"

"How about outside school premises?" His eyes glint mischievously.

"Hell, yes. You want to escape?"

He nods proudly. "I've set everything up, just needed your permission."

"To what?"

"Kidnap you," he answers. Adrenaline wiggles its way into my body. I'm afraid this will mean trouble for both of us, but I need to be alone with him so much it actually hurts. "There are things I can't wait to do to you, and there better be no one around when I do."

The promise in his voice is exactly what I need. I nod.

"Here is what we'll do." He tells me his escape plan in less than two minutes. I ponder over it quickly, but it seems pretty bulletproof. The aftermath will be a disastrous fight with my parents, but right now, I don't care.

I leave first. Paul waits for me in front of the classroom. He throws me a few miserable looks as we walk in silence. I shrug sympathetically, guilt whipping at me for what I'm about to do. I've always liked Paul.

"Let's walk by my locker; there's something I want to take from it." I don't need anything, but it's the only way to pass by the bathroom I need. When we're in front of the ladies room, I say, "I need to go inside. Be right back."

Paul nods, shifting awkwardly from one foot to the other. Once I'm in the bathroom, I break into a run toward the window. It's the only bathroom with a window large enough to climb through. Unfortunately, it's as far away from the parking lot as it gets, and time is of the essence. With my bag on my back, clutching my light jacket tightly in my hand, I climb through the window then jump down. I lose my balance and fall on all fours. Bolting upright, I hurtle across the school grounds, my heart leaping in my throat.

I keep looking back, though there's no way Paul's following me. Still, if he realizes what I'm up to, he has time to stop me. The muscles in my legs pulse from the effort as I force myself to go faster. When I take the last corner, my heart falls back in its rightful place. Damon awaits me on his bike. My breath whooshes out when I reach him. He puts a helmet on my head, and then helps me into his protective jacket. I throw one jittery leg over the bike, mounting it.

"Go, go, go," I urge, and as the bike starts roaring, I cling to him for dear life. From the corner of my eyes, I see Paul arriving in the parking lot, panting and red-faced. His body goes rigid when he sees me. Though I know he can't see my lips, I mouth an apology.

We speed past the school gates and then onto the street. I pinch my eyes shut, the wind tugging at every inch of my body. I feel the hammering of Damon's heart beneath my fingers. This is the most reckless moment in my life, but I feel safe with him. It dawns on me that I haven't asked him where we're going. I only know we're on the highway when the bike lays on speed. I cling to Damon for a long time. When we slow down, my eyes flutter open. I recognize the surroundings. We're not far away from my home, and we're heading downtown.

"Where are we going?" My voice comes out muffled, and the wind covers it. When the bike comes to a halt and Damon descends, I'm baffled. I take in the sight of the familiar restaurant. The first thing I do after jumping down is switch off my phone. Damon does the same. I know we'll face hell after our little adventure comes to an end, but I intend to ignore that fact for as long as possible.

"Why are we here?"

"The best steak on the coast," Damon replies with a grin.

"I know the restaurant, but what are we doing here?"

"I thought you'd like it. You tagged yourself and James here a few times. I saw it on Facebook."

"You stalked me on Facebook?"

"Hey, I was looking at your profile to see if you qualify as girlfriend material. That's totally legit."

"It sure is. Damon...Just because I come here with James doesn't mean we have to go here."

This restaurant is very expensive, and I bet Damon won't let me pay. As if reading my mind, he says, "Don't worry; I've got it covered."

"Take me somewhere you want to go."

"We'd have to travel a long way to do that. All my favorite hangout places are miles away."

"Well then, let's do something else." I notice the giant billboard poster on the other side of the street and an idea strikes. "Let's go see a movie."

"Okay."

"That was easy."

"Look at your smile." He traces the contour of my lips. I hadn't even realized I was grinning. "Nothing makes you happier than a movie, huh? Is there a cinema nearby?"

"Yes. I know where it is. Let's go. We can walk; it's close."

***

This is one of my favorite cinemas. It's an ancient mansion, so it has an old-school feel to it, despite being modern inside. It's pricy because it's in a snobbish area. Since it's three o'clock in the afternoon, it's empty. Damon and I get tickets, popcorn, and soda then hurry in the viewing room. To my disappointment, we aren't alone. There is another couple in front of us, and on the last row, there is a group of five. We take our seats just in time for the movie to begin.

For the first time ever, I'm not paying attention to the screen; I'm too preoccupied with him. I try to be subtle, glancing at him out of the corner of my eye, taking an eyeful only when I grab some popcorn from the bucket. I strategically placed it between us. I'm firmly convinced I'm doing a fantastic job until Damon whispers, "Stop looking at me and watch the movie."

I make myself small, wishing the seat could swallow me whole. The corner of his lip tugs up as he takes my hand, turning it, so my forearm faces up. Looking intently at the screen, he runs his fingers over my exposed forearm, up and down—slowly, gently, his skin barely feathering mine. It sets every inch of me on fire, the sensation of white-hot shivers overtaking my entire body, even though he's only touching my forearm.

"Do you like this?" Damon whispers in my ear. The blow of hot air against my ear pulls a moan from deep inside me. Damon exhales sharply, his hand traveling up to my chin, turning my head until our lips touch. An explosion of sensations overcomes me when he slips his tongue into my mouth, his hand gripping my hair tightly. The ministrations on my mouth spur desire inside me. I'm breathless when he unhitches his lips.

"Dani, stop." He pushes me away a few inches. The air between us is so charged it practically sizzles.

"I want more," I beg. He obliges and my toes curl when he kisses me again, briefly this time.

"Don't tempt me. I am so close to taking you somewhere else to ravage you. I'd kiss every inch of your body and make love to you until you're delirious underneath me." Fire stokes me at his words. It feels intimate and intense; I'm afraid I might combust. My pulse spikes to an impossible rate, the heated void in my lower body climbing to a consuming high. "But we're not alone. When we are, my beautiful Dani, I will rock your world until you scream my name."

Chapter Eighteen: Damon

The foyer of the cinema is milling with people after the movie. "Where did all these people come from?"

"There's a private school nearby," Dani answers. "Their classes probably just ended." We walk through the crowd holding hands, and I tease her for not paying attention to the movie.

"Like you paid a lot of attention," she counters.

I freeze in my steps, my jaw hardening. Dani follows my gaze and then gasps. Gabe is at the entrance of the cinema, propped against a wall, inspecting the crowd.

"What is he doing here?" she asks.

"I don't know. He doesn't live anywhere nearby." Gabe's not the type to go watch movies on his own. He shows no interest in the posters or the various small screens running trailers. He's here for something else. I zero in on the way he looks at people as if trying to weigh them, to decide...what? There's something off about him. His eyes glaze in a funny way, and...

"Hey, does Gabe do drugs?" Dani asks.

"Crap." I pull her closer to me. "Yeah. He sells them, too. Mostly weed. Do you think he's come here to look for customers?"

"That's exactly what I think. Rich suburb, rich kids. That's not gonna happen."

"Dani." My warning tone stops her in her tracks. "Don't get involved in this."

In that precise moment, Gabe notices us and comes our way immediately.

"Well, well, well," he grunts out.

"What do you want, Gabe?" I bark, attracting several ugly glances from those around us.

"Play nice, Damon. This is no way to treat a friend."

"You're not my friend. Outside the ring, I don't give a damn about you."

A vein pulses in Gabe's temple. "Then get the fuck out of here."

"Why, so you can sell your crap to kids?" Dani's voice is a whisper, but several more people turn toward us. Behind Gabe, the guy selling popcorn and drinks jerks upright, staring at Gabe. Damn it, I don't want her to get on Gabe's bad side. That's a sure-fire way to get hurt.

"Your girl here hasn't learned not to mess in other's people affairs. That's just too bad, isn't it?"

I step in front of her, shielding her with my body. "If you have a problem, we'll deal with it in the ring. You can schedule a fight any time."

"My problem is with both of you. Why bother with the ring? This is much more fun. Your girl will see you taking the beating of your life, and you will learn that when you come to a new place, you show respect."

"Fuck off, Gabe. I'll see you in the ring when you aren't high."

Gabe doesn't back off. He just shakes his head, grinning.

"Boys," the popcorn guy exclaims, "whatever brawl you have, take it out of here."

"I don't think we will," Gabe says. The guy's eyebrows furrow, eyeing the phone in front of him nervously. He must have called the police already.

"Dani, go home," I tell her.

"What are you doing?" She steps between me and Gabe, crossing her arms over her chest.

"Listen to me, Dani. It won't go down well. This idiot is high. Go home. I'll call you once I'm out of here."

"I'm not going anywhere," she says.

I want to argue some more, but never get the chance because Gabe pushes her out of the way with a shove. I reach out, but miss her by a fraction of an inch. She stumbles back, right into a group. One of the guys catches her.

What happens next goes on so fast, no one has time to stop us. Gabe and I start fighting.

"Someone break them apart, please!" Dani screams. No one does. Out of the corner of my eyes, I see her get out her smartphone and press it to her ear. There are some big guys in the crowd, and I'm sure they could efficiently break up a high school brawl, but Gabe and I are pros. This is worse than in the ring. We hit with the same ferocity and determination, only this time the determination is a dangerous thing. In the ring, it's about winning, but now it's about hurting him so he can't hurt her. The crowd has formed a large circle around us. I don't know for how long Gabe and I throw punches at each other. Then a guy gets between us, forcing us apart and receiving a punch in the jaw from Gabe. When I see Dani run to the guy, I realize it must be her brother James.

The police arrive a few minutes later, taking both Gabe and me into custody.

"Check his pockets," I say, spitting blood, and I know it's game over for Gabe. He knows it, too, by the look of hatred in his eyes.

The police interrogation lasts for hours. As soon as I spill the beans on Gabe having drugs on him, all Hell breaks loose. He starts talking about the fights, and then the police question us about everything. In the midst of it all, Dani's brother whisks her away, and I'm grateful for it. I don't want her to witness this. She deserves someone who doesn't put her through crap like this. At nine o'clock, I'm dismissed. George is called to take me to his house and the police take Gabe with them.

We stop at a gas station, but George doesn't fill up his car's tank with gas. He goes inside the shop, returning with a pack of ice. He hands it to me, and I give him a silent nod of thank you, and then put it on my split lip. My eye hurts like a motherfucker, so I bet it'll be black tomorrow.

When we arrive at home, I intend to disappear to my room as fast as possible, wondering if it's too late to call Dani, but George stops me.

"Damon, wait. We need to talk."

I lean back against the door of my room, staring at him. This better not be some father-son bonding bullshit from his part. All right, it was decent of him to show up so quickly when the police called him, and to buy me the ice pack, but I'm in no mood for a sermon. He's been backing off for the few past weeks, stopped pestering me to stay away from Dani, so I suppose he's accepting it.

"You've crossed the line," he says.

"I'm not in the mood for this."

"Neither am I. It's late, and I'm tired. I'll make it short. It's obvious I'm not good at this father thing."

"Obviously."

"That's why I'm sending you to boarding school."

"What?" His words hit me like a ton of bricks.

"Isn't that what you wanted? To get away from here?"

I unhitch myself from the door, suddenly alert. "Not at a fucking boarding school. Maybe I don't want to leave anymore."

"Because of Dani."

"That's none of your business."

"It is. I have no control over you. You've done nothing but get into trouble and hurt yourself since you came here."

"She's been helping me," I say, more to myself than to him.

"And this is how you pay her back, by getting her into trouble, as well? You will hurt that girl. You're starting at the new school on Monday."

"But it's Thursday. How did you arrange my transfer so quickly?" I ask. He avoids looking at me. I narrow my eyes, forcing myself to take deep breaths and keep my fists behind my back, so I don't punch him. "You've been planning this for some time, haven't you?"

"Yes, a few weeks now. The principal of the new school is a friend of Dani's father. He sped up the process."

"I bet he has," I say through gritted teeth.

"You'll do nothing but hurt that girl, and you know it." The sad thing is, I do know it, but I won't admit it to him, not in a million years.

"The school is in Canada."

"Fuck you, George."

"You will show me respect, damn you. And you will call me Father."

"As you wish. Fuck you, Father."

"I bought you a plane ticket for Sunday. Don't bother going to school tomorrow. I explained to them today that you'll no longer attend there when they called to tell me you and Dani ran off."

"You can't do this."

"I'm your father. I can do this, and I will."

"How about your promise to Mom?"

"I promised your mother I will take care of you. I'm obviously not good at it, so I'll hand you over to people who can."

"You're washing your hands of me. Don't kid yourself that you're doing the right thing."

And here I was, thinking the lack of conflict in the past weeks meant he was warming up to me. Instead, he was just plotting to send me away.

"Damon." He drops his voice to a calmer note, but it annoys me more. "I'll still pay for your school and whatever else you need. If you decide to go to college afterward, you'll have my full support."

"That's supposed to make me feel better?"

"It won't now, I'm sure, but it will later. Start packing."

Chapter Nineteen: Dani

I spend Saturday morning hiding in my room, as the preparations for Mom's yearly themed party take over the house. The guests will arrive in a few hours, and Mom is in a frenzy. I fiddle with my phone, just like I've done since James brought me home from the theater Thursday night. I hope for a sign—anything from Damon. My stomach drops in disappointment when the phone finally chimes. James is calling.

"Hi," I say.

"You could fake being a bit more enthusiastic about my call."

"I'm sorry, I was just hoping Damon would call. He's not answering his phone."

"You didn't get to talk to him at school yesterday?"

"He wasn't at school, James. I hoped he'd call me, but he completely bolted on me." I take a deep breath. "And Mom and Dad are far too calm about everything. It freaks me out." When James dropped me off at home Thursday night, I was expecting a full-blown fight and got silence in return. It's not unusual for my parents to ignore me, but since they're against Damon, I was expecting a reaction. I don't get an answer from James. "Have they told you anything?"

"Just that they've got it handled."

My stomach drops. "What's that supposed to mean?"

"I honestly don't know," he says. Dread overcomes me, settling over my shoulders with a crushing weight.

"Do you think he had any more trouble with the police?"

"No. The police arrested Gabe only. He'll be going to jail for some months, maybe a year."

"How do you know this?"

"Because I'm paying a lawyer to make sure he gets the jail time he deserves."

"And you're sure there are no charges against Damon?"

"Positive."

"I don't understand why he didn't come to school then." I curl up on my bed, hugging a pillow tightly to my chest. It does nothing to calm me, but I need to hold on tight to something as I feel my love slipping away from me. "He hasn't even called, James."

James huffs into the phone. "What are you doing dating someone like him, Dani? A fighter?"

"He's not even fighting that much anymore. Look, it's not as bad as it looks. "

"Really? He's involved with people who are into things much more illegal than fighting; you don't even want to know. I've talked to Mom and Dad. I know you're doing worse at school."

"You talked to them about me?"

"Yeah."

"They are overreacting. I just got one C in one class—"

"Look, I know how you feel about him."

"Don't do this, James. Please."

"I've had a first love; I know how it feels. But sometimes, it's best to let go." Hot tears sting the corners of my eyes. "He's not good for you, Dani."

"Let's talk about something else, please. Why are you calling?"

"I...er...met someone last night."

"Shocker," I murmur, too low for James to hear me.

"And I've spontaneously invited her to the party today."

"You what?" This is a shock. "James, Mom is going to kill you. You know she makes a fuss about knowing the final number of guests at least a month before."

"I'll deal with Mom. Just make sure she gets in and you find her a dress." Since it's a themed party, everyone brings their costume, but Mom keeps a few as reserve, in case someone has an emergency. "I have some last-minute things to do at the office, and she'll be there before me."

"What's her name?"

"Serena McLewis."

"Let me get this straight. You met her yesterday and today you're inviting her here?"

"Correct."

"Why? You've never brought a date to any of Mom's parties, and God knows there will be enough chicks you've already banged here, willing to do you again. You don't need to drag another poor girl into all of this."

"I'm not sure I like the way you are talking to me." He laughs softly. God, I love my brother. "When did you become so cheeky?"

"Truth hurts, brother. Answer: why did you invite her?"

"Just felt the right thing to do."

At a loss for what to say, I just tell him goodbye, assuring him I'll take care of her. I desperately need something else to think about besides Damon. If this Serena will bring my brother the love he deserves, then I'll make sure she looks breathtaking.

What was it that Hazel's mom always said? The way to a man's heart is through his nose. First take his breath away, then steal his heart. Excellent advice. Unless he breaks your heart first.

***

The party is still in full swing by the time I head to my room, but I have no energy to keep going on. I did all right being Serena's guide before James took over. Now he's doing a fantastic job—at least I think he is. They disappeared from the party hours ago, and his car is still here. This means they're in one of the bedrooms of this house.

I fish my phone out of my purse when I reach the door to my room. There is no call or message from Damon. At this point, I don't know if I'd answer even if he did call. I'm too annoyed.

When I open the door, I intend to head straight to my bed and collapse in it without even changing. But my bed is already occupied. Damon is sitting on the edge, staring at a flyer in his hands, apparently unaware I've just entered the room. Dread creeps under my skin almost immediately. Something is wrong.

"Damon. How long have you been here?"

"Two hours, maybe three." His head snaps up to me, my insides melting when I meet his gaze. He looks like I did before I smeared three layers of makeup on my face: like he hasn't slept at all since we last saw each other.

"Why didn't you say you were here? I waited for you to call." I'm still at the door, afraid to take another step. Whatever brought him in this state...I'm not ready to face it.

"I'm sorry. I wasn't sure if I'd stay here long enough to see you."

"Damon, you're not making sense." Slowly, I walk toward him. "What's going on?"

He rises abruptly, jamming the flyer in the pocket of his jacket. "Will you take a walk with me?"

"Okay. Just give me a few minutes to change."

"Don't. You look perfect."

I raise an eyebrow. I'm wearing a white, extravagant dress which was appropriate for the theme of the party, but will look silly outside. Damon seems oblivious to that.

"I'll just grab my coat then; it's chilly outside. We can use the main entrance. There are so many people downstairs, no one will notice us."

Chapter Twenty: Damon

We walk in silence for ten minutes before she finally breaks it. "Where are we going?"

"There's a planetarium a few blocks away. We're almost there."

"Are we trespassing?" she asks, worry coloring her voice. My heart sinks. The fact that Dani even has to ask this is the last straw. They're all right: her parents, my asshole father. They're wrong in a million other things, but not about this: I am not right for her.

"No."

"I haven't been to this planetarium in a few years, but I'm pretty sure it's not open at three o'clock in the morning."

I take the flier out of my pocket, showing it to her. "It is today. Special night."

"Okay."

I can tell by her wide eyes that she's still waiting for me to explain my behavior. Like the coward I am, I can't find the words to do so. She'll figure it out on her own...I hope.

When we arrive at the planetarium, the man at the reception gives me a skeptical once-over, then ogles Dani's dress.

"What's this, Lady and the Tramp?" I'd punch him if his comment wasn't so ironically spot on. "We're closing."

"On the flier, it says it's open for another hour," I counter.

"I'm closing early. Management thought this would be a brilliant idea. It's been a bust. No one's shown up after twelve o'clock."

"Great. Then we'll have the place to ourselves."

"I didn't say you could go in." He slams his fist on his desk, looking at us angrily.

"What will management say when they hear you've turned down your only customers?"

That shuts him up, and Dani and I go up the stairs, following the signs. I expected to watch stars or some similar shit, but instead, we end up in a room that looks like a movie theater. It becomes dark when we sit down, and images of constellations are projected on the screen, while a voice plays in the speakers, explaining what we're seeing. It's only when I look sideways at Dani that I realize this sends the wrong message. Looking at stars, even fake ones, is something romantic. I'm about to break her heart.

"This is so cool." Excitement laces her voice. I'm doing this all wrong. I should just tell her. But then a new constellation is projected, and I can't bring myself to spoil the moment. I almost forget what tonight is about when the voice mentions Canada. It's like someone dropped a bucket of ice on my head.

"Canada," I whisper, almost hoping she won't hear me. She does, though; I can tell by the tiny quiver in her fingers, like she knows what I'm about to say. My fingers burn with the need to touch and soothe her, but I can't. If I do, I won't have the strength to tell her, let alone get on that plane tomorrow. "That's where I'm going." I don't look at her as I spell out the words, but I hear her harsh intake of air. It cuts through me like a knife.

"You're leaving," she says. I feel her looking at me, and I can't bring myself to turn toward her. I keep looking up as if the damned sky is the most interesting thing I've ever seen in my life.

"My father enrolled me in a boarding school."

"Starting when?"

"Monday."

She chokes out the next word. "No."

"He told me yesterday." I grab her hand gently, rubbing the soft skin of her inner wrist with my thumb. She's shaking badly.

"Your dad couldn't have arranged this so quickly."

"He planned it before."

"Maybe we can talk him into changing his mind." Her eyes are brimming with a tiny bit of hope. I can't stand taking that away from her.

"Trust me; there is no talking him out of anything."

"Let's run away." Her words are like a punch in my gut. They physically hurt.

"No, Dani. That's not what I want for you. You have everything mapped out. You will graduate and go to college in England. I won't take that away from you." For a split-second, I think she'll burst into tears. Her eyes are all glassy, and she's holding her breath. Dani surprises me like she always does. She doesn't cry.

"Okay, well, that's not so bad, really. There are just three months of school left. You can come to England as soon as you graduate. I'll wait."

"You deserve someone you don't have to wait for. A guy who doesn't fight, who doesn't get busted by the police. You could've gotten hurt on Thursday."

The voice in the speaker booms louder, startling both of us, but we don't pay any attention to what it says.

"You want to leave." Her voice shakes.

"I don't know," I say honestly. "I'm just not sure about anything anymore."

"Not even about me?"

"I love you, Dani." Gripping her shoulders, I turn her until we're facing each other. "I am sure of my feelings for you, but not about anything else." She means everything to me; she must know that.

"What happened on Thursday—"

"Is a prime example why good girls shouldn't fall for bad boys. I'm not the guy for you, Dani. Not now, anyway. Maybe someday, when I get my shit together, I will be."

"Damon..."

I kiss her more forcefully than I ever have. I know it's one of the last times I'll get to, so I make it count. Tears stream down her face, making me hate myself for it.

"Stay, please," she murmurs when I pull myself back.

"I can't. My plane leaves tomorrow at noon."

"If you can't stay, then promise me you'll return as soon as school finishes."

She's shaking badly, so I pull her tight in my arms, inhaling the scent of strawberry coming from her hair.

"I promise I will return when I'm able to love you the way you deserve," I say.

"I just want you to promise me you'll come back."

"Only after I get my shit together."

Pulling away from my arms, she says, "I don't want—"

"Just let me finish, okay?" My voice is undependable, but this is it. If I don't say this now, I won't say it at all. I've thought about this since he told me he's sending me away, repeating the words over and over in my head. "When I met you, I was on a cliff, Dani. Thanks to you, I didn't fall over the edge, and I'll never be able to repay you for that. I'm grateful to you, and I love you, but I need to figure everything out on my own."

There was more I wanted to say, but I can't bring myself to, not when she looks at me with wide, fearful eyes, begging me to stop. I kiss her again, and in this kiss, I try to put everything I can't say, because we'll both break. This girl did more for me than she'll ever know. She saved me, and I don't want to repay her by ruining her life. I make myself the promise to return for her. I know this isn't a high school crush, because I've had enough of those. This is different, stronger; I'd bleed for this girl.

"Your hour's up. Out."

The idiot's voice forces us apart, and Dani discreetly wipes her tears away. We walk back to her house in silence, our fingers intertwined. When we reach the gates, I fully intend to kiss her one last time and leave.

Then she says, "Spend the night with me," and I know I will.

Chapter Twenty-One: Dani

The party hasn't died down when we return, but there are fewer people around. If we walk through the front door, my parents could see us. We climb in my room through the window, like we did the first night he came here.

"Dani, are you sure about this?" Damon asks once we're inside.

"Yes."

"I don't—"

"Shh, no talking. No goodbyes." I look him straight in the eyes until he nods.

I fumble with the lace at my back, trying to open my dress, but I pull at the wrong end and it becomes a tangled mess. It doesn't help that my fingers are trembling.

"Here, let me do that," Damon says, but his hands tremble slightly, too. He's better than me at this and before long, my back and shoulders are exposed. He kisses my neck then continues down my spine, leaving a trail of fire on my skin. A shot of breath heats my skin when he pushes my dress down my waist. "You're not wearing a bra," he mutters more to himself than me, continuing to kiss my back, one of his hands traveling to my chest. I gasp when he cups one breast, grazing my nipple with his palm. Then he promptly turns me around. My first instinct is to cover my breasts, but he catches my wrists mid-air, shaking his head.

His green eyes locked on mine, he tilts his head down, taking my nipple gently between his teeth. I draw in a lungful of air, hyper-aware of the wetness pooling between my thighs. It's the most erotic moment of my life. Not breaking eye contact, he pushes the dress all the way down, and I step out of it.

Damon lays me on the bed, kissing me, sliding his arms around me in a tender embrace. His lips tug at mine, prompting delicious impulses through my body. Gradually, his kisses become more demanding. He lures them out of me with a vengeance, claiming each one with more desperation. His hands roam over my hips and thighs, awakening every cell in my body, infusing his desperation in them until I burn for him with such an intensity it almost hurts. I fist his hair, guiding his lips to the places that demand to be touched and kissed. I want to be touched. God, I need it so. When Damon cups my breast again, it almost sends me over the edge. His lips trail down my chest, my stomach, stopping right below my navel. He remains there, blowing hot breaths on my oversensitized skin. All I can concentrate on is the fact that his fingers linger close to the hem of my panties. Next, he slides his tongue up my inner thigh toward my lace thong. Unexpectedly, he places his lips right on the spot where the fabric is wet. I groan in response, and I feel him smile against me. His hands find their way to the hem of my underwear, and he peers up at me as if asking for my permission. I give a silent nod, my palms suddenly sweaty.

"Do you want me to kiss you here, Dani?" He strokes me once over the part of my panties that I completely soaked through, reducing me to shudders.

"Yes," I barely whisper. I sigh when he removes the panties, his cheeks touching my inner thighs. Then he kisses the skin there gently, going higher and higher, stopping at the juncture of my thigh and my intimate spot. His lips rest there while his fingers touch my wetness, coaxing a whimper out of me.

"Fuck," he growls. "Dani."

He touches me gently again, prompting tremors to spread in my entire body. "Damon, please." I'm pulsing with life, with the need for him and his touch. When his tongue lashes against my intimate spot, I fist the sheets, moaning harder than I ever have. He continues the delicious ministrations, every lap of his tongue threatening to send me into overdrive, spurring a million sensations that build up and up and up until I can take no more. The pit inside me grows mercilessly. His tongue should please me. Instead, I grow more insatiable. My breath hitches as a new sensation ratchets through me, starting from somewhere very deep inside me.

"Don't stop," I hear myself pleading. My hips buck forward, driven by a will of their own and a devastating need. I feel one of his hands cupping my breast with greed. He holds my nipple between his fingers, twisting it gently while swooping his tongue across my clit, spurring tremors out of me. Then he does something that is both torment and relief. He dips his tongue slightly inside me while his upper lip rests on my clit. The movement of his tongue drives me restless—in and out, in and out—daring me to imagine how it would feel like if he made love to me. Release shoots through me, racing like lighting, consuming me. I desperately grab the pillow next to me, bringing it to my mouth and biting into it as Damon delivers the stroke that brings on the ravaging orgasm.

I lay with my eyes closed and breathe in deeply when I feel Damon's lips traveling upward until he reaches my neck.

"This was incredible," he murmurs.

"Yes." As he kisses me, I become aware of his erection pressing against my thigh. It strains against his pants, and Damon pushes himself against me, prompting a groan that reverberates from deep inside my chest. The spot between my thighs is soaked anew, a deep craving awakening. Damon stills, his breath wheezing out of him.

He moves his lips down my belly again, then to my thighs, cupping my ass with both hands and pulling me even closer to him. A wave of heat overcomes me when he backs away, his eyes raking over my completely naked body.

"Don't do that," I whisper.

"What?"

"Look at me like you'll never see me again."

"I don't know when I'll see you again, so I want to make sure your beautiful body is branded in my memory."

The next inhale stings, but I try not to show it. "I want the same privilege then. Strip."

Damon gets rid of his clothes in a few seconds. He's beautiful—perfect, really. His erection catches my attention, and not for a good reason. It's huge. How will it ever fit inside me? He chuckles as if guessing my thoughts, and when I bite my lip, he takes it as an invitation, lounging over me within seconds.

Desire sears through me, turning my blood to liquid wildfire, making me squirm under him. Damon drags his fingers between my legs, tapping my folds lightly. I buck my hips, gasping.

"Shh," he says, grinning as he presses his forehead on mine.

"No one will hear us," I assure him.

"No?" he asks playfully. I feel his fingers travel along my slit, sending flaming tingles everywhere. "You are so wet. Fuck." He spreads my wetness around, then dips one finger inside me.

I grit out his name, shiver after shiver raking my body. "Damon. More, please."

"Be patient. I need you to be ready."

"I am ready," I say, though I have no clue, really. Desire blinds me, and this doesn't hurt at all.

"I want to make it good for you; so good you won't forget it." There it is, the bittersweet reminder again. I kiss him so he won't utter one more word.

"Do you have a condom with you?" I murmur when we break apart, wondering what we'll do if he says no.

"Yes. I put it on the nightstand when I was undressing you." He reaches for it, rips the package and slides the condom over his erection. He slides the tip up my glistening flesh in slow motion that turns me crazy, then down again. I keep my eyes glued on him.

I inch my legs wider apart, and hold my breath when he pushes his tip inside just a fraction of an inch. "Ouch." Damon hovers over me, his hands cupping my face, his lips planting soft kisses on my lips and cheeks. Ever so slightly, he lets more of himself inside me, a slicing pain accompanying his move. Tears spring at the inner corner of my eyes and Damon stills, his body rigid. He settles inside me, allowing my body to get used to him. Kissing me languidly, he fists my hair, tugging at it, sending delicious ripples through me. I'm surprised to realize I don't hurt anymore. I push my hips into him to let him know I'm ready for more.

His labored breathing intensifies, and he catches my gaze as he starts moving again, sliding in and out of me with careful strokes. My tight passage still twinges with the slightest pain, but the delicious ripples each stroke sends through me far overrides it. The sensation of him caressing me on the inside is unlike anything I have experienced before. Like all things tonight, our union is bittersweet. Pleasure laces with pain, and when he pins my hands to the sides of my head, interlacing his fingers with mine, smiles mingle with tears. His lovemaking is intoxicating, hearing his grunts of pleasure—addictive. Dragging one hand between our sweaty bodies, he applies pressure on my clit, flicking it with his thumb as he slowly moves in and out of me. That blessed thumb awakens something dangerous inside me. It unleashes an inferno that sets alight every nerve ending in my body, threatening to undo me. The quivers start from deep within me. I clench around his length, writhing and moaning, slamming my hips against him in my frenzy as I ride the wave of my orgasm.

"Dani," he grits, grabbing my ass with his hands, all thoughts of being gentle forgotten. He spasms inside me as he comes, calling my name over and over again. When he pulls out, I feel a sense of loss. Tiredness overcomes me almost immediately, and I suddenly know I won't be able to fight it. The lack of sleep in the last forty-eight hours is finally catching up with me. Damon fumbles with something on the other side of the bed for a few minutes before cradling me in his arms.

"I don't want to sleep," I murmur, even as the tendrils of sleep threaten to steal the last hours I have with him.

"Shhhh, I'll stay with you."

"I want to be awake and talk." My voice is so weak with sleepiness I can barely hear myself.

"You said no talking," I hear him say as I slide away. "I love you, Dani Cohen. You're everything to me."

***

When I wake up in the morning, Damon is gone. My bed is cold. That's it then. There's no point trying to deny the pain. It's so alive; it punches holes in my chest with every breath. It curls around me, ensaring me, dripping in every corner of me, just like a poison would, until I feel his absence in my very bones. I curl, drawing my knees to my chest in the hope of quenching this massive emptiness inside me. Gripping the pillow hard, I can't stop the tears falling on it. I find something underneath my pillow, something silky. Tugging on it, I break into sobs. It's the silk scarf Damon gave me. I stuffed it under my pillow the night after the movie incident. I immediately put it around my neck, covering my mouth and nose with it, breathing in deeply. I search for his scent in it, but it only carries mine. But it also carries something else: whispers from our rooftop conversations and the taste of our kisses. Yes, it holds many dear memories, but now it only causes me pain. I cry and cry for what feels like hours until I feel drained and fall asleep.

The sun still shines when I wake up, and not wanting to fall into crying again, I get dressed and leave my room. I keep the scarf around my neck.

My parents are in the living room, eating lunch together. That's weird. I join them, eating in silence.

"That scarf looks great on you," Mom comments.

"Thanks. Damon gave it to me." I stiffen when I see my parents exchange glances, a sinking feeling forming in my stomach. "Damon leaves for boarding school today. In Canada. Did you have anything to do with it?"

"His father was very unhappy with him," Dad says, stabbing a piece of broccoli with his fork.

"That's not answering my question." Looking at both of them, I get my answer. It's written all over their guilty glances.

"I facilitated his transfer," Dad replies eventually. "A friend of mine is the principal."

"You took him away from me," I whisper.

"What he did on Thursday—"

"This has got nothing to do with that. You've been planning to send him away for a long time."

"Dani, that boy is no good for you," Mom adds unhelpfully. I push my plate away, gripped by the sudden desire to break it along with every piece of china on the table. To avoid that, I cross my arms over my chest.

"He made me feel important and confident," I almost spit the words out. "That's more than the two of you ever did for me." My parents not giving me a shred of love or attention made me wonder if there was something wrong with me. Damon showed me there isn't. It felt so wonderful to be loved. Now he's gone, and I'm alone again, with nothing but a piece of red fabric to remind me I'm worthy of love. "You two have been busy hating each other for more than ten years. You can't tell me a thing about love or who is right for me."

My mother pales, pursing her lips, just as Dad says, "This is no way to talk to your parents." They look stricken, but I'm far from being done.

"I'm the second child you had in the hope of saving your marriage, and then you realized you made a gigantic mistake."

"You were not a mistake." Mom covers her mouth, looking away quickly. I think I spot tears at the corners of her eyes, and guilt overcomes me.

"Really? Great job at showing it, Mom. You hoped that if you ignored me enough, I would eventually vanish into thin air. Well, guess what? I didn't. I'm a real person with real feelings. Damon gave me everything, and you took him away from me. I can't believe it."

When my parents look at me again, I see in their eyes something I never did before: awareness and the recognition they might have made a mistake.

Then my father booms, "You've never been rebellious; this behavior isn't characteristic of you."

I swear something snaps inside me. The moment I stopped being happy with an invisible existence, the moment I wanted something for myself, I became a problem.

Pure anger pours out of me as I say through gritted teeth, "Rebellious? I'll give you rebellious."

One year later

Chapter Twenty-Two: Dani

Drawing in a deep breath, I stare at the gray building of my new dorm at Stanford. Some things you cannot escape, as much as you want to. My father went to Stanford, and my brother went to Stanford; now it's my turn. Still, as I inhale the brisk end of March air, I know I made the right decision to come back. I am home in California, after all.

After Damon left one year ago, all Hell broke loose. I channeled all my pain in lashing out at my parents and James. I wanted to punish them for my pain and for pushing away the boy I loved. It was teenage rebellion at its finest. I had always prided myself in not going through the typical 'teenage phase', yet there I was, squeezing years' worth of rebellion into a few short months. Ultimately, it all came to bite me back. My exam performance took a nosedive, and I missed my grades for Oxford, ending up at another London university. James begged me not to move, but of course I didn't listen. I moved to London and lived there for an entire semester. The best part of my stay there was my kick-ass flatmate, Jessica. The story behind meeting Jessica is quite funny.

Almost exactly one year ago, the night I lost Damon, James found Serena. He fell head-over-heels for her, and they are now engaged, getting married in three months. Jessica is Serena's best friend, and she moved to London at the same time I did and hooked up with my cousin, Parker.

I was only halfway over my rebel phase when I moved in with Jessica, no longer lashing out at my parents, but I continued with a project I started in my rebel days back home: changing myself. I wanted to fashion out a new Dani, one who wasn't a nerd. As a reformed party girl, Jessica was more than happy to help turn this good girl into a bad one. But I never felt right pretending to be someone else, just like I never felt comfortable in London. Turns out the answer to feeling home someplace wasn't moving to a foreign country. I yearned to come back, but pride kept me from admitting to myself and to my family that moving had been a mistake.

One phone call changed all of that.

Before Christmas, James called me during the night with the news that my father had suffered a heart attack and the doctors weren't optimistic. I jumped on the first flight to California, the last words I had spoken to my father playing in my mind over and over again. They had been resentful and mean, and the thought that those might turn out to be the very last words was unbearable. My father was in critical condition when I arrived, but he survived. The doctor ordered him to quit work right away because he was at high risk of having another heart attack. After a heart-to-heart conversation with James and my mother, I decided to return. Despite our differences, we are family, and I longed to be home.

James pulled some strings so I could start at Stanford in the spring, so here I am, in the place I should have been from the very beginning.

"Hazel," I call the second I step into our room. She lifts her head, deep brown curls dangling from her messy bun. She's wearing a baggy t-shirt, and her hands are full with books. Dropping the books, she rushes between the boxes, throwing her arms around me when she reaches me.

"I can't believe you're back."

I inhale one whiff of her familiar jasmine and lily perfume before her hug becomes a tad too tight. "Welcome to Stanford's finest on-campus accommodation," she says. I lived in a luxury apartment in London, but I want an authentic college experience this time.

"Hazel, I can't breathe," I stammer. She lets go. "You have to stop doing this every time you see me." Since I've been back, I've seen Hazel about four times, and she's reacted the same every single time. Truth be told, I can't get enough of her hugs. I missed her like crazy while I was in London. The prospect of experiencing college with my best friend makes me giddy.

"I still can't believe you're here to stay. If you insist I treat you normally, help me unload all of these boxes. We have about four hours. Then we need to start preparing for the party I told you about." She wiggles her eyebrows, and I can't help bursting out laughing.

"I'm sorry to disappoint you, but I have an appointment at the orientation office in fifteen minutes. I'll make sure to come back in time to prepare for the party, though."

"Traitor," she mutters under her breath. "By the way, I need to tell you something." She purses her lips.

"Well?"

Hazel twirls a strand of hair between her fingers, chewing her lip. "I'll tell you when you get back from the office."

"Ah, resorting to cheap tricks to make me help you unpack."

She rolls her eyes, starting to unload yet another box.

I stride through the campus, soaking up the sun. It's good to be back. There is a lot of commotion at the orientation office, and I wait in line for at least half an hour, despite having an appointment. I keep myself entertained by going over the syllabus for this semester again. Thank God American universities basically force you to do a broad selection of courses. In England, you choose one subject and stick with it until the end. I love to read, but it turns out that studying English wasn't exactly my thing. I still don't know what my thing is, but luckily, I have some time to decide before I have to declare my major. I'm still buried in the syllabus when a voice I haven't heard in months reaches my ears.

"How many courses do I have to take if I don't want this one?"

The voice belongs to Damon. My heart does a double-beat, my hands freezing on the brochure. I don't dare raise my eyes for fear that seeing him might prompt a reaction that is best kept out of the public eye. The woman behind the desk explains something to Damon, and he acknowledges it with a short "Thank you." I can't help peeking sideways when he passes me. The air changes instantly, something like an electric shock zipping through me when our gazes meet.

Were this the first time I saw him since he left that dreadful night, I think I might have had to grab the shoulder of the blonde in front of me for support.

I saw him once before when I was in London. I had found out that Damon was in London for a fight. I could hardly believe that after graduating high school he returned to fighting, so I set out to see him with my own eyes. It was a shock to my system to see him in the ring again. I was disappointed and told him so. Our encounter was very brief and bittersweet.

"Why did you never write or call, Damon?"

He gestured around himself as if the mere fact that we were in a fighter dungeon should answer my question. In a way, it did, but I wanted to hear it from him. "I made you a promise when I left California that I will only come back into your life when I get my shit together, and I can't make good on that promise yet." He took my hand in his and pressed his forehead to mine. "I will look for you when I'm able to. I don't know if you'll still want me, but I will look for you."

That was the first and last time I saw him since he left California.

I snap out of my reverie when the woman behind the desk calls my name, the fragmented memories of that night full of heartbreak and hope sliding away in the recesses of my mind. Leaning slightly over the counter, I try my best to pay attention to what the woman is saying. Since I spent the first semester of freshman year in London, and now the second semester at Stanford, I can transfer some credits. Out of the corner of my eye, I see Damon waiting by the door.

He's still there fifteen minutes later when I finish with the advisor.

"Hi," he says.

"Damon," I reply, unsure of what to say.

"Do you have time to talk?"

I lick my lips as I take in his appearance. He was sexy before, but now his sex appeal seems out of this world. He shed the few shreds of boyhood that betrayed his age sometime in the last year. Now he's all man. The green shirt he wears stretches over his shoulders, and I wonder if they were so strong before. Imagining what's beneath the fabric muddles my thoughts.

"Well, I'm supposed to help Hazel unpack..." I squirm in my spot, fidgeting with my fingers, then we move away from the door to a marble fountain. "So, Stanford, huh? Congratulations."

"I have to thank someone for practically forcing me to apply."

"What are you talking about? You didn't apply back when we..." I take a deep breath, letting my words fade.

"No, but you grilled me hard enough about college that I eventually applied for the spring intake."

A grin spreads over my face. "That's great. What about the fighting?"

"No more of that. I quit the day my Stanford acceptance came. I'm looking for an honest-to-goodness job, so if you know of anyone hiring, let me know. My dad is paying for Stanford, but I don't want him paying for anything else."

I nod in appreciation. "Wow, that's a change I never expected. Not in a million years did I think you'd let your dad pay for anything."

"I've learned a thing or two over the past few months. I have pocket money to last me about a week, but I'll gladly give all of it out if you let me buy you lunch." He checks his watch. "Or early dinner."

"I can't," I say truthfully. "I promised Hazel I'd help her unpack, and then we're going to some party." I regret the promise more with every passing second. Damon unexpectedly cheers up.

"I'm supposed to go to a party, too."

"I'm going to a party, no idea if it's the same you are going to. Some guy from the soccer team is throwing it."

"I'm going to the same one."

"See you in a few hours, then." I attempt to pass by him when his hand grabs my wrist. It's a gentle move, but it stops me in my tracks nonetheless.

"I can finally make good on all my promises, Dani."

***

My mind plays his words over and over on my way back to the dorm, sending shivers of anticipation all over my body. This exceeds all of my expectations. Damon attends Stanford, no longer fights, and accepts help from his dad.

A grin the size of California blooms on my face when I enter our room. Predictably, Hazel opened more than half of the boxes already.

"What took you so long?"

"I had to wait in line. Then they took forever to explain everything to me. Oh, and I ran into Damon."

Hazel stops mid-stride, putting down the box she was carrying. "Shit, that was what I wanted to talk to you about."

"You knew?"

"I saw him on campus when I came to do some paperwork yesterday. How was it?"

"Good. Better than I expected." A fluttering feeling forms in my stomach as I remember our conversation, and I try not to get my hopes too high up...but who am I kidding? I'm practically drunk on hope and excitement. "He's meeting us at the party tonight."

"Meeting you, you mean. I'll make sure to disappear at the right moment."

"You will not do that. Let's get with unloading those boxes."

"Are you nuts? You have a date tonight."

"We didn't agree to it being a date—"

"I'm declaring it a date. Come on, let's get you ready."

"You already factored in a two-hour preparation time," I argue.

"Yeah, but that's before this was a date."

My preparation time strongly resembles a spa visit: peeling, moisturizing, shaving...everywhere. Then Hazel and I debate what kind of makeup we want. I decide on a smoky-eyes do. I saw it a few times on Jess, and it looked fabulous. Well, Jess is a wizard with all things makeup, so of course she made it look flawless. But my results, even though they lack Jess's touch of perfection, still look great. Hazel decides she wants a less ostentatious look, just a little pink eye shadow and mascara.

Another hour passes in which we do our hair. I look longingly at Hazel's long tresses. Last year, I started the process of changing myself by cutting my hair very short, which I don't regret, but styling your hair while it goes through all the awkward growth stages is a pain in the ass. Now it brushes my shoulders, and I can't wait until it reaches elbow-length again.

"How was your semester-opening party in the fall?" I ask.

"Interesting. I met a bunch of people, but I'm glad you're here for this one," she says. This time, it's not Hazel who squeezes me in a tight hug; I hug her.

I decide to wear jeans and a fancy silk top, discarding the sexy dress Hazel's mom bought for me as a present. In my rebel days, I would've worn it and hoped I didn't look ridiculous. Maybe Jess infused some of her confidence in me while I lived with her in London, because I'm more comfortable in my own skin than I used to be. There is no point trying to pass off as someone else.

Chapter Twenty-Three: Dani

We meet up with a few friends of Hazel's. A group of three people, two guys and one girl, wait for us in front of the marble fountain where Damon and I talked today.

"I'm Kylie," the girl says, waving at me, the breeze blowing gently through her stark-red curls. It's obvious by the tan complexion of her skin that she's not a natural redhead, but the color suits her. Kylie shudders a bit. Her short black dress doesn't provide much protection against the chilly night.

A hunky, dark-haired and gorgeous guy has his arm around Kylie's waist. "Drew. Hazel's told us lots about you."

"I've heard a lot about you guys, too. You met last semester, right?"

"Last semester's welcome party, to be more exact."

"Aye, aye. Bashes bring people together," the second guy says, and everyone turns to look at him.

"This is Chase," Hazel says. Chase crosses his arms over his chest, a movement that emphasizes his toned arms. He has short, curly blond hair and boyish blue eyes. I can imagine that if he wants to, those eyes can be a weapon to bring any woman to her knees. By the way his eyes drink in Hazel's body, he must know this very well. "Chase, please behave."

"Don't I always?" he says in mock offense. Hazel rolls her eyes at him.

"Hey, I've known Dani for thirty seconds. Usually by that time, I'm already sticking my tongue down a girl's throat. I haven't so much as made one move. I'm on my very best behavior."

My mouth falls open. "Is this the way you usually talk?"

"You haven't seen anything, trust me," Drew adds, shaking his head in amusement. He pulls Kylie closer to him, planting a small kiss on her neck. Hazel and I exchange a furtive glance. She mentioned a few times how, ever since these two hooked up, they can't seem to be able to keep their hands off each other. I think they're cute.

"Enough talking," Chase says, jamming his hands in his pockets. "If we're too late, the line to the bar will be huge. I'll have to flirt with the bartender again so we can get some beers. I'm hoping to avoid that this time. There's only so many times I can do that before he realizes I'm not playing for the other team."

"I thought we were going to a house party," I point out. "There's a designated bartender?"

"There is when the captain of the soccer team is throwing the party," Chase says.

"The bartender is very cute, but not into girls," Kylie explains. "Anyone who thinks you're into anything but girls isn't right in their mind, Chase. But it did get us drinks without waiting, so..."

"Is everyone on campus attending the same party?" I inquire.

"No, the cool kids attend it. Couldn't care less what the others do. Safe to say that everyone is attending a party. It's just the way things work around here, love."

Chase puts an arm around my shoulders, drawing me close enough to him that I can inhale the whiff that tells me he's been busy with pre-drinking before he got here. "Study hard, party harder."

"But the classes haven't even started yet," I point out, pushing him gently away so I can inhale some much needed fresh air.

"Oh, that's right." Rubbing his chin, he adds, "Then I guess we should correct the saying: Party hard, study if you have time left."

"That's his mantra, Dani." Hazel looks at the arm Chase is holding around my shoulders. The longing in her gaze makes me squirm. "Please don't listen to him."

"Hey, I had a better GPA than you last semester," Chase retorts. "So far, seems like my way is the way."

"And what's your way, Chase?" Kylie inquires. "Charming poor Ms. Ember and Ms. Lawrence? We all know you're not above that."

"I'm not, but cougars aren't my thing. I prefer fresh meat. Can't help it if they can't resist my jerk-charm, though."

"You're disgusting," Hazel tells him.

"Some call me charming. It's a matter of taste."

"Or how much alcohol they've had," Drew points out.

"You're such a borefest since you got into Kylie's pants. Hazel, Dani, please don't get into relationships. It turns perfectly normal people into insufferable bores."

"Let's go, shall we?" I interject. "Or the line to the bar will be so long that even if you offer to do the bartender, we won't get drinks any time tonight."

"Bossy. I like it." Chase puts his other arm around Hazel's shoulders, pulling her so close to him she might get drunk just by inhaling the puffs of alcohol on his breath. I look at her with raised eyebrows, but she doesn't notice me. She's too preoccupied with Chase; her eyes are fixed on him with a yearning I recognize. Yep, my beloved friend has the hots for what looks to be Stanford's designated man-whore. He seems like good fun, though, and guys can change. My brother proved that by leaving his man-whoring days behind him. Drew and Kylie lead the way, holding hands. The three of us trail behind them, Chase holding both Hazel and I close to him.

The party surprises me. I haven't been to many house parties, but I imagined them to be pretty laid-back and improvised a lot. This one looks planned down to the last detail. No wonder it's popular. One thing becomes painfully clear: the line to the bar is so long, we won't be getting drinks any time soon.

"Chase, you and I are in charge of drinks," Drew says.

"Oh, come on, that's not fair. I'm the one waiting in line every time. Why can't Kylie wait with you?"

"You should learn how to be a gentleman. Besides, no bartender can resist your charm," Kylie says. With that, Kylie, myself, and a very conflicted Hazel leave Chase and Drew at the bar, making our way through the crowd. Men and women swing their hips to the roaring sound of the music, sweat glistening on their skin in a sexy way. Laughter stretches across their faces, and were it not for the music, it would be echoing all around us. The music is electrifying, the rhythmic bass making even the air pulse with life. The whole atmosphere is infectious, and when Kylie and Hazel start dancing, I don't hesitate in joining them, barely containing my grin.

I'm usually uncomfortable in crowds, especially when we're so squeezed together that one wrong movement is all it takes to touch butts with someone. Some of that uncomfortable feeling still lingers in the recesses of my mind as I swing my hips, laughing as both Hazel and Kylie mimic grabbing someone's ass. There's this one other thing that bothers me, though...How will Damon find me here? I make a full turn in my spot trying to gauge him in the crowd. No luck.

Chase and Drew arrive an eternity later with our drinks. Chase hands me one of the glasses.

"What's this?" I yell in his ear.

"The barman's specialty. Tequila Sunrise with extra tequila." We all clink glasses.

I eye mine suspiciously then sip from it, squinting as the alcohol burns down my throat. Drew immediately pulls Kylie to him and they start dancing. Their intimate moves make me blush and look away. Chase pulls both Hazel and me to him, slinging an arm around each of our waists. I push him away because I have the nagging suspicion Hazel wants to have Chase all to herself. My friend has gone all sneaky on me. All those times she talked to me about her new friends, she never once mentioned she has a crush on Chase. I dance on my own, trying not to spill my drink on anyone. I study Hazel and Chase. For all his womanizing air, he doesn't dance nearly as provocatively with Hazel as other pairs around. In fact, he seems determined to keep a few inches of distance between them. Weird.

I've nearly finished my drink when I feel a familiar presence behind me. I don't know what alerts me to it, but I whirl around just as Damon says, "Dani."

***

My breath hitches as I stare directly into Damon's stunning green eyes. He takes my hand, placing a small kiss in my palm, making my toes curl. It's here, in the dimness of the room, with neon red and blue lights dancing across his features, that something becomes clear. Damon has changed. It's as if a veil has been lifted off him, and the burden he was carrying on his shoulders when I first met him no longer weighs on him as much.

"You look beautiful," he mouths to me. His eyes rake over my body, drinking in every inch of me. I don't return the compliment, but that's just because I'm too busy admiring him.

The bad boy vibe coming off him is so strong; I can almost touch it. I'm not the only one mesmerized by him. A group of women to our right point at him, giggling. Damon must know the effect he has on women, yet he only has eyes for me.

"Can I get you another drink?" he asks.

I nod, a familiar feeling of longing springing inside me as Damon takes my hand, leading the way. Delicious tingles form in my palm, traveling up and down my body, sending hot and cold shivers through me. The gentle squeeze of his hand bestows confidence and a sense of empowerment. It's not the first time his presence has made me believe that with Damon next to me, I could do anything. When we arrive at the bar, I'm pleasantly surprised to notice the line isn't nearly as large as it was before. When our turn comes, Damon asks, "What do you want to drink?"

"Tequila. I've already had a Tequila Sunrise, which had an overdose of tequila in it, and I'm sticking to the 'only one type of drink a night' rule."

"Smart rule." His lips curl upward to form the smile I fell for.

We walk with our shot glasses in the opposite direction from the dance room, into a darker part of the house. It's also quieter, though the bass still pounds heavily around us. Holding the glasses to eye level, we clink them.

"To what are we drinking?" I ask.

"To the girl who made me want to change," he answers. I tug at my lower lip with my teeth, trying to hide the devastating effect his words have on me.

"I can't toast to myself, Damon."

"To us, then." There is no hesitation in his voice.

"To us," I agree. The mere word makes me dizzy with elation; no tequila needed. Us. The possibility of us haunted me since our first kiss. When it became a reality, I was convinced it was a dream. When the dream turned into a nightmare, I wanted to forget. Now I'm ready to dream again. We take the orange slice off the edge of the glass then down the liquid, keeping our gazes interlocked the whole time. Tequila burns my throat, but Damon ignites every other part of my body.

"I wonder if the bartender needs help with other bartending gigs," Damon says, switching the topic.

"You're super smart. You should apply for some jobs in Silicon Valley. I know from James that companies there always look for programmers."

"I have. Meanwhile, I also applied for nearly every job on campus."

"I'm very proud of you." I lean on the wall behind me, jumping a bit as the cold concrete touches my skin. Silence dons between us for a few seconds that stretch into minutes.

"Dani?" Damon says tentatively, but I stare insistently at my feet. "There is something you want to ask me. I can sense it."

"Why did you never call, Damon?" I know I asked him before, in London, but his answer wasn't enough. "Even if it was just to say you never want to see me again."

"Precisely because I did want to see you again, but I was in a bad place when I left, Dani. It felt like I would never get out of it, and I didn't want to drag you down with me. I didn't know if I'd finally get my shit together or end up in jail like Gabe." Leaning toward me, he adds, "I want a second chance with you. I will make it right this time."

My head spins from the impact of his words and his intoxicating scent. I put my palm on his chest, gently pushing him away so I can whip my thoughts in order. Feeling his defined muscles beneath my fingers has the opposite effect, unleashing memories I tried hard to forget. The night we spent together flashes before my eyes, the hunger he awoke in me then ravaging me now.

"You're taking things a bit too fast, Damon. I didn't even know you were back until today."

"Okay, let's start with baby steps. A date?"

I chuckle, twirling a strand of hair between my fingers. "That's a giant step."

"A dance?" Damon holds out his hand, giving a theatrical bow as if inviting me to a turn-of-the-century dance.

"That would be nice," I say. "Let's stay here, though. There are too many people in the other room."

"I was going to suggest the same. I like it here. It's more...intimate."

The moment I place my hand in his, he pulls me to him, twirling me around until I'm no longer facing him. He pulls my hips against his with such force that he steals my breath away.

I try—and fail—not to think about the fact that my bum presses on his crotch as we start moving to the inviting rhythm of the music. Intimate, indeed.

"Relax, Dani," he whispers in my ear. Every muscle in my body surrenders to his command, liquefying. I give myself to him, allowing him to guide my moves, to own my body. His fingers descend from my hips, intertwining with my fingers. The skin-on-skin touch is electrifying, zipping through me and awakening every inch of me. His grasp tightens as we lower ourselves toward the floor during the refrain, then rise back up, our hips glued to each other the entire time. I've always found this move a challenge for everyone who has mediocre coordination skills—like me. Somehow, I know Damon will never let me fall. Pushing my hair to one side, he bares my neck to him. I think he might kiss me there. His breath on my skin and the proximity of his lips drive me crazy with anticipation. I know I'll combust the second his lips touch my neck. Except they don't. Such a tease. But two can play at this game, so I start moving more provocatively, pressing myself more into him as we dance. The effect is immediate; his breaths come out in short, intense puffs. I continue my ministrations, relishing when a deep groan reverberates from his chest. It gives me a weird sense of power to know that I can undo him this way. The music changes, the rhythm becoming even more inviting and the lyrics so explicit they make me blush.

"Dani, stop." He twirls me around. His eyes are hooded with desire, their electrifying green a few shades darker. "You can't do this, or I'll come in my pants."

I giggle, tugging at my lip. "That's how everyone around us is dancing."

"Well, maybe they've gotten more action than I have in the last year. My right hand isn't much to brag about," he says. I look at him in confusion. "I haven't been with anyone since you. Have you...?" A somber look takes hold of his features as his words trail away as if they're too painful to utter. "Forget I asked that. It wouldn't matter. It was your right to date other people."

"No," I whisper. I cup his face, forcing him to look at me. I want him to know this is the truth, to have no doubt. No matter what happens between us, I need him to know this. "I haven't been with anyone else. A few guys asked me out in London, but it didn't feel right..."

"I've thought about that night so many times, Dani." He cups my face, too, our arms intertwining. The space between our lips is so small...it would take very little for us to kiss.

"At times, I felt guilty for having made love to you. I wasn't sure how much the memory hurt you, but I couldn't bring myself to regret it. It made your memory too real and too raw. When I was in those dark places, Dani, all I had to do was think of you, and I'd go on."

"You really haven't been with other women?"

"No." He presses his forehead to mine, closing his eyes. "Is that so hard to believe if you didn't?"

"Men are different from women."

"Not when we love," he says. My breath hitches, my heart thundering in my chest. Everything around us fades. The music, the people, the party altogether. Time seems to stop too, or at least pause on this very second. Yesterday seems like a lifetime ago, same as all the days since his lips last touched me. "I know the rule is that first kisses come after first dates, but then again, we've always made our own rules."

His mouth covers mine so completely I'm sure he'll take my breath away, but the opposite happens. It feels like this is the first time I'm breathing in months. I lose myself in his kiss and the warmth of his arms. He coaxes my lips open, slipping his tongue into my mouth. Sighing, I welcome him, allowing him to probe me on the inside, exploring in turn his delicious taste. The primal dance of our tongues lights up an impulse deep inside me that travels right between my thighs, turning my intimate spot tender and wanting. His kiss drives me to the edge, and I find myself returning to that happy place I had memorized and revisited in my dreams.

We gasp for air, our breaths skittered.

"I haven't asked for permission," he says in a husky voice. "Do I need to ask for forgiveness?"

"Wow, Damon. We need to slow down. You cannot just waltz back into my life and declare your love for me. You're making me hyperventilate."

He chuckles lightly, but his stare loses none of its intensity. It smolders me. "I got my shit together, and I want you, Dani. I will accept nothing less. I will fight for it, and I won't play fair all the time. I need you. This year has proven to me how miserable I am without you. So, how about that first date? What do I have to do for you to agree to it?"

"This can be our first date," I offer.

"Not a chance. Last time, I did it all wrong."

"I liked it," I say in all honesty. "I think a little adrenaline was just what I needed at that time."

"Regardless, had I been more careful, maybe things would have been different. This time, I want to do everything the right way."

"Okay."

"Let's go back to your friends."

"Why?" I ask, startled.

"Because if it's just the two of us here, I'll damn all rules, and do more than just kiss you senseless."

"Oh." Heat creeps in my cheeks, and somehow Damon notices it even in the dim lighting.

"Stop blushing, or I will not be responsible for my actions. I always did think you were irresistible when you blushed."

"Let's go," I murmur.

When we find the group on the dance floor, Chase immediately puts an arm around my waist, as if we're old friends.

"If you want to keep that arm, you'd better put it elsewhere," Damon tells him. His tone is half-joking, but the glint in his eyes is dangerous. Even in his advanced state of drunkenness, Chase recognizes an alpha claiming what's his and backs away.

"Didn't realize she's yours," Chase slurs, removing his hand. "My bad."

"Now you know it. She's mine." Damon pulls me into him, and we begin to swing our hips to the rhythm of the music. We spend the rest of the night dancing with the group, laughing and joking. Damon never lets go of me.

***

When the night is over, Damon walks Hazel and me back to our dorm while Kylie and Drew carry a drunk Chase to his room. Tiredness sweeps into my bones, yet when I slide under my covers, I remember the touch of Damon's lips before he said goodnight. A delicious shiver shakes me. Suddenly, I know sleep won't come easily. Hazel twists around in her bed, too. I bet I know what keeps her awake.

Clearing my throat, I ask, "What's the deal with Chase?"

"He's the world's biggest man-whore," Hazel declares. "And I am totally in love with him."

"Of course you are." I punch my pillow into a more comfortable mass then turn on one side toward Hazel. "You are finally meeting your mom's prophesy of dating a bad boy."

"Not exactly. I'm not dating, just daydreaming about a bad boy."

"Did anything happen between the two of you?"

"You mean besides me drooling whenever I see him?"

"I'm pretty sure there's some drooling on his part, too."

"Nope, that look he gives me is just him exercising his eye-fucking muscles." There is disappointment in her voice; my heart breaks for her. "Don't read anything into it. I did last semester and was bitterly disappointed."

"But why are you into him? I mean, he's good-looking and fun, but seems a bit of an asshole."

Hazel gets out from her bed, groping for the door in the darkness.

"Where are you going?"

"This talk needs chocolate," she says.

"True that." I follow her, driven by the promise of chocolate. Nothing better to prolong the afterglow of a kiss than chocolate. I turn on the small lamp on our couch table, though Hazel seems to be able to find her way to the chocolate piling place even without light. That's what I call commitment. She whisks out a new package and we both sink on the couch, ripping it open.

Hazel sighs over-dramatically while taking a bite. "Other college kids have beer stacked up everywhere, and we still swear by chocolate. Do you think we might do college wrong?"

"Absolutely not." I savor the chocolate, the caramel melting in my mouth and the pepper giving it just the right amount of kick.

"I don't get the appeal of beer. It's bitter and makes you fat. Why not eat chocolate instead? Anything that fits the saying one second on your lips, a lifetime on your hips should at least have the decency to be sweet."

"Amen."

We chew on our guilty pleasure for a while before I bring Chase up again. "So...every good girl has to fall for a bad boy, right?" I say, remembering her mother's words of wisdom.

"Yep. My turn has come, it seems. I just wish it would fade away soon. I'm tired of hyperventilating every single time I'm around him."

"Have you tried...you know, making a move on him?" I ask tentatively. Knowing our history with boys, it's unlikely.

"He sort of made it clear last semester that he only sees me as a friend." She plays with the hem of her pajama top, rubbing her thumbs together.

"Oh."

"Yeah. We had that talk."

A loud bang coming from the direction of the corridor makes us both jump. "Should we go outside and see what happened?"

"Nah, probably just someone who partied too hard tonight. You'll get used to it." We listen for a few more seconds, but no other sound comes.

"Do you think Chase meant it?"

Hazel throws up her hands in frustration. "How the hell do I know? He keeps giving me that stare and hangs out with me during all our classes—he insisted we take the same classes because he says I'm a good study partner. But when we go out, he makes it his mission to either ignore me or keep an embarrassingly large distance between us if we dance. You'd think I develop some incredibly dangerous virus as soon as I'm in party clothes, and he can't come closer than an arm's length."

"Hmm..." I make a mental note to study Chase closer.

"Do you want to talk about Damon?"

"Not really. I'm still trying to convince myself I haven't just imagined the whole thing," I answer. Hazel sashays across the room, returning with a new chocolate package. "Give that here. It's my favorite chocolate in the world."

"I know," Hazel says proudly. "Lucky your parents own the company producing it."

I lean my head back, closing my eyes as I take the first bite.

"God, I think I am in love with chocolate," Hazel announces. "I think Facebook should have the option to put as a status, In a relationship with chocolate, and it's not complicated at all."

Chapter Twenty-Four: Damon

I look at the glass and steel skyscraper for a few good minutes. Meeting James Cohen on his territory will be a challenge, but I'm up for it. The last time I saw him, I was beating someone and putting his sister in danger. I'd be surprised if he doesn't have his guards kick me out of the building or punch me. Doesn't matter. James Cohen is the only person who has the resources to help me, and Dani's safety is more important than anything—including my damn pride.

"What can I do for you?" the receptionist asks.

"I'm here to see James Cohen." I use my best unapologetic, no-questions-allowed tone since I don't have an appointment. I lift my lip in a half-smile and look her straight in her eyes. She holds my gaze for a few seconds then looks away, blushing.

"Sixth floor," she murmurs.

What is it with women that this tone and smile always work on them?

"Thank you."

I slip in the elevator, surprised at the mix of business suits and ragged jeans and t-shirts inside it. When I step out on James's floor, a bunch of the fellow jeans-wearing dudes follow. So this is what an office full of techies looks like. There are more than three dozen people typing away on their laptops in the open-space office. The sound of typing is occasionally interrupted by cheering or laughter.

I spot maybe two people wearing suits, but everyone else looks as though they've just put on whatever they found first this morning before coming in to work. They look like me. The muscles in my neck loosen a notch.

"I'm looking for James," I tell a dude passing by.

"Corner office in the back. Are you new? Haven't seen you before," he says. I give a noncommittal shrug. There are enough people around that I can get lost in the crowd, and I look the part of a newbie, so I go along with it. "He's pissed. I suggest whatever you have to ask him, ask someone else or he'll eat you alive."

Just my luck. "Thanks for the warning." I head to the back office with determined strides. I knock twice and go in after I hear a brisk, "Later."

"I said later," James says. He sits at his desk, his head bent over some papers. He's not wearing a suit, either. There is a tall brunette next to him, gesturing heatedly and pointing to something on the paper. I've seen photos of the two of them in a magazine. That must be Serena, his fiancée. He angles his eyes at me then stands up so quickly he nearly topples the papers in front of him. "You have the nerve to show up here?"

Well, this is going as expected, minus the punch. "I have to talk to you."

"Are you Damon?" Serena asks. To my astonishment, she's smiling.

"Yeah."

"Excellent," she says.

James turns to her, frowning. "You knew he was coming here?"

"No, I'm just happy to finally meet him. Hi, Damon. I'm Serena."

I smile at her, nodding curtly.

"Good, you two met. Now get out of my fucking office, Damon."

"You'd better listen, James," I say. "It's about Dani's safety."

This stuns him for a few seconds. "That shouldn't be an issue if you stay away from her."

"Not true."

James stares at me, but remains quiet. I take that as an invitation to continue. No reason to soften the blow, so I just say it bluntly. "Gabe seems to be plotting some stupid vendetta. He's pissed at both of us; on me for ratting him out for the drugs, on you for hiring the lawyer."

"Why now?" James asks.

"He's out of jail. I'm back. Dani's back. And he's targeting her. He told me so."

James swears loudly. "Why?" he asks through gritted teeth, though I'm sure he knows the answer as well as I do.

"Because she's your sister," I pause, "and because he knows I love her."

He swears again.

"He's keeping a low profile. Gabe's not stupid. I learn from my mistakes, so I won't underestimate him again."

"What's your plan?" James squints, his jaw clenched.

"You have him watched. You have resources to do that, right? My...sources tell me he's into drug dealing for real. Heavy stuff. If we manage to get the police to catch him and lock him up..."

"And your part in the plan would be?"

"The bait."

"No." His tone is so firm Serena flinches next to him. "Let me ask you this: what are your intentions regarding Dani?"

"Um, James...how is that your business?" Serena asks.

"I'm making it my business. She's my sister. The last time he was in her life, he screwed everything up for her then left."

It's my turn to get angry. "Not by my choice. I didn't leave her. I was carted off."

"You stayed away from her after you graduated high school. That was your choice."

"Yeah, after graduation...thought that was for the best."

"What changed?" he inquires.

"When I met Dani, I was at the lowest point in my life. I was dragging her down. It was a series of fucked-up circumstances, but still, I brought them on. When your dad and my dad arranged for me to be shipped away like a piece of pork, I gladly wanted to strangle them both. But then I thought, maybe it's a good thing. Maybe Dani would be better off without me. I hadn't planned a future for myself, or at least not one that would be worthy of Dani. After I finished school, I got into fighting again. I tried to live my life the way I had before I met her. It didn't work out. When I saw her in London, I realized I didn't want to stay away from her anymore. I wanted to change. I applied to Stanford and got in. I know I am not the man you want for your sister, but I want to become that man. I owe it to my mom, to Dani, and to myself."

"That was a swoon-worthy love declaration," Serena announces. "If you haven't told all of this to Dani, I will chase you with a gun."

I grin. "I like you, Serena."

"Serena," James exclaims, throwing his hands up in the air, "you are not helping." Turning his attention back to me, he continues, "Say this business with Gabe doesn't come to a resolution. What then?"

I take a deep breath. "That's not an option."

James gives me a loaded look. I hold his gaze. He and I both know what will happen if locking up Gabe fails. I will have to disappear from Dani's life for good. It won't solve the issue, but it'll hopefully make Gabe leave Dani alone. My presence here is a provocation for Gabe.

"Have you told Dani about Gabe?" James asks.

"No, I wanted to talk to you first."

"That's a change." His tone holds appreciation.

"I want to make things right this time."

"I'll put some detectives on it immediately. It's best if you talk to them first and tell them everything you know about Gabe's current activities. They'll be here within an hour."

"How do you know?" I ask. "You haven't even talked to them."

He gives me a pointed look. "They will be."

"You know detectives who can be here in an hour?" Serena asks half-amused, half-incredulous. "Who am I marrying?"

James makes the call, and then he and Serena look over some papers again. I catch the words 'chocolate factory' and 'father'.

"I heard your father suffered a heart attack," I say.

"He did," James replies, without looking up from the papers, "and the doctor ordered him to stop working. He actually listened and now Serena and I are looking for someone to take over the reins of the factory."

"Why don't one of you do it?"

"I don't have time, and Serena already has a job."

"What do you do?" I ask her.

"Investment banking," she replies, just as someone knocks at the door.

"Later," James bellows.

The door opens, and James looks up exasperated. I have a hunch the word 'later' doesn't mean much around here. Two twenty-something guys who look like they haven't slept for a while stand in the doorway. One of them carries a laptop.

"We know you're busy, but this is urgent," one of them says. "If we break through this, we could advance by a month. We need your input on the code."

"Okay, come in." James gives Serena an apologetic look, but she waves him away good-naturedly, continuing to look over the papers by herself.

"You still code yourself?" I ask, impressed. James is something of a legend in Silicon Valley—an exceptionally skilled coder who started his company when he was a few years older than me. I figured he's doing only business stuff by now, leaving the coding to minions.

"Sometimes," he answers.

The guy carrying the laptop places it in front of James while the other one grabs a marker and starts scribbling some lines of code on the whiteboard. James scans the laptop intensively for a few minutes, and then the three of them huddle in front of the whiteboard, each writing snippets in an attempt to find the piece of code they need to move forward. James is very good, but looking at the lines of code, I realize they're missing something.

I grab a blank sheet of paper and a pen. Blocking out their voices, I focus hard and start writing down possible solutions.

"How about this code sequence?" I hold up the paper.

The three men stop mid-talk, turning to me. James copies the sequence on the board as the other two still look at me in surprise.

"Nah. The repetition happens one sequence too early. It won't—" James stops mid-sentence, drawing a double-headed arrow between two of the lines of code. "But if we inverse this sequences, then it will work. Great job, Damon. Chris, John, what do you say?"

Chris and John stare at the whiteboard suspiciously. Then the guy called Chris says, "I have to run it in the program, but I'm ninety-nine percent sure it will work."

"Is he another prodigy, James?" the guy named John says. "Where do you find them?"

"This time, he found me." James grins at me.

"Get him to work for us. Maybe we'll be able to keep him, unlike the last one." With that, John grabs the laptop from James's desk, and both he and Chris leave the room.

"You're smart!" James exclaims.

"That surprising tone is not offending at all."

"I didn't mean that I thought you were stupid. Dani said you were smart, and you did get into Stanford, but you're not average smart, you're very smart. Are you looking for a job?"

"Yes," I say without hesitation.

"Then you're hired. I'll take you to Francine, our HR head afterward. She'll help you with the paperwork. Take as many hours as you can. When can you start?"

"Right away, since classes don't start until tomorrow. Why did the other guy leave? The other prodigy."

"He started his own company. That's the best reason to lose employees. I don't mind, though the team always feels that's a betrayal of sorts." The door opens. "Ah, detectives, you're already here. Good. Let's start."

Chapter Twenty-Five: Dani

The first day of classes is hectic. I grab a coffee and a donut for lunch and still make it to the first afternoon class with only a few minutes to spare. I take a deep breath in the doorway then start looking for Hazel in the classroom. Even though the auditorium is large enough to seat two hundred students, there are only twenty or so in attendance, so I find Hazel quickly. She sits next to Chase, of course.

"We saved you a seat at lunch," she says when I sit on her other side. "Where were you?"

"The history teacher kept us a little longer to explain something about an assignment."

Chase grimaces, shaking his head. "Why are you taking history? It's the most boring class in the history of the world. No pun intended."

"Because she's taking a variety of classes." Hazel picks up the schedule I've printed out. A strand of her hair has caught in the corner of her mouth, but she's oblivious to it as she looks at the piece of paper incredulously. "Are you insane?"

"No, I am testing out the classes. The advisor said that's what the first weeks are for. I can drop any classes I'm not interested in afterward."

"I am pretty sure the advisor didn't mean you should sign up for every class," Hazel insists.

"I didn't sign up for all of them, just more than average."

"The average is three," Chase says.

"No, it's five." Hazel turns to him with her eyebrows raised.

A sheepish grin spreads on his face. "Yeah, well, I totally brought that number down last semester when I signed up for zero classes before you kicked my ass."

"I'll keep five courses at the end of the period," I promise.

"I hope you will, Miss Indecisive."

Her comment stings, but I mask it with a smile. She knows me too well. Miss Indecisive is the perfect description for me right now, and it kills me. I prided myself during all of high school that I knew what I wanted to study. After discovering in London that I don't like it as much, I feel lost and confused. That's why I want to try everything, even business courses like this one, even though I've never been particularly interested in business.

The professor comes in. He's a plump man in his fifties with too much mustache and too little hair. Still, despite his almost comical appearance, he exudes authority because the murmurs die down immediately. I listen to him for a few minutes before I feel something. I can't explain it—it's like a magnetic pull, and I turn sideways. My heart does a somersault as my eyes find Damon sitting on the opposite row, all the way back. He smiles my favorite smile, the one where he gets delicious dimples and his lips curl in a way that says I am preparing for mischief. His gaze rakes over me, sending flaming darts shooting through me as I remember the way we danced two nights ago and how it felt to have his lips on mine again. I force myself to look at the professor and take notes, still feeling Damon's gaze on me.

I can't help stealing a glance at him every now and again. He's a different boy than the one I met in senior year. He had a perpetual look of anger on him, and he seemed so lost. Now he's eager and focused. I might be lost, but he isn't. Damon is not a boy anymore; he's a man. And just like in high school, he attracts stares from about every girl in the room. Some of them try to be sneaky, only looking at him every now and again. Some don't bother at all with manners, gawking at him like he's in the room for the sole purpose of fulfilling their fantasies. I get jealous only imagining what they're thinking about. His devil-may-care appearance exudes sexiness. It's like a magnet. I can hardly blame anyone else for staring at him when I can't keep my own eyes off him.

Midway through the lecture, the professor announces that the class will be graded based on a project that will last the entire semester and that we are to complete in groups of two. He suggests we start looking for a partner sooner rather than later, and that if we plan to drop this class we do so now and not waste his time for two weeks. I automatically turn to Hazel, but Chase puts his arm around her shoulders before I even open my mouth.

"Sorry, love, but she's the only person who likes me enough to spend an entire semester working on a project with me."

"She's my best friend," I retaliate, as if this somehow nullifies what he just said.

"You took off to London for half a year. You snooze, you lose."

"You're impossible. Hazel?" I eye my good friend closely, though I know it's a lost cause. My phone buzzes, saving Hazel from telling me that to my face.

Stop trying to separate the lovebirds. How about you and me pairing for the project? I peer at Damon out of the corner of my eyes, squirming in my seat when I realize his gaze is fixed on me. I am very good at Googling and picking up wine for late nights, which we'll spend studying, of course.

I try to ignore the delicious shiver running through me as I text back. I'm not a wine girl. Anyway, Hazel and I have enough junk food to last us a year's worth of study nights. If you behave, I can even give you some pussies. After I press send, I look at him anxiously behind my shoulder. For some reason, he bursts into laughter as he reads my text. I look again at what I wrote. OMG. I meant cookies!!! Cookies. Stupid autocorrect.

My phone chimes again, spiking my blood with that wonderful adrenaline that flirting brings. Do you want me to believe you still haven't learned to turn off autocorrect after all this time? I think it's easier if you admit you want me. Even your autocorrect thinks you should.

I barely concentrate as the professor wraps up the class.

"I was hoping you'd argue over Hazel some more." Disappointment colors Chase's tone. "You're so much fun when you get all bossy. Did the cat get your tongue?"

"No," Hazel intervenes, pointing at my phone. "Damon did. I bet he asked her to be his project partner."

"Ah, that explains it. I bet he'll be eating something else before long."

"You are gross," I say, but as we make our way to the door, I can't help remembering how it felt having Damon's mouth down there all those months ago. Damon himself waits outside the class, propped against the wall. Chase wiggles his eyebrows, looking from Damon to me, and Hazel punches his chest lightly.

"You didn't answer," Damon says. "Do we have a deal, partner?"

"Yes, we do," I say confidently.

"Fantastic," Chase announces. "Now, can we all grab a coffee?"

"I have fifteen minutes before I have to go to the next class." I check my schedule. Out of the corner of my eyes, I see Damon's jaw drop as he peers at my schedule. I know he's taking fewer classes; James informed me yesterday that Damon started working for him. He didn't give me many details, so I can't wait to question Damon.

"Exactly how many classes are you taking?" he asks.

"Never mind," I reply, jutting the piece of paper in my bag.

"He's just worried he won't have enough bang time between classes," Chase adds helpfully.

"He's practically begging me to kick his ass," Damon mutters under his breath as Hazel and Chase walk away. "So, about that date you promised me...when can I kidnap you?" Damon says in my ear, bringing back all my dirty thoughts from earlier.

My voice is a whisper when I say, "Friday."

Chapter Twenty-Six: Damon

"I don't think we've ever had an intern who works this much," Francine, James's HR head, comments on Thursday night. Francine, James and I are inside the elevator—the last ones to leave the office. I'm used to hard work; I've been doing it for years. It's a welcome change to spend my time doing something where I can use my brain instead of my knuckles.

"I won't stay as long tomorrow," I tell James. "I have a date with your sister."

James narrows his eyes. "If you hurt her, I will beat you up."

"I used to fight, remember? I'd knock you out in no time."

Francine's eyes widen. "He's got a mouth to match his brain," she says. The elevator doors open, and we get out. There is a guard behind the reception, nodding at us before we exit the building.

After Francine leaves, James grabs my arm. "Take care of Dani."

"I will," I assure him. He lets me go reluctantly, heading to his car while I mount my bike.

I can understand his skepticism, but I won't make any mistakes this time. The year I've been away from her has been excruciating.

The stint in boarding school was just what I expected it to be. A bunch of over-privileged teenagers stuck together twenty-four-seven...the level of snobbism was astonishing. There was no way to let out steam through fighting while I was in there, so once I got out in June, I threw myself into fighting with a vengeance. I travelled all over Europe, using the money from fights to finance myself. Until I met Dani in London last fall.

The thing is I knew I didn't want to keep fighting, and I desperately wanted Dani back, but I wasn't doing anything to change my situation. I travelled a lot, and met more people than I can keep track of, but I missed her every day. Seeing Dani again was a wakeup call. I applied to Stanford for the spring intake the day after I saw her.

Now I have a job I'm proud of and am about to get my girl back. This time, I'll do everything right.

Chapter Twenty-Seven: Dani

"What are you going to wear?" Hazel asks as we inspect the clothes I laid out on my bed.

"No idea. He didn't say what we're doing." It's Friday, and my date with Damon starts in one hour.

"Oooh, he does have a knack for mystery, doesn't he?" She fiddles with the hem of a light pink dress. It's cute, but who knows what Damon has in mind.

"You can say that." Finally, I decide on black jeans and a pink shirt with long sleeves. "This should be safe for everything, right?" I ask Hazel after putting the clothes on.

"Well, Damon's seen you wearing tent-sized t-shirts. This isn't bad, but it's not first date material. Why don't you sex it up a bit?"

"I have. I'm just not showing it." Flashing a smile, I push down the waistband of my jeans half an inch, revealing the upper hem of my thong.

"Dani Cohen," Hazel says, clutching at her chest dramatically. "Are you wearing lace lingerie?"

"Yes, I am," I declare proudly.

"My, my, my...teens these days."

"It makes me feel sexy, even if I'm not showing it."

"How long till he'll be here?" Hazel props herself against the windowsill.

"Half an hour. I'm a bit too eager." I already put makeup on, and perfume, so I'm ready to go.

Looking out the window, Hazel says, "I think you're not the only one who's eager. He's already here."

"What?" I hurry to the window. My heart does a somersault when I see Damon leaning against his bike. He has on a leather jacket and messy hairdo. His casual appearance screams, I'm sexy and I know it. My knees go weak, my body aching for him, especially the parts covered in lace.

"A bad boy through and through, isn't he?" Hazel asks in amazement.

"I hope so." Every nerve in my body lights up with excitement and fear.

"Go. Don't make him wait."

My legs seem to have turned to lead, and Hazel practically has to shove me out the door. With every step I take, my heart hammers stronger against my ribcage, and when I get outside, I have the distinct impression it will burst.

Damon stands up straight when he sees me, taking his hands out of his pockets. "Hi."

"Hi," I whisper back. When I see the desire burning in his eyes, I feel naked in front of him. "Nice ride."

"Did you miss it?"

"Yeah." I missed him more. "You love your bike, don't you?"

Lolling his head to one side, he grabs my hand, pulling me to him. His hands slide around my waist, entrapping me. "I don't love my bike. I like it. I love you."

I melt on the spot; I truly do. His intoxicating proximity and his words spike my blood with fire. He tilts my head up, caressing my lips with his thumb, then kisses me. With this one kiss, I know I am his entirely. No matter how much time has passed, or how much we've both changed, this hasn't.

His kiss wipes away every anxiety, every doubt. When he pulls back, I'm left with a cold sense of loss. "Time to gear you up."

I slip on the jacket and helmet he hands me.

Once we're both on the bike, I ask, "You're still not going to tell me where we're going?"

"Nope, but we won't ride for long."

"Can I guess?"

His lips twitch. "You can try."

The next half-hour passes in a rush. We pull off the highway, driving for another fifteen minutes and then stop in a parking lot where there are three cars. The place around us is deserted, except for closed stores and a gas station. From somewhere in the distance, the ripple of a river reaches my ears, barely audible. Damon takes my hand without hesitation, leading the way. I let him guide me without a shadow of a doubt. His hand feels smoother than I remember—there are no recent marks from fights. They've healed nicely, just as Damon has. We trudge through the open field for several minutes. I suspect our destination is the hill rising in front of us, though I can't imagine why. I bite back the temptation of asking if he has a plan, but then we reach the hill, walking around it. When we stop, all I can do is stare.

"I knew you wanted to go bungee jumping for your birthday, but someone told me you didn't."

"Hazel." I take in the giant platform rising high, very high up in the air, squinting to see the few people milling around at the top of the platform.

"James, actually."

"Right. You're working for him...You and my brother are getting a little too cozy already. I'm not sure if I like that."

"Why not?"

"You are both strong-willed and very smart. If you two put your heads together, you'll be unstoppable."

"Why's that bad?" His green eyes bore into mine with an intensity that makes the air ripple with a wave of hot tension. It's so thick and palpable that I could bite into it.

"It's not. Let's go up."

"I'm actually going to wait for you here. I'll bring the bike around; didn't realize there was space for it here."

"Aren't you jumping?"

"No way in hell. I'd pee my pants on the way down."

"Hohoho, you ride a death machine on two wheels and fought for a living, and you're afraid of bungee jumping?"

"Hey, everybody is afraid of something. I have a fear of heights."

"The fearless Damon Cooper is afraid of something."

"I always thought people misunderstood the word fearless. If you think about it, it means fear less. Doesn't mean no fear at all."

"Okay," I say, fighting to keep a straight face. "Wait for me here."

"You'll kick ass. Go."

As I make my way up the platform, a pang of fear sprouts inside me. Eventually, I reach the top, and a guy my age greets me. "I'm Max. Dani Cohen, is it?"

"Yes. How do you know my name?"

"Your boyfriend mentioned it when he made the reservation," he says. Warmth travels all over my body at the word boyfriend. I pinch myself to make sure I'm not dreaming, and then grit my teeth to stop a yelp. I overdid the pinching, and it hurts like a bitch. Max wastes no time getting the gear ready.

I look up in the distance while he gets me prepped, trying to find Damon. From up here, I have a direct view of the parking lot beneath. He already brought the bike here, but he isn't next to it like I expected.

"Ready? Your boyfriend seems eager for you to get back down."

"What?"

"He's down there, possibly thinking he can catch you if the rope breaks."

"No, he doesn't." I giggle. "That would be silly." I approach the edge of the platform, looking down. So that's why he wasn't near the bike. He holds a poster-sized paper above his head. I'll catch you if you fall is written with huge letters on it.

Excitement bubbles up in my chest, getting out in a roar-like laughter attack. Max laughs with me, too, shaking his head. Deep inside my belly, butterflies wake up to life. Damon might not be able to catch me now if the rope breaks, but I know he'll be there if anything else goes awry. Another staff member appears next to Max as he nods, indicating everything's set, but I don't move, fear suddenly gripping me. This is insane. I eye the ground again, trying to calculate the distance. Why did I ever think this was a good idea? I try to remember what twisted logic led me to want to be up here. Oh, yeah, I wanted to get out of my comfort zone. Bad, bad idea. People flirt with strangers or have a Brazilian wax when they try to get out of their comfort zone. They don't decide to jump from God knows how many feet up, possibly to their death.

"Is there any chance of the rope breaking?"

"Less than one in a million."

"But there is a chance," I say through gritted teeth.

"You can jump whenever you're ready," Max calls. He and the other guy are right behind me, waiting for my signal so they can get me started.

I don't move, stuck to the edge of the platform, without the courage to go forward. I am so not ready. But sometimes getting unstuck means taking a jump even when you're not ready, so I do. I signal Max, raising my arms to the sides and leaning forward, gasping as my feet leave the platform. The fall is quick, a hole springing up in my stomach, getting bigger and bigger the lower I go. I hurtle toward the ground like it's nobody's business, and when the air is so cutting that my eyes water, I close them. That very second, I feel a pull around my waist, and I bounce back upward. Cold panic grips me, making my heart beat with lightning-quick speed. The up and down movement goes on for a while, and when I open my eyes, the world is upside-down. At first, I can't make sense of anything. I try to hone in my eyes on a familiar point in the sea of unknown, but even trees and roads look foreign when viewed upside-down. Eventually, my eyes settle on the only unchanged point: the sun.

My heartbeat steadies as I use the sun as a point of reference and then slowly place everything else. Mental note for the future: when everything looks upside-down, it's enough to find one point to ground myself. Then things become clearer.

As I am pulled up toward the platform, something much more dangerous replaces fear. Nausea. I close my hands over my mouth, tasting bile at the back of my throat, breathing in deeply as I'm being pulled up.

"You okay?" Max asks when I'm on the platform and he removes my gear.

"Yep, but I thought I'd throw up."

"Happens to some people," he admits.

"Well, thank God I wasn't one of them. Can't spoil my date." Realizing I'm completely out of the gear, I wink goodbye. "It was nice meeting you, thanks."

Five short minutes later, I'm on the ground, running straight into Damon's arms.

"This was fun." I grin as he pulls me into a hug. I lose myself in it, inhaling his scent, ruffling his hair as I peek at the jumping platform. It's not something I'd do again, but I discovered something interesting when my feet left that platform to plunge into nothingness. Something exquisite lies beyond fear: freedom. As Damon tightens the hug, I become certain of one thing: whatever happens, no matter how upside-down things look, I can count on him to ground me.

"Ready for the next part?" Damon murmurs in my ear.

"Absolutely."

"There's something I want to tell you first." The seriousness in his tone makes me stand up straighter.

"Okay."

"You remember Gabe?"

"Yes." A hollowness forms in my stomach, rising all the way up to my throat. "He's out of jail?"

"He got out a month ago."

"Did you run into him?"

"He sought me out."

"Why?" A hundred different reasons pop up in my mind, one less plausible than the other.

"He wants revenge on James and me for sending him to jail."

"His illegal behavior sent him there."

"Yeah, well, he needs someone to blame." Taking a deep breath, he reaches for my hand. "He threatened to hurt you."

"W-why?" I squeeze his hand tightly, my chest heaving restlessly.

"It's the easiest way to hurt me and James, because we both love you."

"That's why you met with James." It all makes sense now.

"Yes. The job was a pleasant side effect. I know Gabe's involved in drug dealing right now, and James and I are looking for some proof. He should be locked up for a long time if we succeed. In the meantime, I want you to be careful. If anything looks suspicious, I want to know, okay? Keep your eyes open, but don't worry too much."

"Okay."

Once we drive away, I cling to him tightly, playing his words in my mind. We both love you. I take in as much of his presence as I can. As always, it's intoxicating, and by the time the bike pulls to a stop, I am drunk on him. It's only after I descend from it and get out of the jacket and helmet that I snap back to reality.

"What the—?" I gasp, looking wearily at the familiar venue. "Prom and the graduation party were here."

"Exactly."

"What are you trying to do, Damon?"

"I can't make up for all the times I wasn't here with you, but I want to make up for all the special dates I missed."

"My birthday—"

"Prom, graduation. I missed a few good ones. Come on, let's go. I don't know about you, but I'm starving," he says. I'm about to remark that this is an expensive restaurant, and he's broke, but he adds, "I sold some old stuff I didn't need. I received good money for it." I don't protest, but I still feel bad that he's spending that money on me.

The second we step inside, the waitress comes up to us smiling.

"Mr. Cooper. Ms. Cohen, welcome. I'll take you to your table."

The restaurant has two floors and a terrace on top. It's lined with window walls so it can be used even when it's not warm enough outside. She leads us all the way up to the terrace. There are fewer tables here. It's more intimate. As she guides us to our table, a detail makes my pulse ratchet up.

"Christmas lights," I whisper as we sit. "They're everwhere. Let me guess. This is prom, graduation, and Christmas all rolled into one?"

"Yep. I thought of doing them one by one, but then I realized it would take forever to get to my favorite part of the night."

"Mmmmm." I bury my face in the menu to hide my blush. Then I realize...where will we go after dinner? He has roommates; I have a roommate. I could almost face-palm myself. Why didn't I sort this out with Hazel? This is a disaster waiting to happen. As discreetly as I can, I text her. Is there any chance you can stay out later tonight?

Her reply comes almost instantly. Relax, I've got plans until the wee hours of the morning.

"Who's that?" Damon asks.

"Hazel." I push my phone away, giving Damon my undivided attention.

"Okay, so, since we're celebrating so many things, how about a food festival?"

"You know me; I like to eat," I reply.

"That's my girl."

"Tell me about your dad," I beckon. "I think he stopped working with mine some time ago."

"Yeah, apparently my dad found someone who paid more for his stuff, and yours found someone who was cheaper. Everyone's happy," Damon says, shrugging. "He's in London right now; I think he'll stay there for a few months. I don't talk to him often."

We order everything. Appetizers, roast beef, turkey, and top it all with cake. By the time the waitress brings us the cake, the button of my jeans threatens to pop open, and I feel sleepy.

"I need a break. I can't eat this right away," I say, eying the delicious chocolate cake in front of me. I can't believe it, but I might have to pass on dessert.

"Let's skip it altogether." His voice is low and rough, sending a delicious jolt right through me. I press my thighs together in an involuntary attempt to curb the ache there. In the flash of a second, my sleepiness vanishes.

"Yes."

***

The ride to the dorm passes in a haze. When we reach the door to my room, I suddenly have a lump in my throat. I know what follows next, but I'm unsure how to do this.

"Come on in."

"Is that an invitation?" His green eyes lock on mine.

"Yes," I breathe.

"Be careful, Dani. Once you let me in, I don't plan on leaving."

"That's what I'm hoping, even though Hazel will return eventually." I fumble in my bag for my keys, feeling Damon's breath at the back of my neck.

. Heat radiates from where his breath brushes my skin, spreading on my shoulders, down my arms, chest, and further down, until my intimate spot is pulsing. "Damn it, where are they?"

Damon lays an arm around my waist, pulling me gently to him.

"Relax, Dani," he whispers. I nearly giggle in relief when I find the keys.

"Here they are."

I unlock the door and welcome Damon in our living room.

"This place is huge compared to my dorm," Damon comments, and I can tell he's trying to make small talk to put me at ease.

"Hazel's mom made sure we got one of the largest units available on campus. Our bedroom is pretty small, though. Wish we'd gone for a unit with separate bedrooms." I open the door to the bedroom, experiencing the same feeling of nervousness I did when I first welcomed him in my room back home. After Damon left, I started reading steamy novels—part of my rebellion. I found out I really liked them. I really hope my reading will substitute my lack of experience.

"See? Tiny."

"You're blushing." Damon runs his fingers over my neck, then down my chest. "That makes self-control very hard for me, you know that, right?" He bows his head, and I moan when his lips touch my neck. I fist his hair, willing him to continue. "I missed you. God, I missed you," he mutters against my skin. His hands roam over my back, their touch making my nerve endings shimmer. I slide my hands under his shirt, caressing his rippled muscles. Every single one is as contoured as I remember.

I become putty in his hands, a mere slave to my need, driven by desire. He nibbles at my lower lip then tugs at it with his teeth. He removes my top, leaving me only in my bra. Sitting on my bed, I pull his jeans down, biting my tongue as I take in the sight of him in his boxers. Then he gets rid of them, and I suck in a deep breath. I want to caress his thickness, but have no idea how to do it right. Focus, Dani. You've read enough romance novels. You can do this.

Just as I gather some courage, doubts overcome me again. Sure, I've read enough novels, but they didn't specifically say how hard to squeeze, or exactly how fast I should move my hand. Damn it. Why doesn't sex come with an instruction manual?

"Dani, stop looking at my dick as if you're about to dive into a science experiment."

I glance up to find Damon looking at me. Oh, crap. How long have I been staring at his shaft? He grins, beckoning me to touch him. I wrap my palm around his thickness.

"That's right. Now move your hand up and down," he says huskily. Furrowing my brows, I do as he says.

"Is this okay? Should I do it faster, or—"

"You're doing great." His eyes are locked on mine, his chest moving up and down faster than before.

"Show me." I say the words in a whisper so low, I fear he might not hear me. But he does and places his hand over mine, pressing on my fingers. I tighten my grip. Then he changes the tempo to more rapid movements. When he pulls his hand away, I continue. Following my instinct, I stroke him even faster. He grunts out my name. I keep my eyes focused on him, drinking him in as he tilts his head back.

His nostrils flare as if he's forcing himself to breathe in and out. He's coming undone at my touch.

"Enough," he grunts, pushing my hand away. Locking his darkened eyes on me, he pushes me gently on my back then removes his shirt. I run my hand hungrily over his granite-like abs, tracing the lines angling toward his pelvis. "Remove your clothes," he orders. I push my jeans down my legs, doing my best to appear seductive. "All your clothes," Damon continues. I obediently get rid of my bra and panties. My nipples pucker, aching for his touch.

"You are beautiful, Dani." His eyes travel over my body desperately, as if he can't get enough of me. The feeling is mutual, and I beckon him to climb on the bed. I inch my legs apart invitingly. He props a knee between them then leans over me, grazing my nipple with his teeth. I arch my back, gasping, and reach for his shaft again. When I touch him, I feel a few drops of warm liquid on its tip. Warm wetness pools in my intimate spot immediately. On cue, Damon reaches into his discarded jeans for his wallet, retrieving a condom. He rips the package open and slides the condom on, biting furiously at his lips while doing it.

"It might be uncomfortable in the beginning," he warns me, "since you didn't ...you know."

I nod, bracing myself for the sharp pain I felt the first time. When Damon positions his tip at my entrance and pushes inside, I sigh. There is no pain, just a sense of discomfort as he slides in. He puts his hands on my sides and I happily rest my palms on his biceps, reassurance filling me. All the discomfort is gone. He slides out and in again with measured strokes, coaxing whimper after whimper out of me. His muscles contort violently under my fingers as if it takes effort not to ravish me.

"It doesn't hurt." My legs cinch up his waist to give him better access. "You can let loose, Damon."

"Not a good choice of words." His labored breathing leaves no room for misinterpretation. The next second, his strokes become merciless as he pounds inside me with ferocity, his lips covering my neck and breasts with kisses. A liberating sensation spreads inside me, dissolving the pain I kept hidden, leaving place for hope, bliss, and the conviction that together we will bloom into something beautiful. The heat between my legs becomes singeing as his groin presses on my clit with every move, making me writhe and moan underneath him.

"Dani, God, you feel so good." He makes love to me for a long time until tension erupts deep inside me, causing my hips to buck. I plant my legs firmly on the bed, meeting his desperate thrusts with fervor. The tension turns unbearable, flaring through me, alighting every part of me until my body begs for release.

"Damon," I murmur, tugging at his hair and pulling him into a kiss. I feel him widen inside of me, his body going rigid while my orgasm shatters me.

With one last deep kiss, he pulls out of me and sits on the edge of the bed, still panting. He discards the condom while I trace the tattoos on his arm, wondering if I should shower. My hair sticks to my sweaty neck, but I'm not sure what the after-sex protocol is. I fell asleep last time, and I want to do things right now.

"Should I shower?" I ask tentatively.

"You're not going anywhere." He fixes his green eyes on me then slides in the bed next to me. Nibbling my shoulder, he adds, "Turn around; I want to do some spooning."

"Do guys actually use that word? I was under the impression it was an activity men avoid like the plague."

"Idiots, maybe," he says with an air of superiority, winking. "I get to feel your cute little ass against me."

Grinning, I turn around and grind against him. To my surprise, he's hardening again. There is something unbelievably sexy about both of us being sweaty and messy. "You lasted a long time for someone who was afraid he'd come in his pants from merely kissing me."

"I...prepared for this." He slings his arms around me, pulling me even tighter to him until I can feel his cock pressing against the crack of my butt, giving me hot flashes.

"What's that supposed to mean?"

"I jerked off a few times before our date." He says the words with complete nonchalance.

"You...umm...wow." Imagining him touching himself makes me burn for him again. I press my thighs together, trying to suppress the need.

"You want me again, don't you?" he whispers in my ear, sending shivers down my spine.

"Yes," I answer.

"Good to know I'm not the only addict. I can't get enough of you, Dani." He flicks one of my nipples between his fingers, grazing my earlobe with his teeth. I become hyper-aware of how hard he is. Unexpectedly, he pushes me up on all fours, my ass sticking up in the air. Positioning himself behind me, he swipes his tongue from my neck down my spine, prompting me to shiver.

"Damon."

He cups my ass, spreading my cheeks apart, dipping his tongue between them, touching the sensitive skin there briefly. My thighs quiver and I fist the bed sheets for support. Sweet God, this man will be the death of me. He is just reaching for another condom when the door opens, and for a moment the whole scene freezes.

Hazel walks in, her eyes widening. Damon and I are both stark naked, and my bottom sticks up in the air. To make matters worse, Damon leaps from the bed, giving Hazel a full frontal view. He seems to acknowledge his mistake and turns around, giving her an eyeful of his butt, as well. I groan, wishing we had turned off the light.

"Will you turn around?" I ask her, because she seems far too perplexed to realize that's the thing to do.

"Oh, yeah." She swirls around, giggling. Damon dresses faster than I blink. "Oh, my God, I will never be able to unsee this. Damon, you have spoiled me for other guys."

"Thanks for the compliment." His clipped tone puts a smile on my face.

"Poor guys. I will always keep everyone to your ass's standard. Not to mention your other endowment."

"Hazel," I say, mortified. "Can you drop it?"

"Well, it's true."

"I am so not hearing this conversation," Damon says.

"I thought we had a texting code going on, Hazel."

"Well, you texted me when you left the restaurant. That was hours ago. I thought he left. Were you at it the entire time?"

"Aaaaaand I'm out." Damon plants a kiss on my lips. I think it was meant to be quick, but his lips linger until my breath ratchets.

"Should I leave again?" Hazel interrupts. We immediately pull apart.

"See you tomorrow." Damon stomps out of the room.

I pull the sheets up to my chin as Hazel rushes to her bed, watching me curiously. "I want to know everything."

I tell her, though I still resent her for interrupting us. Hazel giggles and covers her mouth, as if she's watching a movie. The only thing missing is a bucket of popcorn.

"You are a bit too excited, you know that, right?"

"I've had zero action all year." She sits up straighter on the edge of the bed, watching me solemnly. "I'm living through you."

"You have to stop doing that."

"Are you kidding? Now that I've seen how well-endowed Damon is...How is that even legal?"

"Why don't you make a move on Chase?" I ignore her comment about Damon.

"I've been through that once, last semester. Not happening again." After an awkward pause, she tucks herself into her bed, still fully dressed. "I'm too tired to change into my pajamas."

"Give another guy a shot."

"We'll see," she says vaguely.

"You do know you'll have to get out of bed and turn the light off, don't you?"

"But the switch is closer to you," she protests.

"Yeah, but I'm naked."

"Gross. I didn't want to be reminded of that." Grinning, she gets up and turns off the light. She falls asleep the second she returns to her bed, but I'm awake for a long time, replaying the events of tonight in my mind. I wish Damon had spent the night with me. Being in his arms felt so good, so right. I reach on the nightstand for my phone and look at the picture the waiter took of us. It brings a smile on my face and makes my ache for him so much harder to stand.

I text him on a whim. Are you asleep?

My phone pings almost immediately. No. I can't stop thinking about tonight. I swear my heart swoops out of my chest. Another ping. I wish I could have slept next to you.

Me, too, I type back quickly.

We need to find a sleeping arrangement where I can be with you. I try not to swoon too much and play it cool, but my toes curl all on their own.

Arrangement? You've just started working with my brother and already sound like him.

I already miss you, he texts back. We need to get any inconvenient roommates out of the way.

I allow myself to swoon just a little. Make sure Hazel doesn't hear you call her an inconvenient roommate. She might just let our entire dorm know how well "endowed" you are, and then all the sorority girls will want to jump you.

His reply comes right away. Don't worry, I'm all yours.

Now I allow myself to swoon all the way.

Chapter Twenty-Eight: Dani

When I get up on Saturday morning, I tiptoe out of bed, careful not to wake Hazel. I've learned from our countless sleepovers that she sleeps like a rabbit. One wrong move and she's up, and waking up Hazel before noon on a Saturday is a course of action to be avoided at all costs.

Peeking through the window at the blinding sunshine, I take the clothes I'm planning to wear in the living room and then head to the shower. Once I step in and let the warm water spray over me, I become aware of how sore my body is, especially between my legs. Damon's smell still lingers, but the overwhelming aroma of lemon from my shower gel washes it away. I'm visiting my parents and would rather keep my nocturnal activities a secret. I step out of the dorm in a flimsy dress and ballerinas, ready to soak in as much sun as possible on the way to my car, only to immediately start shuddering. Okay, total misjudge of the weather. The sun shines bright, so I can practically picture myself on the beach, feeling the grains of sand scratch my skin lightly, but a rush of cold wind prompts me to hurry to my car. I'll just throw something warmer on once I get to my parents' house. I've left enough clothes there. I get into my car, and as the engine roars to life, I inspect the parking lot through the rearview mirror, checking if the coast is clear to leave.

It is, but that's no surprise, given that the cars' owners are probably sound asleep inside the dorms. Every car is empty.

Except one.

I wouldn't have noticed it had an occupant, if he weren't staring at me so insistently. I wince, as if someone just dropped an ice cube down my spine.

The person sitting behind the wheel is Gabe.

My body reacts before my brain has time to process what this means. In a haze, I drive out of the parking lot, my hands shaking on the wheel. My heart slams in my chest, a sudden heaviness descending upon the nape of my neck. The weight of fear keeps me from looking back up in the rearview mirror to check if Gabe is tailing me. Eventually, I do look up, and my stomach constricts with pain. He's right behind me. I assess the situation as best as I can. My car is better than Gabe's. This can give me an advantage in the speed department. I press the pedal, sinking in my seat as the car lunches forward with a vengeance. I head straight in the direction of the highway, but it'll be a while before I reach it. Right now, I'm on a two-lane street, one lane for each direction. The only cars in sight are mine and Gabe's. Empty shops and sleepy houses line up the road on both sides.

Gabe's car roars from behind as he closes the distance between us. What's his deal?

As he comes side by side with me, I realize what he wants: to drive me off the road. At this speed, a collision with anything would cause a lot of damage. I hit the gas pedal again, which is stupid and dangerous—I'll lose control of the car before long. Right now, all I want is to get rid of Gabe. I put a few feet between us again, but as the speed indicator alerts me to my very precarious situation, I realize Gabe only needs to crash into my car lightly, and I wouldn't just drive off the road—I would overturn.

Gabe's about to catch up with me again when the sound of a police siren reaches my ears. Their car shows up a fraction of a second later in the distance, speeding toward us from the other direction.

I barely blink away from the police car, when I realize Gabe takes a sharp turn to the right, disappearing on one of the side streets.

When the police car passes me, the two officers inside it don't even glance my way. They must be having an emergency wherever they're heading, or they would've fined me for the speed. I reduce it somewhat, until I'm certain I have full control of the car. Gabe doesn't make an appearance again.

It's only after I get onto the highway that I realize how stupid I've been. I should have alerted the police to what Gabe did, but in my haste to put as many miles between him and me as possible, I let the chance slip.

Cursing, I pull out my phone and call Damon. He picks up after the first ring and I tell him what happened. I'm not sure how coherent I am, because fear still muddles my thoughts.

"Do you want me to drive up to you?" he asks.

"No, it's okay. I'm going to my parents' house. I don't think he'll come back. Can you tell James what happened? I want to concentrate on driving, and I don't feel like repeating the story for him."

"Sure, I'll take care of it. Be careful."

"I will."

My heartbeat only regains its normal rhythm after about an hour of driving. I try to concentrate on the upcoming hours, and how my visit will go. I decide not to tell my parents anything about this morning.

A contradictory feeling of nervousness and warmth rears its head. It does so every time I visit my parents since I returned. Part of me still can't get over how much they've changed. They'd entered the hospital as strangers and came out determined to save their relationship. I had heard my parents used to love each other very much, but didn't believe it. Now I do. Their priorities changed completely. Dad handed over the reins of the chocolate factory and has no plans to return to work. Mom cut back on her charity work a lot and spends most of her time with Dad and on the phone with me. They're also determined for us to become a real family. I love spending time with them. They are finally the parents I wished for my entire childhood. I contemplate calling James to ask him if he'd like to come, and then decide against it. He makes it to the weekly Thursday dinners, but rarely has time for more visits. I don't blame him; the three hours' drive to our parents' home isn't much fun.

Just as I get out of the car in front of the house, the massive oak doors of the entrance open and my mother appears.

"Dani, you must be freezing." She throws me a worried look. "I'll get you a coat. Your father is in the glasshouse." With that, Mom disappears back inside. Despite the chilly wind, warmth spreads through my limbs. She really makes an effort to pay attention to me, and I appreciate it.

I make my way to the glasshouse, sucking in a deep breath when I find my father. He still bears the marks of his heart attack. He's thin, pale, and has sunken eyes. But he's livelier than I've ever seen him, smiling, and even chuckling occasionally. He's immersed in the book he's reading and doesn't see me come in. Just the fact that he's reading a book blows my mind.

I don't remember ever seeing my father do that, unless it was a book by some famous business guru. When I take a closer look at what he's reading, I do a double-take. Yep, Dad holds Harry Potter and the Sorcerer's Stone in his hands.

"Dad, what are you reading?"

His head snaps up to me. "I found this in your room. It's brilliant."

"I know," I say. He closes the book as I sit opposite him, putting it on an empty chair. "There are seven of them, and they're all brilliant."

"I'll look for the second one in your room as soon as I finish this one."

"Who are you, and what have you done with my father?" I make a mental note to scour my room and take with me every single steamy romance book I own.

"I only have twenty pages left." He put the book away, but eyes it with an almost comical longing. I'm jealous. Nothing comes close to the excitement of reading the Harry Potter series for the first time.

Mom arrives carrying a tray, one of my old hoodies and sweatpants hanging on her arm. I snatch them, throwing them over what I'm wearing in a heartbeat.

"Oh, breakfast," Dad says. "Looks great." He glances up, beaming at Mom. She smiles back shyly, as if she's a tad ashamed. My parents are rediscovering how to love each other one step at a time. It's beautiful to watch. I barely withhold a groan when I see what's on the tray.

"I made your favorite breakfast, Dani," Mom declares proudly. "Pancakes with mashed banana." Now, here's the thing. I don't have any memory of ever liking, let alone loving this. After Dad came back from the hospital, we viewed some old photo albums. In a lot of those, I was eating this awful stuff and looked happy doing it.

Mom concluded I must have loved it, and makes it for me every time I'm here. It's gross and slimy, but I'm not about to tell her that. I had given up hope a long time ago that she'd cook anything for me, so this is almost a miracle. I take a bite, hoping it'll taste better this time. Nope. Forcing a smile on my face, I gulp the thing down. If my parents had a dog, this would be the moment when I'd slip him the food under the table and pray for him to eat it.

"Eat up. There's more if you want," Mom says. Okay, new resolution: I must buy my parents a dog, preferably one who likes mashed bananas.

"I just learned that Dad started reading. How about you, Mom?"

"Me, too. I found some books in your room." She motions with her head to the lounge chair a few feet away from the table. My heart stops. Lying there with a bookmark between its pages is one of the steamiest romances I own. "It's great."

"Perfect," I mumble, feeling my cheeks heat up even though Mom looks completely unfazed.

Dad reaches for one of my pancakes. "I haven't tasted these." There is no way to warn him, so when he takes the first bite and winces, throwing me a questioning glance, I bite my tongue to stifle a laugh. Luckily, Mom's looking away.

"Tell us about your first week. How is the accommodation?" Dad says, skillfully avoiding Mom's gaze as he puts the pancake back on my plate. I wet my lips, inhaling deeply. After years of silence from them, this feels weird. But then I remember that Mom reads steamy novels and Dad devours Harry Potter. Asking me to tell them about my week is the most normal thing I've heard since walking through the door.

"The bedroom is on the small side, but we'll manage."

"Hopefully Heather doesn't snore," Dad says.

Mom elbows him. "It's Hazel."

"I know that." He flinches in his seat, throwing me an apologetic look. "I swear I do. I'm just bad with names."

"She doesn't snore, Dad."

"So you moved in with Hazel. Go on." Squaring his shoulders, a sharp breath whooshes out of him. He suddenly looks very business-like. I imagine this is how he used to be in meetings, recapping what had been discussed and prompting everyone to move forward. Since he got out of the hospital, he alternates between trying to play the cool dad and moments of lucidity when he realizes he has no idea how to do that. For some reason, this puts me at ease from my own difficulties in communicating with them. Even adults have to wing it sometimes.

I grin and start telling them about the classes, my crazy schedule.

"Wait, why are you taking so many classes?" Mom asks.

"Well, I just want to try out as many as I can, so I figure out what I like."

"Oh, I see," Dad says. "It's time you lost that chip on your shoulder. You dropped out of your London Uni after one semester because you didn't like your subject, so what?" When I don't answer, he continues, "Dani, listen. Everyone goes through a soul-searching period at some point in their lives. Don't sweat over this. You're young; you have time to figure things out."

"But—"

"You are the most responsible kid I know," he says. "You have a huge trust fund and chose to live in a dorm and drive a cheap car. Ask James what he was doing when he was your age."

"I know what he was doing," I say. James was the only person in our family to burn his trust fund, and he managed that in three years. "But I missed my grades for Oxford, all because I was too busy rebelling against you and Mom," I challenge.

Mom folds her arms, leaning back in her chair. "Well, you were bound to rebel. Most teenagers do that for years. I was one of them. I gave my mom hell. Your months of rebellion were nothing in comparison, really."

I eye her suspiciously. "You were very alarmed at the time."

"We'd become used to you being a good kid. You just threw us in for a loop." She and Dad exchange a gloomy look that tells me they haven't fully forgotten those months, but want to let the past go.

"Just enjoy college." Dad winks at me and Mom nods in approval. "Anyone up for a game of charades?"

"Sure." As Mom brings the game, I add, "Damon's back. He's at Stanford, too." Dad goes rigid, and Mom pauses in the act of reaching for her chair.

"He's not fighting anymore," I add quickly. "At all." My throat goes dry as the silence stretches and my parents exchange furtive glances.

"Good for him," Mom says eventually. As she drops in her seat, I grow uneasy.

"What are your intentions regarding him?" Dad asks. His tone is now all business.

"We went on a date. He seems changed," I say. When skepticism stretches on both their faces, I add one last piece of information, hoping to soften them. "He works for James." Instantly, their eyes widen. I bite my lip, imagining how they will grill my brother about this.

"We can't tell you what to do or not." Uncertainty tinges Dad's tone.

"Just be careful," Mom says.

Well, all in all, not the worst reaction.

We focus on the game of charades after that, playing it for hours. Mom babbles about her newly discovered love for reading—she's devoured most of my steamy collection—then tells me all about organizing James and Serena's wedding. She pretends to be upset they don't help her much, but I know she's secretly happy they're letting her do whatever she wants. The sun is almost setting when they walk me back to the car. I'm still wearing my hoodie and sweatpants, and I've decided to keep them on so I won't freeze my butt off.

"Hey, we should all go to the factory soon, like we did when I was little."

"Your dad still tires very quickly, so he won't leave the house for a while," Mom says apologetically.

"But we can give you a set of keys. Maybe you can go with some friends," Dad suggests. "It closes to the public at eight o'clock; I can tell the guards to keep it open for you and your friends."

"Okay, I don't need keys then."

"No, you should have your set," he insists. "It's yours, too, after all."

I'm grinning ear to ear when Mom brings me a set of keys. "Is there any chance you can visit me on campus any time soon?"

"Only after your father feels better."

"Okay. I just don't know if I'll be able to make it this Thursday to dinner. I'll come next weekend for sure, though."

"Good." Mom grins, pulling me into a hug. "I can make more mashed banana pancakes."

"How do you eat that stuff?" Dad mouths to me, and it's all I can do not to burst out laughing.

I return my mother's hug tightly. Trying mightily to keep a straight face, I suggest innocently, "Guys, what would you say about buying a dog?"

Chapter Twenty-Nine: Damon

"The factory is ours for the night. I'll give you a tour," Dani says. It's been two weeks since our first date, and between my work and her crazy schedule, we haven't had time for a second one. We hang out in classes, during breaks, and half-clandestine night escapades, but I've yearned to have her all mine for an entire evening again.

The police said there isn't anything they can do against Gabe for the stunt he pulled with the car. James says they're simply following the law. I say they're incompetent, and told them so to their faces. In the meantime, we keep an eye out for Gabe. Dani's been beyond brave through all of this. If something happens to her, I won't be able to live with myself.

As we step inside the building, her eyes are alight with excitement. Her happiness has more to do with this place than with me. "When's the last time you were here?"

"Last year, when they added a museum to the factory. When I was, like, four or five, my dad used to bring me here every Sunday. It was my happy place. I was surrounded by chocolate and had the undivided attention of my family. Well, almost. Dad was working, but at least we were all together. Then things between him and Mom got worse, and our weekly trips stopped."

"How are your parents now?"

"Huh, you'd think Dad has had a heart transplant or something. They are so in love; it's just weird, but I'm happy for them. Look, this is the main entrance to the museum."

"I thought we were going to see the factory."

Dani shakes her head, unlocking the front door. We step inside. "The museum shows the entire production process, but we'll see it through a glass. Come on."

We spend the next hour touring the museum. Dani gives me the entire history of the company besides telling me about the processes. She knows everything inside out. I only half-listen to her, because I am fascinated by the expression on her face. She's more radiant than I've ever seen her. This place is good for her. "You love it here."

"Yeah, I do. I know it's strange, but I feel more at home here than in my parents' house." She smiles as we move to the next room. Before speaking, she hurries to the small chocolate containers, taking a few pieces. So far, there was chocolate in every room, and Dani indulged in it every time. She closes her eyes after popping the chocolate in her mouth, savoring it. When she opens them again, she catches me staring at her.

"Quality control," she says confidently.

"How much chocolate can you eat?" I ask.

"That is a question you must never ask a woman."

"Duly noted." The tour ends in a room with flowing chocolate. There is even a plate of waffles. "How come the river is still flowing this late?" The word 'river' isn't fitting, but that's what the shield says. There are actually two small rivers, running on both sides of the room. There is a railing on either side.

"I asked someone from maintenance to stay late today. They'll turn it off after we leave."

"Ah, I see. Asking for favors because you're the boss's daughter."

Punching me playfully in the chest, she leans over the railing, dips a waffle in the flowing chocolate, then takes a bite. I follow suit. The chocolate is warm, not hot, and it's good, but I've never had much of a sweet tooth. Watching her enjoying it is more fun.

"You're no fun; you barely ate. I should come here with Hazel. She appreciates all of this. What's the point of visiting a chocolate museum if you don't eat chocolate?"

Leaning in from behind, I push her hair to one side, revealing her neck. "Tasting you." Dani squirms under my touch, goose bumps forming on her arms. "Can anyone see us here?"

She giggles nervously, leaning her head on my shoulder, looking up at me. "No."

"Are you sure?" My cock already throbs in my jeans. I press myself against her. She lets out a sigh, reaching behind her, popping my button open. Then she slips her hand inside, palming my cock. I can feel the slight tremor in her arm.

I love this about her. She keeps that innocence that made me fall in love with her, but when pleasure overtakes her, she gives herself to me with abandon. In that moment, she trusts me enough to let herself be free and wild.

"This room is safe. I have it on good authority that James also...fooled around here."

"I so didn't want to know that." Gritting my teeth, I fight to maintain my composure as she pumps along my length. I rake my eyes over her, studying her from head to foot, then back up. She's wearing a light pink dress with a delicious amount of cleavage and a decent length. It covers her all right, but I can see all the potential it has for me to touch her skin without having to undress her.

I cover her mouth with mine, slipping my tongue between her willing lips. With one hand, I unclasp her bra. As her breasts spill free, I lower myself to their level, turning her slightly to me. Pulling aside the fabric covering her breasts, I take one puckered nipple into my mouth, suckling on it while watching her coming apart. Dipping my thumb in the chocolate river, I run it across her lips, smearing them. Then I kiss her hard. I push my tongue into her mouth in quick, precise moves, mimicking the act of making love. At the same time, I touch her intimate spot over her panties. She's breathless when I pull away. Perfect. Just the way I want her.

"Turn around," I order. "I want to take you from behind." I can practically see how the commanding tone makes her eyes dilate with desire, demanding to be pleasured. I bet she's dripping wet, too. Placing my hands on her hips, I turn her around. I push my hands under her dress and discover her thong has ribbons to the sides. Pulling at the ribbons, I undo them, and the panties fall to the floor.

I drip my fingers in chocolate again, and I'm sure she expects me to smear her breasts, but I like to surprise her. I place my fingers between her legs, on her slit. She lets out a moan as I move my fingers rhythmically, chocolate mingling with her wetness.

Then I get on my knees, pushing her dress up. She fists the fabric, giving me full access.

I press my palm on her back, indicating to her to lean forward, so her ass sticks up in the air. Spreading her butt cheeks apart, I lick her folds from the front all the way back. Her thighs quiver as she grips the railing to steady herself.

"Damon!" The way she grits out my name undoes me. I need to be inside her this very second. Rising to my feet, I take my wallet from my back pocket, retrieving a condom. Sliding my jeans down and the condom on takes a few seconds. I cup her cheeks, playing with the tip of my cock across her folds, teasing her though I can barely keep it together. When I slap it across her clit, a shudder shakes us both.

"So wet and ready," I growl. "What am I going to do with you?" I watch her lean her head back on my shoulder, licking her lips. This is my favorite moment—the most delicious one—even more so than an orgasm. The moment when raw need and desire subdue her inhibitions. She's a few strokes away from turning wild and passionate in my arms.

"Please. I need you," she says.

"Fuck, you're sexy." I slide inside her, feeling her tightly around me. Gripping her hips, I slam against her, filling her. "You like this?"

"Yes," she answers. I slam harder. "Yes." Her knuckles turn white as she clasps the railing more forcefully. I enter her like a man possessed. Sweat forms on my forehead, falling in heavy drops on her back. Her moans are intoxicating, driving me over the edge just as much as her spasming pussy. Looking down, I observe my length drilling in and out of her, then tip forward, nibbling at her neck. Dani's skin is soft and carries a sweetness I can get high on.

My hand reaches her clit, flicking it. I listen to her breath as I probe her wetness with my fingers, until I see what she likes because I love giving her exactly what she needs. It's not long before she bucks, grinding against me like a woman who's about to claim her orgasm. Then she tightens even more, driving me over the edge, too. Need skims over me, starting at the base of my spine, rippling through me. I force myself to keep my eyes open, wanting to see her fall apart.

A violent blush spreads over her skin as she tips her head back, crying out with pleasure. I last about two more seconds before my release ravages me. Resting my chin on her neck, I lose myself in her scent, listening to her shallow breath. I belong to her, like this. It's not just the post-orgasm bliss talking, but the year I spent away from her in which I felt like part of me was missing. I need this woman.

I will not lose her again. I can't.

Chapter Thirty: Dani

"I can't believe we let ourselves be talked into doing this," Hazel says, clutching a cup of coffee with one hand, trying to hide her yawn with the other. We are a few days before Spring Break, and there is a fair about majors taking place in the green space next to our dorm. Our dorm supervisor approached us last week, begging us to spend our day behind this booth, because the people who were expected to do it bailed. We accepted. It didn't seem like much trouble, until we were told we were expected here at six a.m.

"Yeah, I know. It's nine already, and I still feel like there's a hammer inside my head." And I already drank two coffees. The bright side is that the place is buzzing with people, meaning it's not for nothing. The sun isn't burning yet, so all in all, not too bad.

I'm about to pour myself a third cup from our flask when a pair of arms slide around my waist from behind.

The fragrance of ocean and mint overwhelms my senses, the underlying scent of man weakening my knees. My man.

"Hello, gorgeous," Damon says into my ear, then trails his lips downward, planting a kiss right on my neck.

"People are looking at us," I whisper, smiling at a couple of freshmen who inspect the brochures at our booth.

"So what? They'll see you're mine." His grip on my waist tightens with his last word. This is Damon. He takes what he wants, when he wants. I wouldn't have it any other way.

When he finally releases me and steps in front of me, I let out an involuntary sigh. The sight of him will never cease to amaze me. He wears black jeans and a burgundy shirt with the top button open, as if he just threw the clothes on him without bothering to look in the mirror. He makes carelessness look so sexy. The shirt hugs his tapered waist and I can almost make out the v-shaped stripes of his pelvis. It mortifies me that everyone else can, too.

"Hazel, mornings don't suit you," Damon teases her.

She offers a yawn as response. Then her eyes widen, as if an idea popped into her mind. "Can we talk you into taking over the booth?" she asks Damon.

"Nope. You two should learn the value of saying no," he replies. "Look at me; I do it all the time."

Hazel rolls her eyes. "Like anyone ever asks you to do stuff like this."

"They do. I just give them precise instructions of all the holes where they can shove their activities."

"That's very nice of you," I tell him, but there isn't much severity in my voice. He works very long hours with James; he should do whatever he likes in the few spare hours he has.

He leans in to me, his proximity causing my breathing trouble. "Oh, but you didn't fall for me because I'm nice, did you?" His eyes bore into mine, daring me to contradict him. I don't. "You did because I'm a bad boy."

"The two pigeons," a cold voice says from our right. Both Damon and I turn to face Gabe. I haven't seen him since the day of the car chase. I was hoping he gave up. Looking at Hazel, Gabe adds, "And the third wheel."

My legs turn to jelly at the implications in his statement. Has he been watching us?

Damon wastes no time stepping in front of the booth. Towering over Gabe, he grabs him by the collar.

"You piece of shit," Damon says through gritted teeth, attracting stares. "If you ever pull a stunt like that—"

"Careful, Damon," Gabe says. His arms are limp by his side. He's not even attempting to defend himself. "If the police interrogate me, they'll be very interested in you if I tell them you threatened me."

I grab the stand for support. I remember Damon telling me the police specifically told him and James not to engage in fights with Gabe, or make threats. But how does Gabe know this?

"Damon," I plead. "Let him go. He's not worth it."

Damon pushes him away, his eyebrows pinching together. Gabe throws me a glance that tells me I'll find you alone again then walks off without another word.

Cupping my cheeks, Damon whispers, "I will not let him hurt you. I promise."

I nod, sliding away from his grasp as new students stop at our booth. In the distance, Damon and I see Gabe slide into his car. Damon punches the booth, swearing loudly.

Hazel hands Damon some ice, then tells me, "You can take the bad boy out of the fighting ring, but you can't take the fight out of the bad boy, can you?" She smiles, but the tinge of worry in her voice makes me shudder.

I cannot exactly accuse Gabe based on a look he gave me. He doesn't show up again the entire day, but I know he's watching.

Chapter Thirty-One: Dani

The next weeks pass in a whirlwind. I'm doing five courses, and that still proves to be a full-time job. Damon's doing four, but also works a lot of hours with James. Thank God we're on the same team in the business project. Otherwise, I'd barely see him.

"I need a break, or my brain will explode," Hazel complains. It's three o'clock in the morning, and Damon, Hazel, Chase, and I are in our living room, busting our asses to get the presentation for our business class ready. Hazel and Chase sit under the window with their laptops in their arms, while Damon and I have taken over the opposite corner of the room. "I can't believe we're having exams already. How are you guys doing?"

"Bickering over who will present tomorrow," I say.

"No bickering," Damon says in a final tone. "We'll both present."

"But I hate presenting and you're great at it."

"You're good at it, too. It's just out of your comfort zone. You've worked hard on this project. If you don't present, you'll sell yourself short. Everyone always remembers the presenter."

"Is this another piece of wisdom you got from my brother?"

"Yeah, but it's true, and you know that."

The thing is, I do. "I'm scared," I say quietly, staring at my knees.

He lifts my chin with his fingers, so I have no choice but to look him in the eyes.

"You are great; you just let your fears keep you back, and sometimes you need a little push. I volunteer to do that. You push me, too. Hell, I'm at Stanford because you pushed me to apply. You're never going to get out of your comfort zone if you don't try to break through it."

"You're right," I say.

"Do you remember Rhetoric & Public Speaking class?" A mischievous smile plays on his lips.

"Yeah, I wore the red scarf you gave me."

Leaning into me, he says. "Let's try the panties trick now." The commanding tone and the scent of his skin—impossible to ignore when he's so close—are almost enough to make me lose my trail of thought and accept. Almost.

"Damon Cooper," I say under my breath, "I am not going to stand in front of a class full of people without underwear. Forget it. But I will wear the red scarf again."

"You still have it?" The emotion in his voice tugs at my heartstrings.

"Yeah, I kept it after you left. It reminded me of you."

"God, you two are adorable," Hazel says, making us both jump. She's standing a few feet away. I hadn't realized she was this close. Judging by the uncomfortable look on Damon's face, neither had he. "I would have been severely heartbroken if you hadn't gotten back together. I need to find you a couple name. "

"What?" Damon looks at her as if she's speaking pig Latin.

"Don't open that can of worms ...it's a girl thing," I say.

"It's difficult because both your names start with D," Hazel continues undeterred. "Maybe I can use your middle name, Gemma. You could be Gamon or Demma."

"They both sound terrible," I interject.

"How about D&D?" Her eyes light up.

"I refuse to have a couple name that's a stand-in for Dungeons and Dragons," I say heatedly.

"What is going on?" Damon asks, looking at Hazel and me as if he fears we might be losing our minds.

"Nothing. You'll just be the perfect power couple," she announces.

"Shouldn't you go back to your presentation?" I ask.

"We're taking a break." She puts her hands on her hips, tilting her head to one side and then the other one. "My neck is stiff."

"You've taken a break every hour," I accuse.

"Yeah, Chase is convinced his neurons will get fried otherwise." Chase is watching a YouTube video.

"He'll ace the presentation tomorrow. He always does. I need more coffee," Hazel complains.

"That's not a bad idea," I mutter as Hazel is already walking with determined strides to our coffee machine.

"We've run out of coffee," she announces. "How is that possible? We don't have chocolate, either."

Chase jumps to his feet so fast I swear I hear his knees snap. "I'll go to the vending machine real quick and get you a coffee," he says to Hazel.

"How considerate of you," I say.

"Trust me; I've seen Hazel low on chocolate and coffee. Not pretty."

"Very funny," Hazel says. "I'll come with you. Anyone else want coffee?"

Both Damon and I raise our hands. As Chase and Hazel leave, I can't help but wonder what his deal is. It's obvious he likes her. He attends to her every need, from carrying her books to making sure she has her coffee, and still he won't ask her out.

"Let's take a break, too," Damon says, massaging his temples. He leans on his back on the floor, propping his head on a book. "What's with all these brochures about majors?" He points to the shelf behind me.

"I'm just doing a bit of reading, trying to decide what I'll pick."

"Relax, Dani. You don't have to declare a major yet."

"Yeah, but I already want to know what I want to do so I can work toward it. I'm used to knowing what I want."

"You're too harsh on yourself. That's what the first part of college is for. Soul-searching. Well, between parties and assignments. Haven't you heard the phrase, Not all those who wander are lost?"

I stare at him in amazement. "That's from The Lord of the Rings." I don't say anything else, at a loss for words.

"Yeah. After I left, I…" He looks away, but I catch a glimpse of his glassy eyes. "Well, you liked it so much, I wanted to see the movies. And then I thought, if I do it, I'd better do it right. I read the books first."

"And?"

"You were right. The movies are cool, but the books are way better. Also, I will never call you my precious again," he says. I burst out laughing and Damon joins me, the clouds in his gaze dissipating. Our separation didn't leave marks only on me. Between the red scarf and the books, we both carried each other's absence with us. It weighted like a rock and hurt like a punishment. "So, about that quote."

"If they have a map, they don't get lost. That's what I want. I don't want to know exactly how my future will look. I just want a map. You have one."

"I do?"

"Yes. You're a talented programmer and one day, you'll have your startup, probably in healthcare."

"What?" Soft laughter escapes his lips as he sits up straight.

"You're not the only one talking to James. He is my brother, you know."

"I have no recollection whatsoever of ever telling James that. Did he say I said that?"

"Well, no. He said you are very interested in the healthcare industry and are super good at what you do—in fact, so good, he thinks you might leave his company soon and start your own. That was just he and I reading between the lines."

For a few seconds, Damon just stares at me, but then his face splits into a grin. "Dani, I think you just gave me my map. I'll help you find yours."

"Okay," I say. His grin is so contagious I can't help laughing, too. "Where the hell are those two with our coffees?"

"Let's go check on them."

There is a vending machine down the hall, and we find Hazel in front of it. She's chatting with a guy who lives on the second floor of our building, Anthony. He's on the soccer team and hovers around Hazel whenever he gets a chance.

"Where's Chase?" I ask.

"This machine's run out of anything but watered-down cappucino, so he went to check the one in the next building." On cue, the doors open and Chase comes in carrying four cups. Damon and I hurry to him, relieving him of two of them, while Hazel and Anthony stay back, talking about Anthony's upcoming game.

Chase acknowledges Anthony with a forced smile, saying loudly, "Okay, everyone, break's over."

Hazel jumps slightly, running her hands over her arms as if she's suddenly cold. "It was nice talking to you, Anthony. I have to get back to work."

"Sure, me, too. Nothing like cramming the day before the exam. So, listen, why don't you come to my next game? It's at the end of the week. We can go grab dinner afterward."

Hazel's eyes widen, but before she manages to get one word out, Chase shoves her cup of coffee in her hand, putting an arm around her shoulders. "We still have exams next week; she'll be busy studying."

Anthony looks taken aback for a second, but then his eyes narrow on the way Chase plays with a strand of Hazel's hair.

"Well, I'll see you around, Hazel," he says.

Hazel pushes Chase away just as Anthony disappears up the stairs. "What are you doing? He was asking me out."

"Yeah...he's a soccer player, which equals dumbass," Chase replies.

"You don't know that."

Chase takes a sip of his coffee. "Everyone knows that."

"He has a point," Damon says to Hazel, then turns to Chase, "but it's still her call if she wants to go on a date with him."

Chase shrugs, drinking up again. He's trying to play it cool. It's high time for me to have a little chat with Chase.

***

My chance to corner Chase comes the next day after the presentation. I didn't do badly at all. I spot Chase sitting at a table in the cafeteria, eating a sandwich all by himself. He gulps down large bites while reading the textbook lying on the table. Since I am still wearing the red scarf from the presentation, I feel particularly bold.

"Is this how you trick everyone?" I ask as I approach him. "You tell them you don't need to study at all for exams then cram all by yourself?"

He looks up, his nonchalant expression firmly in place. "I do plenty of studying with Hazel, too."

"Glad you brought her up." I pull up a chair and sink in it without an invitation. "I want to talk to you about her."

"Oh, going all bossy on me." He slams the book shut, leaning over the table and giving me his most charming smile. "I'm all ears."

"You like Hazel."

His eyes widen infinitesimally, but otherwise, he displays no signs that I took him by surprise. "I like girls. Hazel is a girl," he says in a clipped tone.

"Don't play mind games with me. I'm immune to your jerkish charm." I lean forward, as if to prove that he doesn't affect me even when I'm close.

"No one is immune." His words are faltering, and he starts eyeing the door as if plotting his escape. Perfect. My instinct was right. I'm onto something.

"You like her more than a friend."

He jerks violently in his seat as if I've just poked him with a needle. I have shaken the great Chase.

"Did she tell you that?" He picks up the pen lying beside the book, twisting it compulsively between his fingers. A vein pulses in his temple.

"No, she told me the exact opposite, but I've seen the way you look at her."

His demeanor changes in an instant. He drops the pen, his usual conceited smile making an appearance again. "Oh, right, and you're an expert on dating?"

"I'm not, but I am Hazel's best friend."

"Just drop this, okay?"

"If you like her, why don't you ask her out?"

Chase runs a hand through his hair, shaking his head. "I'm the kind of guy every girl wants to bang and then move on to someone better. Despite my best efforts, it never takes more than a month for me to screw up. Hazel is the only girl who's stuck next to me for more than half a year. I refuse to screw that up by screwing her. Yes, I like her, but she deserves a better guy."

I stare at him for a long time, trying to read him and gauge whether he's telling the truth.

"Well, then stop throwing death stares at every guy she meets."

He jerks his head up, searching me with desperate eyes. "Is it that obvious?"

"Yeah, it is for anyone who pays any attention."

"I can't help it." Chase wets his lips, shaking his head. "Just the thought of her doing another guy makes me want to rip someone's head off."

"Look, Chase," I say firmly. "You either ask her out or step aside and let someone else do it. You have to decide; you can't have it both ways."

My talk with Chase turns out to be a failure of epic proportions. Instead of making a move on Hazel, he ditches her the next evening when they were supposed to watch a movie together, as friends. We start watching said movie in the living room of our quarters and end up doing a movie marathon, ordering pizza, eating chocolate, and calling Chase all the obscenities we can come up with.

It's past midnight when someone knocks at our door.

Chapter Thirty-Two: Damon

When she opens the door, I cradle her head with my hands, kissing her hungrily.

"Hello to you, too," she murmurs, smiling against my lips.

"Hi." I kiss her again, pulling her up close. "Had a rough day. Can I crash here tonight? The guys are having a mini-party back in my room, and my brain will explode if I don't get some sleep."

She pulls away, placing her hands on her hips. "Have you been with James ever since we finished the presentation yesterday?"

"Yes, but—"

"I need to have a talk with my sweet brother. He's completely overworking you."

"We made some real progress on a project, so it wasn't all for nothing."

"Like that's an excuse." She softens a bit. "Come in."

One look at Hazel makes it clear I'm intruding on a girls' night. "Err, is it really okay if I crash here?"

"Come in, Damon," Hazel answers. "You'd better prepare yourself to be surrounded by so much estrogen, you might grow boobs."

"Ewww, Hazel, come on..." Dani complains.

"I'll take what I can get. If it means I can get some time with my girl." I shrug then notice the open box lying on the floor. "And eat pizza. Can I eat that?"

"Yep."

I gulp down the pizza, looking from Hazel to Dani and back.

"So what kind of progress did you and James make today?" Dani asks.

"Some investors came to us today with a shitty offer. I told them I can smell bull from miles away, and they stink so bad, my eyes are almost watering."

Dani gapes at me. "And James is okay with that?"

I nod. "He knew their offer would be shitty, but he must remain diplomatic. He gave me the go to call bull when I see it. That way, it won't impact his relationship with them on the long term. After all, I'm just an intern with a big mouth—"

"And even bigger balls," Hazel says. "Is this sort of a 'good cop, bad cop' thing?" She raises an eyebrow.

"Exactly like that."

"And it works?" Dani asks.

"Yes. They sent us a higher offer a few hours later. James is considering it."

Dani bursts out laughing. "I can imagine you in James's office, playing off your bad boy charm with women and telling off anyone who crosses you."

"No one bosses me around," I say. "Not even your brother's trying it."

"Yeah, well, James is smart. I'm glad you two are getting along so well."

The conversation fades after that, and Dani and Hazel exchange glances.

"Whatever guy troubles you're having, spill it, Hazel," I say.

"What?" Hazel sputters.

"Is it that obvious?" Dani asks.

"Now you just confirmed it. Maybe he was bluffing," Hazel says, elbowing her.

"He wasn't bluffing."

"I wasn't. It's written all over you. Don't you want a guy's opinion? I'm here anyway." When Hazel still looks unsure, I add, "Is this about Chase?"

Slumping her shoulders, she pulls her knees to her chest, leaning her head on the backrest of the couch. "Great."

"I think Chase likes you." At her surprised look, I add, "Wasn't that obvious?"

"That's how guys treat a girl when they like her? How do they act when they hate her? And they say girls are hard to understand." Hazel huffs.

"I don't know him well, but I bet he's never been in a serious relationship. He just doesn't have the balls to ask you out."

"This might be a good time to tell you that I talked to Chase yesterday and told him exactly that," Dani confesses, looking miserable.

Hazel pales. "You...why did you do it?"

"He needed to hear it. I thought I was helping. Sorry."

Several minutes pass in awkward silence, and then Hazel says, "I'm going to bed." Dani opens her mouth, but Hazel cuts her off. "I'm not mad at you, Dani. It's been a long day. Are you coming to sleep, too? Damon, do you need a pillow or something?"

"I don't need a pillow," I say. "Dani, can you stay with me a while longer?" I crack a knowing smile, my gaze dipping to her nipples, which have turned to hard nubs, pressing against her flimsy t-shirt.

"I'll be wearing ear plugs," Hazel announces from the doorway.

"Hazel," Dani says, mortified.

"It's because the hotties above us snore loudly sometimes." By the way Dani narrows her eyes, I can tell no one above them snores. "So, in case you two...you know. No need to worry about me." With that, she disappears into the room. Dani looks after her, stunned. Well...I suppose their friendship has just reached a new level if Hazel pre-emptively uses earplugs.

"Come here," I beckon, moving from the floor to the couch, and Dani immediately straddles me. I wait all of two seconds before sliding a hand under her shirt and cupping her breasts.

"I thought you were tired." A deep throb starts in my jeans. She moves her legs to sit more comfortably, and as she settles over me, she feels my erection pressing against her.

"For this?" I push her shirt up, uncovering her breasts, then take a nipple between my lips, running my tongue over it. "Never." She shudders in my arms as if an electrifying tingle strikes right through her center.

I push her on her back, and she loses her balance for a split-second, but then firmly lodges her feet on the couch as her back lands on the soft cushion. I run my tongue from one nipple to the other, then descend to her navel and linger at the hem of her shorts. She arches her hips, eager for more. Unhitching my lips from her skin, I stand on my knees. I caress her ankles in a sensual gesture, my head tilted to the right. I lift her right leg up, pushing it toward her, my eyes not leaving hers. Then I plant my wet lips on the skin behind her knee.

"Damon," she gasps, her legs wobbling so strongly, I might have kissed her directly on her folds.

"You like that?"

"Yes," she says in surprise.

"I know something you'll like even more."

"Oh, yeah?" she challenges. "What?"

"Mmm..." I dip my fingers in the elastic band of her pajama shorts, pulling them down her legs in slow motion. I blow a whiff of air over her dripping slit and she closes her eyes, biting her lower lip hard.

"Oh," she growls when I spread her wetness up and down her slit with my fingers.

"I want to kiss you here." I press my thumb on her clit, prompting her to dig her nails in the cushion beneath her. Need flares through both of us. I open her knees, settling between them, looking up at her beautiful face while I bury my lips in her crotch. My tongue laps up and down her wetness while my fingers pinch her clit playfully, then dance in a rhythmic swing that drives her blind with pleasure. She closes her eyes, as if lightheaded and hoping to pull herself together. I won't give her that chance.

I plunge my tongue inside her while my fingers continue to circle her clit.

"Oh, no, no, no..." She groans. My thoughts scatter as I watch her, my pulse ratcheting up to an impossible speed. I become painfully aware of the tension building at the base of my spine. "Pillow," she mutters. "Need...pillow." She dislodges one of the pillows, pulling it over her face and biting into it hard as her orgasm erupts inside her, making her burn and spasm around my tongue.

A few minutes later, she discards the pillow, throwing it on the floor, drawing in a lungful of air. I watch her chest heave up and down and then kiss my way up to her neck, and then finally hovering over her mouth. I get rid of my clothes. My rock-hard erection presses against her inner thigh.

"I want you so badly," I say raggedly. She palms my erection, pumping her hand along its length. I swallow hard. "I don't have a condom."

"I started birth control pills ten days ago. We don't need a condom," she says. I hesitate, though my entire body is rigid with the effort of controlling myself. "You don't trust me?"

"Of course I do." Tapping my fingers on her shoulder, I plant a soft kiss on her cheek, trailing my lips to her ear. "It's just that I've always used a condom."

"Then this will be the first time. I finally get to be your first at something."

"I had many firsts with you, Dani." I catch her earlobe between my teeth, tugging at it gently. "You are the first woman who made me feel alive, the first one I've fallen in love with. And you will be the last one," I whisper. She tips her head up, kissing me, answering my unspoken question. She wants me to be her last love, too. She guides my erection to her entrance, even though her body is still recovering from the orgasm.

"God." I bury my head in her neck as I slide inside her, cupping her ass cheeks with both hands. "Dani... Oh, fuck." My next words stumble out in an incomprehensive sentence. Dani isn't doing any better. She seems unable to breathe properly, let alone talk. The feel of skin on skin, caressing her inner flesh without barrier, is out of this world. "You feel so good. We are never using condoms again."

"I'm right there with you." Her words come out in such a weak whisper I almost don't hear her. I pull out of her and lift her legs on my shoulders, positioning a cushion under her ass. I plunge inside her again, deeper than ever, making her thighs quiver. My hands graze over her legs, my nails digging in her thighs while I cover her ankles with lavish kisses.

Then I tilt slightly forward, changing the angle. It drives her crazy. Sweat forms on my forehead, falling in small drops right above her clit. It's such a turn-on, I almost come this very second, but I force myself to breathe in and out, to last longer.

"Touch me," she begs, looking at me. Her eyes widen, but she is beyond shame at this point. I flick my fingers over her clit, slowly making us both come undone.

"You are so sexy," I growl.

My orgasm hits fast and hard, and I have no time to bite into any pillow before it shakes me. I'm still lost in it all when I hear Dani cry out.

I rest my chin on the crook of her neck, and after a few minutes, she says, "This was..."

"Intense," I finish for her.

"I hope Hazel's earplugs work," she says, giggling. "We should get dressed, though." She collects our clothes from the floor, and we put them on fast.

"Stay with me," I say.

"Okay." She lies down again. "There's plenty of space for both of us." A loud bang comes from the corridor, followed by the sound of someone throwing up. Another few minutes pass in silence, and then she asks, "Have you heard from Gabe lately?"

"No." My heart stings as I feel her tense beside me.

"Maybe that means he's just dropped the whole thing."

"Yeah, maybe," I say evasively. Or maybe not. James is having him watched, but so far, nothing. He hasn't made an appearance since that morning weeks ago, but I know him. He won't give up. Not while he's free, anyway.

"So, how come you didn't stay at the party in your room? How could you say no to that?" she asks, in an obvious attempt to change the subject.

"I wouldn't want to be anywhere else but here. I love you, Dani."

"I love you, too," she says. I smile against the back of her neck, giving her a tight hug. She falls asleep, but I remain wide awake, thinking about Gabe and everything that can go wrong.

Whatever happens, I will not let her go again.

Chapter Thirty-Three: Dani

My parents visit me on campus the weekend after the most hellish exams week, which means I have to skip the lazy day at the beach I had planned with Hazel. Chase, who was looking for a way to make up for ditching her last week, offered to keep her company the second I bailed, so I don't think she was too disappointed. They took off for the beach this morning. One hour ago, I received a text from Hazel with strict instructions to get rid of my parents at seven o' clock at the latest. She and Chase were invited to a party off-campus and she immediately agreed on mine and Damon's behalf. I never thought I'd say that, but a college party feels exactly like what I need right now after exams. When I text Damon about the party, he sends back, Bring it on, along with an emoticon of a champagne bottle. I guess he needs to let loose a bit, too.

My parents arrive at noon, and I show them my room and the campus, then we watch one of Stanford's drama groups rehearse Romeo and Juliet for two hours. We end up in the cafeteria for an early dinner.

"Why is this place so empty?" Dad asks as we take our trays to one of the numerous empty tables.

"It's the weekend and exams are over. Most people are on the beach. Except for Damon. He's working."

"James is not going easy on him at all, is he?" Mom shakes her head as we sit at a table.

"The two found each other. Two workaholics," I say.

"You should save Damon while you can," Dad points out.

"Says the recovered workaholic." I smile at him, loving seeing him relaxed and happy.

"Better late than never."

"Speaking of workaholics who found each other, I don't know what to do with James and Serena. They left their entire wedding organization to me."

"Mom," I admonish gently. "You love throwing parties. Don't act like you're not enjoying that James and Serena pretty much left you to your own devices."

"You just wait for it." Mom's face splits into a contagious smile. "The wedding will be epic."

"Epic, huh?" I wonder where my mother's picking her vocabulary from these days. "Dad, your food is getting cold."

Dad draws in a deep breath as if bracing himself to eat what's on his plate. His food consists of steamed broccoli and fish. I didn't even know the cafeteria had this kind of food. As my mom goes on and on about the wedding, I watch my father glance over his shoulder, and then under the table with a guilty look in his eyes I know only too well. He hopes to find a way to get rid of his food. I press my lips together.

"How were exams?" Dad asks eventually, after forcing himself to swallow some broccoli.

"I have a good feeling. I have this very interesting business course—"

"Wait, you took a business course?" Dad gapes at me as I nod. "And you liked it?"

"I loved it." I tell them more about the course as we eat, then Mom gives us some more details about the wedding.

Dad keeps his eyes trained on her, absorbing every word. I'm not sure if it's the words themselves he's absorbing, or just her presence. From time to time, he drags his hand over the table toward her, as if he'd like to take her hand, but doesn't quite dare to. Yet.

"Tell us more about Damon," Mom beckons as if reading my thoughts. I gulp, playing around with my fork.

"Yeah, we hear more about him from James than from you," Dad adds.

"This is news to me." I squint. "What's all this you hear from James?"

"That he has an excellent work ethic and is very determined." Mom rubs her chin, pinching her brows together. "And talented," Mom adds.

"I used to think Damon was very bad for you." Dad says this so matter-of-factly, I can't help laughing.

"Now you don't anymore?" It's not like his opinion of Damon would change my feelings for him, but I'd be less tense when they eventually meet each other.

Dad holds his hands up, as if saying, I'm not sure. "According to your brother, he's changed a lot from the rebel with self-destructing tendencies he was in high school. I will give the benefit of the doubt to anyone who's willing to put so much effort into turning his life around."

Mom leans over the table, dropping her voice to a conspiratorial whisper, "Your brother has been lobbying Damon a lot."

I am so happy right now I could hug them. "I think you two can finally meet Damon."

"So, this was a test?" Dad grins.

"Yes, sir. Can't have you scare off my boyfriend."

Dad shrugs, pleased with himself, then tries to steal a slice of beef from my plate. Mom slaps his hand, frowning at him.

"You're not allowed red meat, you know that," she says.

"I can't be condemned forever to a life of fish and vegetables. I need some toxins in my system."

"You're not eating that." She glares at him while pointing at the tiny piece of beef stuck in his fork.

"Okay, okay." Dad puts the beef back on my plate and resumes eating his food. Mom makes a point of looking at him until he gulps down the very last bite. He looks up at me hopefully a few times, silently pleading for me to help out. I love my dad, but I draw the line at steamed broccoli and fish. I just give him my most sympathetic look.

"Did we tell you we plan to move?" Mom asks.

"No. When? Where?"

"Nothing's set yet, but somewhere next to San Francisco, so we'll be closer to you and James."

"We're thinking of buying a small house, maybe a bungalow," Dad fills me in.

I stare at them. "You live in a palace and want to move into a bungalow?"

"Our house is just too big. We don't need that much space," he explains. "It's just the two of us now."

"Wow. Do you have any other life-changing news to share?" I ask.

"I'm thinking of selling the chocolate factory, too."

"No way." It feels like a punch in my gut. "Why?"

My father starts explaining his reasons, and I can't say he's wrong, but I feel a deep sense of loss at the news.

"Well, I think you had enough bad news for today," Mom says after everyone finishes eating.

"But it's only six o'clock," I protest.

"Your dad is getting tired." She watches him wearily. "And surely a freshman has better things to do than hang around with her parents on a Saturday night?"

"I'm going to a party," I admit sheepishly, "but it's not until later."

"Well, use this time to get prepared. Enjoy it. A little fun never hurt anyone."

"True," I agree.

We couldn't be more wrong.

Chapter Thirty-Four: Dani

My head still spins from my parents' news when I arrive at the address Hazel texted me. The two-story house is remote. That's good. The wild dancing on the porch and the booming music wouldn't get love from any neighbors. Hazel is not outside, and I brace myself before going inside. I recognize a couple of people from campus, but there are mostly strangers here, which makes me uneasy. I find Hazel in the main room, dancing her ass off with Chase, who has his hands firmly on her hips, holding her very close to him. Well, well, well. Not one to want to interrupt a love story in the making, I peek around to see if I can find someone I know until Damon arrives. Before I can disappear, Hazel sees me and motions for me to come to them. Chase gives me a smug grin as he places a soft kiss on Hazel's shoulder, not letting go of her waist.

"What's wrong?" Hazel asks, swinging her body with an energy that makes me think she's had one too many tequilas.

"Dad wants to—" I begin, practically yelling into her ear. She pushes me away, shaking her head.

"Dani, I am a bit drunk, not deaf."

"Dad wants to sell the chocolate factory," I say in a more measured tone.

Hazel's eyes bulge. "What, why? Let's go someplace quieter." Turning to Chase, she rises on her tiptoes and speaks into his ear.

"I'll just wait for you around here. Don't be gone for long." He looks at Hazel with such a heartfelt longing that I am practically swooning.

"Okay, let's go." Hazel takes me by the arm, and we manage to navigate out of the room without bumping into anyone.

"Are you two on a date?" I ask once we're on the corridor. I blink, looking around startled. I swear there are twice as many people inside than when I walked in a few minutes ago. When did all these people arrive?

"Yes." Her gaze is dreamy and full of hope.

"We can talk later. I don't want to crash your first date."

"No, it's okay; I was hoping I could get to talk alone to you." Blushing seriously, she adds, "Let's find a quieter place. I need some advice on something."

"Hazel!" I come to a halt, doing my best to give her a death stare. "It's too soon for sex."

"Gee, could you have been louder?" One look around us proves that no one's paying any attention to us.

"Sorry," I drop my voice to a whisper, "but it is too soon."

"I wasn't going to ask about sex, just about...doing other stuff."

We find refuge on a dark and narrow staircase everyone ignores. The main staircase that everyone uses to get to the upper floors is only a few feet away, but that's far enough. No one can overhear us.

"Spill everything, right from the start."

"Well, I owe it to you. We talked today on the beach, and he said you verbally flogged him, and he realized he was an idiot. The next part is a bit fuzzy. He asked if I want to date him, and I panicked so I'm not sure if my answer was intelligible at all, and then he kissed me."

"On the beach?"

"Yep," she says with a big grin, straightening her shoulders and pushing her chest out a tad.

"I'm so happy for both of you."

"So..." Her expression becomes sober again, and she lowers her eyes to the floor. "I've known Chase for more than half a year."

"Yeah, but trust me, it's too early for sex. What's the rush?"

"Well, he's been with a lot of girls, and I just think he expects..." Her voice trails away as she starts rubbing her palms up and down her thighs as if they're suddenly sweaty.

"Did he say something?"

"No, I'm just assuming that."

"Of course you are. We're best friends for a reason. I thought the same thing when I met Damon." Hazel snaps her gaze up, looking half-relieved, half-skeptical. "Look, if he cares about you—and I think he does—he'll be happy to wait until you're ready."

"Dani, Hazel." I whip my head to one side. Damon hurries toward us, sporting a panty-melting grin. He kisses me the second he's close enough, and the desire to be alone with him hits me hard and unapologetic. By the way his lips linger on mine, I can tell he feels the same. "Why are you two hiding here?"

"We wanted someplace quiet," Hazel says quickly, blushing even more furiously than earlier. "Where we could talk..." Damn Hazel and her pearl-white complexion. In a fraction of a second, her face gets a violent shade of red, and I jump in before Damon can figure out what we were talking about.

"So I could tell Hazel why Dad wants to sell the chocolate factory. I might lose my best friend. Sometimes I think chocolate was the only reason Hazel decided to be friends with me."

Hazel elbows me gently before admitting, "No bonding like that over chocolate." Wrinkling her nose, she asks, "Is this weed I'm smelling?"

"Ugh." I acknowledge the scent.

"Definitely," Damon says.

A tall, athletic-looking girl materializes out of nowhere. She looks like she had something stronger than weed.

"Well, this is one classy party," I mutter as the girl leaves.

"I'll leave you two and go back to...dancing," Hazel says. I give her a pointed look before she walks away, then Damon and I sit on the stairs. He pulls me into his lap, kissing my mouth hungrily. My body responds to him immediately, my thighs pressing on him. I fist his hair as Damon's lips descend to my neck, nibbling hungrily.

"I want you." His voice is rough as he cups my chin, looking at me so intensely I start burning on the inside. We launch into another kiss, more passionate than the first one. Heat pools low in my body, more so when Damon cups my ass over my dress, pulling me even closer to him until I can feel just how much he wants me.

A loud burst of laughter behind us makes us both jump and come to our senses. I climb out of Damon's lap, carefully rearranging my dress as I sit on a stair. Next to me, Damon draws in a labored breath. I can't help smiling, but I force myself to look anywhere except at the bulge in his pants. We can't jump each other again.

"I didn't know about the factory sale," Damon eventually says in a strained voice. "James did mention your dad wanted to talk to him, but gave no specifics."

"I talked to Dad earlier and he dropped the bomb."

"But why does he want to sell it? It's doing great, even if he isn't heading it."

"He intended for it to be a family business, and since James has no interest in it and Dad is getting old..." I lean back on the stairs with my hands under my head. "It's such a shame. I love that factory. I always hoped it would stay in our family."

"So, why don't you do something about it?" Damon asks.

"What do you mean?"

"You're part of your family, you know. If James doesn't want it, you can take charge in a few years."

"I never thought about that...the subject never came up." But now that I'm thinking about it, the excitement starts trickling in my veins. I bounce to my feet, no longer able to sit.

"You aced the business course, and you looked like you had fun doing it," Damon continues, evidently encouraged by my reaction. "With the right training—"

"I could work part-time during the term and then full-time during summers," I say, more to myself than to him. "I'd learn my way up. No favors for being the boss's daughter or anything."

"That sounds like a good plan."

I grin. "I just found my map."

"Why don't we go celebrate? Just the two of us."

"You seemed excited about the party when I texted you."

"I know, but now I just want to be with you." He leans into me, dragging the back of his fingers on my cheek. "I love you, Dani."

"I love you, too, and I'd love to celebrate alone with you."

"Let's go."

"I just need to go to the ladies room, and then find Hazel to tell her we're leaving."

"I'll find Hazel," Damon says. "Meet me on the front porch when you're ready."

I groan when I see the line to the bathroom. I wait in line for ten minutes before I give up. A house this big must have a bathroom upstairs. It might not be polite to snoop around, but neither is peeing myself. The music is as deafening upstairs as it was in the dance room, and I quickly identify the culprits for this: two speakers. I inspect the place carefully, looking for a line—the clearest sign of a bathroom—but don't find one. There are at least a dozen couples around me making out, so when my bladder threatens to explode, I finally just say to hell with it and go to the nearest couple. I cringe when I tap the girl on the shoulder. She's too preoccupied with the kiss to budge. I tap harder. Finally, she looks up at me.

"Bathroom?" I mouth, trying to appear as apologetic as possible. She nods toward the door at the end of the corridor, and I all but break into a run toward it.

When I get out a few minutes later, the music seems to have gotten even louder, and the light on the corridor dimmer. Much dimmer. I take out my phone from my purse, using it as a flashlight of sorts. I only make it a few feet before someone grabs both my arms forcefully and pulls me into a room.

Chapter Thirty-Five: Dani

My head collides painfully with wood as my aggressor pins me against the door once we're inside the room. Panic shoots through me. I try to make sense of what's happening. It's pitch-dark, and the only thing I'm aware of besides the pain in my head is the whiff of alcohol coming off him.

A drunkard. I try not to let the panic cloud my thoughts.

"You have it all planned out, don't you?" a familiar voice asks, freezing the blood in my veins.

"Gabe," I whisper, my stomach churning so violently I fear I'll throw up.

He jerks me away from the door and further inside the dark room. "Funny how things work out. I've wanted to get you alone for months, and then you walk right into this party."

"You're selling drugs here." Remembering the girl downstairs, I taste bile at the back of my throat.

"Why, yes...excellent deduction skills." He jerks me forward, causing me to stumble and lose my balance. I bare my hands in front of my face, expecting to hit a wall, but it's my knees that take a full sting when they collide with the metal railing of a bed. I crash in it with a loud cry, clutching my knees tightly, blind from the pain. Light suddenly assaults my eyes. Gabe has turned on a bedside lamp.

In the split-second it takes me to realize this is my one shot to run away, Gabe is already over me, pinning me into the mattress. With the light on, the horror becomes even more real.

"What do you want, Gabe?"

"Cutting right to the chase, aren't you? I'll show you what I want." One of his hands shoots up under my dress, groping my inner thigh hard while his other hand keeps my wrists over my head.

"You don't want to do this," I beg.

"Oh, but I do, and I will."

"I will scream."

"Please do. Who do you think will hear you over the music?"

No one, that's who. And no one knows I'm up here. Sure, Damon will start looking for me if I don't show up soon, but that still gives Gabe plenty of time to have his way with me. I swallow hard, forcing myself to keep my head cool and consider my options. I weigh about half as much as him, and with my hands trapped, I can't push him off. His knees are pinned at either side of my legs, his crotch right above my knees.

"You think you're tough, don't you? Cornering a girl, using your strength to subdue me?" I push my head up to him as much as I can, sharp pain twitching in my arms. It achieves the effect I was hoping for. Gabe takes his hand away from my thigh, groping my chin instead.

"You—" he begins. I swing my left knee upward fast and hard, hitting him squarely in the crotch. "Fuck!" Gabe screams every profanity at me as his body involuntarily bends, releasing his grip on me. I push him off me, slamming my elbow in his jaw. I scramble out of the bed, my feet trembling dangerously. I make a run for the door, and almost make it.

Even though I know no one will hear me over the deafening music outside, I scream for help.

No one arrives. I hear Gabe behind me, but I'm less than a foot away, and my hand shoots forward, clasping the doorknob. Then Gabe fists my hair, pulling me and throwing me on the bed again. My head lolls back, giving me whiplash. By the time I see straight again, Gabe is on top of me already. "Bitch." Something's not right, though. He doesn't have me trapped like before. Yes, he's leaning over me, but my hands are free. That's when I feel something against my neck. It's cold and sharp—the blade of a knife.

"If I were you, I wouldn't move."

"I won't," I assure him, dread creeping deep into my bones. There is no fighting him off now. My breath comes out in a rush.

"So, the rich girl had an existential crisis, didn't she? Didn't know what to do with all that money you've got, and now you'll finally be Daddy's girl?"

"You were spying on Damon and me?" Maybe if I make him talk long enough, I can get him to change his mind.

"I didn't want to let you out of my sight. No one will help you. Not Damon, not even James. It will kill him to live with it...the almighty James Cohen couldn't keep his sister safe. It will serve Damon a lesson, too. Let's see if he still wants you after I'm done with you."

"What do you have against James and Damon?"

"I spent a year in jail because of them."

"You went to prison because you broke the law," I say coldly.

"You rich people always have an answer. Everything comes easy for you. It's great, making plans, isn't it?"

Something about his controlled composure sets off alarm bells, sweat forming on my palms. His face tightens, and his eyes come alive with hatred. "You know who didn't get to make any? My sister. Because your brother and Damon killed her."

"What are you talking about?"

"When your precious James put me in jail, I had a lot of debt toward dangerous people. You're a smart girl, tell me...do you think I could pay them back if I were jailed?"

"No," I whisper.

"No. These aren't patient people. They don't give second chances."

"I don't understand—" I begin, but Gabe cuts me off abruptly.

"I'll explain. They took it out on my sister," he says. Cold fear runs through me as Gabe leans in closer to me. His weight crushes me. "They raped and beat her." Pain flickers somewhere behind all the rage in his eyes. "She killed herself two days later."

"I am so sorry, Gabe." I barely get the words out. My chest heaves, each breath slicing through me.

"You should be. I wonder if you'll do the same after."

"You don't want to do this. It won't bring your sister back," I say with as much calm as I can muster.

"I don't care."

My body starts shaking uncontrollably, beads of sweat forming on my upper lip. Images of what my life would look like if Gabe rapes me flash through my mind with a nauseating speed. My heart slams against my ribcage so violently it blocks out any other sound, including his voice. I don't hear what he says next. My eyes fix on the burning anger in his eyes, on the way his jaw clenches.

"Answer," he bellows, moving away the knife and shaking me so violently that yet another whiplash hits me.

"I didn't—I didn't hear what you said," I stutter. Gabe presses the side of the blade deeper into my skin again, his other hand groping the inside of my thigh, moving higher and higher.

The next seconds pass in a blur. When Gabe's hand reaches the hem of my underwear, the pressure of his knife on my neck weakens. My senses kick into overdrive. I suddenly become aware of every muscle in my body, every weak point of Gabe's, anything that could provide an escape. It's all or nothing now. I'll be damned if I'll let him have anything at all. With a force I didn't even know I possess, I shove his blade-holding hand away. When it touches his chest, Gabe yelps, moving back, looking at his knife in disbelief, checking if I've cut him.

I didn't because the blade was sideways, but this split-second of confusion offers me my one shot. I push my elbows in the mattress, propelling myself upward, then throw myself at Gabe with all my force. He falls back on the bed, ripping a shred of my dress in the process. I try to jack myself out of the bed when I feel his hand close on my ankle. My stomach churning violently, I kick him with my other leg. I don't turn to look where I've hit him, but he growls in pain. I just push myself forward, landing on all fours on the floor.

Half-crawling, half-running, I barrel to the door. The crackling floor behind me announces to me that Gabe is out of the bed, lurching toward me. I barely have time to process the thought when Gabe jams me into the door, squishing my breasts against the wood.

"You bitch." He pushes himself into me, pinning my hands just above my head, holding them with one hand.

"Let me go," I grit through my teeth. My whole body becomes clammy with sweat when I hear him unzip his jeans.

I force myself to breathe in deeply, but pain slices through my chest with the next inhale. My nails graze at the door, hoping against hope it will attract someone's attention. Gulping down hard, I push the next words past my lips. "That's how you're gonna do it? You don't even have the guts to look at me?" I grasp desperately at words, something to halt him.

Gabe flips me around. "Problem solved," he says. I glance down at his unzipped jeans, and any hope of fighting my way out of this crumbles, fear overpowering me. I wish I had the power to turn off my senses. That way, I wouldn't hear his ragged breath in my ear, or smell the whiff of alcohol. I wouldn't feel his hand pressing my wrists above my head so hard it's like he's wrapped them in barbed wire. I wouldn't hear him pushing down his jeans. I've never been this afraid. I once read that fear paralyzes you, dulling the senses. It has the opposite effect on me. I sense everything in the most ruthless detail.

All of a sudden, the music stops, startling Gabe. Then the door bangs open, sending both me and Gabe stumbling forward. I regain my composure, but Gabe, whose dropped pants limit his movement ability, falls flat on his face. I grip the railing of the bed to steady myself as I take in the scene before me. Damon storms inside.

"You bastard," he spits.

Gabe rises to his feet, pulling his jeans up. Then he launches himself at Damon, wielding his knife like a sword. Damon deflects Gabe's arm with such force the knife flies out of his hand, colliding with the wall and dropping on the floor.

"I don't need a knife for this," Gabe says. His face contorts into a grimace as he and Damon start fighting. Both men fight to kill. I scream as Damon receives almost as many punches as he throws.

"They're in here," Chase's voice resounds from the corridor. He and Hazel burst into the room, followed by a police officer. The officer immediately takes Gabe on, putting shackles on his wrists.

Damon hurries to me, wrapping me in his arms.

"Did he—"

"No. If you hadn't arrived, though..." I don't finish the sentence, unwilling to voice those words. I let all his wonderful warmth envelop me, the smell of his skin fill me. I lose myself in him for a few seconds, maybe even minutes, shutting out everything else. I'm still shaking when Hazel pats me on the shoulder lightly, arranging my hair, sniffing silently.

"Hazel, don't cry." I take her hand in mine, squeezing it slightly. "I'm okay. It was just a scare." Both Damon and Hazel stare at me in disbelief. One look at myself reveals why. I hadn't noticed just how ripped apart my dress is. I look like I've been in a life-or-death fight. Behind us, the police officer escorts Gabe out of the room. Gabe recites every profanity he knows, most of them directed at Damon, and some at me. I even hear James's name a few times. Damon fists his hands, his knuckles turning white. I can tell he'd love to retaliate, but he's making an effort to remain by my side. I appreciate it greatly.

"Officer, what are the charges for beating the crap out of a rapist, drug-selling asshole?" Chase inquires.

"Don't worry, young man. He'll get a lot of that in jail. Go to your friends."

"How did you find me?" I ask.

"Damon had us check every room in the house when you didn't come outside," Hazel answers.

Chase looks out the door after the police officer and Gabe disappear through it then glances at us over his shoulder. "Let's get out of here."

"Yeah, let's go," I say. Without warning, Damon lifts me in his arms. I rest my head on his chest, playing around the buttons of his shirt with my fingers, trying to block out everything else. It's a challenge, given that the house is full of unhappy drunkards because the party was shut down. Still, I try. I close my eyes and take deep breaths. When he puts me in the safety of my car, I open my eyes again.

"The police officer wants to talk to you," Damon says.

"Okay."

The officer comes my way and I talk to him for a while, recounting everything. Then Damon secures my seatbelt and places a kiss on my forehead before shutting the door. Hazel and Chase are right outside the car, Hazel tearing up and Chase wiping her tears away, holding her tightly in his arms. I wave at them, forcing a reassuring smile on my face. Behind them, the mayhem of the busted party doesn't paint a pretty picture.

"What happened?" I inquire once Damon's in the car, too. "How did the police get here?"

"Someone alerted the parents about the party." The engine roars to life, and every muscle in my body unclenches. We're finally leaving this place behind.

"A neighbor?"

"Must have been someone from the party because they also knew about the drugs, so the parents came with the police."

"What will happen to Gabe?" A shiver runs down my spine, gooseflesh forming all over my thighs. I do my best to cover them with my dress.

"He'll go to jail again, but for a few years this time."

"Did you know what happened to his sister?"

His eyes narrow infinitesimally, his hands clasping tighter on the wheel. "I found out right after my return. I met her briefly when I first came to California. She was a sweet girl, but had the misfortune to have Gabe for a brother. When he went to jail, he told his creditors his sister was their guarantee that he'd pay everything."

"What? Why did he do that?"

"Desperation."

"He blamed you and James."

"It's always easier to blame others. You are so strong," he whispers, caressing my cheek. "I'm sorry. This is what I wanted to avoid right from the beginning."

"And you did. Gabe didn't hurt me, and now he'll go to jail for years. There is nothing to worry about anymore."

"I'll take you to your dorm and take care of you."

"You're more hurt than I am." I jolt as I take in his wrecked knuckles and tender lip. "I'll take care of you."

"We'll take care of each other."

Damon strokes my hair lightly. I lean in, searching for his lips, needing them to soothe me. When he brushes my lips, I sigh in his mouth, shifting closer to him, needing the warmth of his body. Worry laces his kiss, and he frowns when he returns his attention to the road. I pull my knees to my chest and rest my head on them, remaining cocooned like this for a long time until I drift off to sleep.

Chapter Thirty-Six: Dani

"Are you ready?" Damon watches me with a grin the size of Texas as I descend the steps outside the dorm three weeks later. I'm quite proud of my choice of clothing: a gorgeous, red gown. The shoes were a bad idea. The heels are about two inches too high for me, and every step I take feels like it'll be the last one before I fall flat on my face.

"You look great in a suit. Should wear one more often." He's wearing a black suit and a white shirt, looking more elegant than I've ever seen him, and completely breathtaking.

"It's your brother's rehearsal dinner, and I am officially meeting my future in-laws today. I must make a good impression."

"They'll both be in a frenzy because of the wedding. No one will pay you much attention, trust me."

"That's encouraging. Are you going to talk to your dad about the factory today?"

"I'm certainly going to try." Now that I know what my dream is, I intend to go full steam to get it. "Don't worry about meeting my parents. James lobbied so hard for you since your return that they worship you. Now, let's get to the in-laws bit."

"Did I say that out loud? Whoops." He opens the door of my car, helping me inside.

"You won't hear more about it for another four years, at least. Where are Hazel and Chase?"

"Right here," they both say from behind him. When we're all inside the car, I glance in the rearview mirror at Hazel and Chase, holding hands and smiling at each other.

Then Chase looks at me pointedly. "So, how come Hazel and I are invited to the rehearsal dinner? I thought this would be Damon's awkward meet-the-family day."

"Hazel's invited, and hence, you, too," I say.

"You're coming to make it less awkward," Damon groans, pushing the gas pedal.

"Oh, and you are also meeting Hazel's parents," I point out matter-of-factly.

"What?" Chase looks wildly from Hazel to me, and it's all I can do not to burst out laughing. "You're not serious. Is she serious?"

Hazel nods, grazing her lips with her teeth in an effort not to laugh. "They spontaneously decided to stop by."

"And you all decided to spontaneously give me a heart attack?"

Chase's clumsy attempts to get out of the whole thing punctuate the three-hour drive to my parents' house. For the last part of the journey, Chase and Hazel start bickering. I'm grateful no one brings up the incident with Gabe at the party. In fact, no one's mentioned it at all in the weeks that passed. I had to visit the police station once. Things aren't looking good for Gabe. The officers were throwing around terms like 'seven to ten years imprisonment'. I shake my head, dispersing the thoughts of the incident. It's over; that's all that matters.

When we arrive at my parents' house, the parking lot is full with guest cars.

Damon parks, and then we make our way around the house toward the garden where the official entrance to the ballroom is. When I say official, I mean it. There are arrows with James and Serena's name pointing toward it, as if there's any chance someone might end up at another wedding. I snicker, imagining how much fun Dad made of Mom because of these arrows. The garden looks utterly amazing. With twinkle lights around the trees, it's like we've stepped into a fairytale.

"Are you sure this is the rehearsal dinner and not the actual wedding?" Hazel asks. "There are so many people."

It becomes clear real quick that despite all the hired wedding organizers, my mom is the official whip-cracker here. She's snapping at the service people continuously, and we stay out of her way. Chase and Hazel hover around us. Serena is nowhere, but I do spot James and Dad in the doorway of the ballroom. Parker is with them, which means Jessica is around, too.

"Dad, this is Damon," I point out unnecessarily when James and Dad come to greet us. They shake hands, smiling. No one says anything, and I sneak a glance at James, silently pleading for him to come up with an ice-breaker. Chase was supposed to fulfill the ice-breaker role, but he's too stressed looking around for Hazel's parents.

"Dani has something to tell you." James grins at me. I gulp...well, that wasn't what I had in mind as an ice-breaker.

"Well, I..." My words wither as I notice Dad's smile growing wider. I'm certain he knows all about my plans to work at the chocolate factory.

"You told him," I accuse James. I told James about a week ago.

"Guilty."

My father gives me a bear hug, the kind James always gives me, saying, "I'm sure you'll do great."

"I have thought it all out," I start, ready to recite the speech I've prepared. "I'll start as an intern. I don't want any favors—"

"Dani," Dad interrupts with a good-natured chuckle. "I'm sure you made a ten-year plan. We'll discuss it after the wedding, and you'll tell me everything. Your mother might just have all of our heads if we talk business today. Now, I'd very much like to talk to this gentleman." He looks up at Damon, who's gone suddenly pale. Chase puts his fist in front of his mouth to hide his smile.

That's when Hazel elbows him, pointing in the distance. "My parents have arrived; let's go say hi." Chase goes even whiter than Damon.

I look after Dad and Damon, my stomach squirming tightly. "What does Dad want to talk to him about?"

"Quit the scared face, kid."

"Don't call me kid, James."

"That's right; you're not a kid anymore. Look at you, showing up at my wedding rehearsal with your boyfriend and an agenda to take over the chocolate factory. You once told me you're entitled to life-long cuddling because you're my younger sister. Can I still hold you to that?"

"Yes, but only if you go save Damon. Look, Mom's heading in their direction, too. They'll gang up on him."

"If I go there, she'll corner me."

"What for?"

"Oh, she has an entire list." He runs a hand through his hair, looking more agitated than I've ever seen him. "Have I checked Parker's best man speech, does Serena need any help, are your and Jessica's bridesmaid dresses all right—you name it, it's probably on her list."

"James Cohen." I put my hands on my hips, pulling myself taller. "You're a grown man. You can handle Mom."

"Not when she's overseeing my rehearsal dinner and wedding," he says.

I tilt my head to one side, drilling him with my gaze. "Go."

"Okay, okay."

To my astonishment, James manages to split up the group pretty quickly. He, Mom, and Damon head inside the venue, while Dad walks my way.

"What's the verdict?"

"Verdict? You barely let me talk to him."

"What?" I ask, feigning innocence.

"You think I don't know all the tricks? Should've seen me when I first met your mother's family. I'll say, Damon is doing quite fine," he says. I breathe, relieved, beaming at him. "Any man who makes my daughter feel like she can grab the stars is a man I respect. I don't like to be wrong, but I'm happy I was concerning him. You two are good for each other. You show each other how to find your strengths."

"Thanks, Dad."

We both head inside after that. With the weight of the awkward meeting off my shoulders, I can concentrate on the fact that this is my brother's rehearsal dinner. It takes place in the large ballroom of the house where Mom used to host her charity parties. The decorations surpass anything I've seen before; lavish silk garlands and rich bouquets of orchids fill the entire place. My mother put her heart in this. I find Damon talking to Parker in front of the small bar.

"Cousin, look at you." Parker takes my hand and twirls me around twice. My head spins when I come to a halt. Thankfully, Damon slings a firm arm around my waist. "I must say, I never expected you to walk in here wearing a bright red dress. You seemed too shy for that."

"Well" I glance at Damon, grinning, "things change. How is your best man's speech coming along?"

"It's perfect," Parker says proudly, then takes off with a curt nod to join Jessica. She's talking heatedly with Hazel and Serena, who looks radiant.

"Hey, where's Chase?" I ask. Damon shrugs and we both scour the crowd for him. It's not easy spotting him, but eventually Damon points toward him on the opposite side of the ballroom. Hazel's parents flank Chase, and by the look of it, they're grilling him. "What do you think, should we go help out?"

"Nah, it's more fun watching. I can't believe so many people showed up to the rehearsal dinner. "

Leaning in to him, I whisper conspiratorially, "I know a quiet place not far away from here where we can escape for an hour or so. You might know it; we snuck up inside it twice. If we're careful, no one will notice we're gone."

"Mmmm, that sounds tempting." He tilts my head up, kissing me gently. "Sneaking around again?"

I flash my most mischievous smile. "Some things don't have to change."

Epilogue: Five years later

Damon

"Nervous?" James asks. We're in the living room of the beach house he and Serena own near San Francisco. I look over my shoulder before answering, but Dani is well out of earshot. She and the other girls went on the terrace about ten minutes ago.

"Not at all. I have everything planned down to the last detail."

"Believe him, he really means the last detail." Chase shakes his head, prompting James and Parker to chuckle. After pouring himself a drink, he joins the three of us on the couch.

"If you give me that look again..." Chase warns me.

"What look?" I feign innocence.

"That look that says, Chase, you've been dating Hazel for five years. Get your sorry ass down on one knee and propose. Just because you've decided to doesn't mean I have to."

"He knows the whole repertoire." Parker flashes a huge, shit-eating grin. "That's a laddie."

I raise my hands up in sign of peace. "I won't say one word."

"I will," James offers.

Chase groans. "Please, don't."

"I find married life great," James continues, undeterred.

"Since we're going down that slippery road," Parker adds helpfully, "I also think it's great."

"Let's focus on our boy here." Chase leans back on the couch, raising his glass in my direction. "Wouldn't want him to get cold feet."

"He won't. He knows if he does, there will be nowhere to hide from me." James is smiling while saying this, but I know he's only half-joking.

"See, that's why I'll wait for a while before I propose. Don't want any overprotective brothers hustling my ass."

"Hazel doesn't have any brothers," I point out.

"I'm sure some long-lost ones will show up the second I propose," Chase replies.

"So you have thought about it," Parker teases.

"Shut up," Chase says.

We all do as the door to the terrace opens and the girls come in. Jess is first, carrying her three-year-old daughter, Sarah, in her arms, followed by a highly pregnant Serena, who's talking to Hazel. Dani comes in last. She's wearing a strapless, short white dress that looks gorgeous on her tan skin and hugs her slim curves deliciously. When she looks up at me, she takes my breath away.

Yeah, she still does that five years later, and I'm sure she always will. My girl turned twenty-four today, and we've all gathered here to celebrate. We've had the cake already, and now it's time for her to open her presents. They're all piled up right next to the couch, except mine. It's in the pocket of my jacket, waiting to finally rest on her finger. I've waited long enough for this, and twenty-four seems the perfect age to propose to her. I've wanted to do it since our freshman year at college, but I knew we still had a bit of growing up to do.

Dani worked at the chocolate factory during college, and after graduating, she became the right hand of the CEO. I founded my company during my second year at Stanford. I won't lie, I didn't build it up all on my own; I've had lots of help from James and Parker. But I've learned that taking help doesn't mean I'm weak. It means I'm smart.

Almost unconsciously, I pat my pocket, wondering if Dani will like her ring. I asked James and Parker for tips when I went shopping for it because they bought decent rings for Serena and Jess. At least they both seem happy with their rings. They all look the same to me: big, white, round stone in the center. Turns out James and Parker were as clueless as I was. They pointed me to the shop they bought it from, owned by a friend of theirs. They also pointed me to the same personal shopper who helped them pick theirs. I look at Dani's ring finger again. Yeah, that diamond will fit her just perfectly.

***

Dani

"Anyone else want a second piece of cake?" I help myself to a second serving, watching Jessica trying to braid Sarah's hair. Parker watches them from afar with a dreamy smile; Jess and Sarah wear light pink dresses. The fabric is identical, but the design differs. They look freaking adorable.

"No, thanks," Hazel says. "If I eat anything else, I'll explode."

"Mommy," Sarah asks loudly, looking at Hazel crestfallen. "Why do all these people talk so funny? Didn't they learn how to spell proper words at school?"

"Ah, we're all just lousy Americans," Chase says.

"Sarah, you can't say that," Jess admonishes her. "It's rude."

"Mommy, you are saying it wrong. It's ruuuuuude." Her little mouth curves to form the long u. I bite my tongue to stifle a laugh.

"Ah, that lovely moment when your daughter corrects your accent." Jess plants a huge kiss on her daughter's cheek. "Off you go, your hair's ready." Sarah runs right into my presents pile and starts playing with my gift boxes. Jess and Parker both stand up, but before they can stop her, I motion them that it's all right.

Damon walks up to me, leaning from behind to whisper in my ear, "Can I get another piece of cake?"

"Not until you give me my gift."

"How do you know it's not in the pile?" he asks. I turn around to face him. "You haven't opened the presents."

"I know it's not," I reply. He's hiding something. I've known it since we arrived here a few hours ago. The others are in on whatever he's hiding. They smile at me for no apparent reason like they're all enjoying a private joke or something.

"Let's take a walk."

"Okay." A light flutter settles in my stomach as he takes my hand and leads me outside to the terrace. The mid-July sun burns intensely, making my skin prickle with heat. We descend the staircase to the beach, tossing our shoes aside before we step onto the sand. "I don't see you carrying any gift," I tease.

"It's a small package." Leaning in, he drops his voice to a knowledgeable whisper. "Strong essences are kept in small bottles."

"You bought me a perfume?" I inspect his jacket, looking for the contour of a mini-bottle. It's hard to disguise my curiosity.

His face splits into a grin. "I love this about you."

"What?" Caught off-guard, my eyes snap up to him.

"Your curiosity." He drags his fingers down my cheeks. "The way your eyes light up when you look at me."

My insides melt and I fidget in my spot, sinking half an inch in the sand. Damon takes a step back, dipping his hand into the inside pocket of his coat. I expect him to snatch out a miniature perfume bottle, but his next move whips my breath away. He drops on one knee at the same time he whisks a small jewelry box out of his pocket.

"Not perfume," I whisper, my legs suddenly weak.

"Dani Cohen..." His voice quivers slightly. "You've meant everything to me almost from the day I met you—"

"Surely not. I insulted you that first day."

Damon smiles, cutting through my rambling. "They were good insults; I deserved them. Besides, that's why I said almost. Now, can I finish the question?" he asks. I nod, a strange sensation overcoming me. It's like I've just drunk an entire bottle of champagne by myself and all the bubbles have cumulated low in my stomach. "You will always mean everything to me. Will you marry me?"

The bubbles inside suddenly burst, filling me with euphoria. I stare as he opens the lid of the box, revealing the most beautiful ring I've ever seen. The stone is an emerald, like the color of his eyes. Tearing my gaze from the ring, I look at Damon, drinking him in. I love this man more than anything in the world. Every day, I learn to see the perfection in his love and the beauty in his mistakes. He is mine, and I am his. It's only when I see apprehension creeping in his eyes that I realize he's still waiting for my answer.

"Yes, yes, yes." Once the words are out of my mouth, the euphoria explodes, painting a wide grin on my face. As he slides the ring on my finger, a vision of a mini-me wearing a dress similar to mine, like Jess and her daughter do, flashes before my eyes. "I don't want to ever take it off." I'm practically squeaking.

"You're not supposed to."

"Let's go tell the others. Oh, wait, they already know, don't they?"

Rising to his feet, Damon grins, sliding his arms around my waist and planting a soft kiss on my lips. I'm surprised to discover I'm trembling slightly.

"Nervous?"

"Like it's our first kiss all over again."

"Mmm," he murmurs against my lips. "I remember how delicious that first kiss was." A look of mischief takes hold of his features. "Do you remember what else we did that day?"

Smiling, I turn to look at the beckoning waves of the ocean.

"Skinny-dipping," we say together.

***

THE END

***

Dear Reader,

If you want to receive a FREE copy of my full-length romance Found in Us (retail price $3.99), please type in your browser: http://laylahagen.com/mailing-list-sign-up/

Other Books by Layla Hagen

Titles in the Lost Series

Novella Lost
Lost is a FREE is a prequel novella to Lost in Us and can be read before or after.

Whatever might help him forget his past and numb the pain, James has tried it all: booze, car races, fights, and then some. Especially women. College offers plenty of opportunities for everything. . . Especially when you have a trust fund to spend.

Serena spirals deeper and deeper into a hurricane of pain. But no matter how far she falls, there's no redemption from the overwhelming guilt.

Two souls consumed by their pasts fight to learn how to survive. But all hope seems to be lost.

Until they meet each other.

<u>Available at all online retailers.</u>

***

Lost in Us
The story of James and Serena

Serena has learned to live with her past, locking her secrets and nightmares deep inside her. But when her boyfriend of six years abruptly leaves her, she's catapulted back into pain, nursing a broken heart. When indulging in mountains of chocolate doesn't work, Serena decides the best way to deal with her shattered heart is to indulge in something else. A rebound . . .

The night she swaps her usual Sprite for tequila, she meets James. The encounter is breathtaking. Electrifying. And best not repeated.

James is a successful entrepreneur in Silicon Valley. A man who has amassed a fortune by taking risks. A man who has shunned commitment completely, and still does. He's the exact opposite of Serena. But sometimes opposites attract. Sometimes they give in to burning passion. Sometimes opposites are perfect for each other.

James is everything her damaged soul could want. His kisses are intoxicating, his touch out of this world. He makes her forget. He grants her peace from her pain. But as they grow closer, Serena discovers she isn't the only one with a past.
James carries the scars of a past much darker than hers. One that has left him damaged, hurt, and wary of love. A past that gives him the power to shatter her.

Now James and Serena must find a way to mend one another. Or risk losing each other forever.
<u>Available at all online retailers.</u>

***

Found in Us
The story of Jessica and Parker

Jessica Haydn wants to leave her past behind. Hurt by one too many heartbreaks, she vows not to fall in love again. Especially not with a man like Parker, whose electrifying pull and smile bruised her ego once before. But his sexy British accent makes her crave his touch, and his blue eyes strip Jessica of all her defenses.

Parker Blakesley has no place for love in his life. He learned the hard way not to trust. He built his business empire by avoiding distractions, and using sheer determination and control. But something about Jessica makes him question everything. Not only has she a body made for sin, but her laughter fills a void inside of him.

The desire igniting between them spirals into an unstoppable passion, and so much more. Soon, neither can fight their growing emotional connection.

But can two scarred souls learn to trust again? And when a mistake threatens to tear them apart, will their love be strong enough?

***

Withering Hope
USA Today Bestseller

Aimee's wedding is supposed to turn out perfect. Her dress, her fiancé and the location—the idyllic holiday ranch in Brazil—are perfect.

But all Aimee's plans come crashing down when the private jet that's taking her from the U.S. to the ranch—where her fiancé awaits her—defects mid-flight and the pilot is forced to perform an emergency landing in the heart of the Amazon rainforest.

With no way to reach civilization, being rescued is Aimee and Tristan's—the pilot—only hope. A slim one that slowly withers away, desperation taking its place. Because death wanders in the jungle under many forms: starvation, diseases. Beasts.

As Aimee and Tristan fight to find ways to survive, they grow closer. Together they discover that facing old, inner agonies carved by painful pasts takes just as much courage, if not even more, than facing the rainforest.

Despite her devotion to her fiancé, Aimee can't hide her feelings for Tristan—the man for whom she's slowly becoming everything. You can hide many things in the rainforest. But not lies. Or love.

Withering Hope is the story of a man who desperately needs forgiveness and the woman who brings him hope. It is a story in which hope births wings and blooms into a love that is as beautiful and intense as it is forbidden.

<u>Available at all online retailers.</u>

***

Excerpt from Withering Hope

Chapter 1: Aimee

My last flight as Aimee Myller starts like any other flight: with a jolt.

I lean my head on the leather headrest, closing my eyes as the private jet takes off. The ascent is smooth, but my stomach still tightens the way it always does during take-offs. I keep my eyes closed for a little while even after the plane is level.

When I open up my eyes, I smile. Hanging over the seat in front of me, inside a cream-colored protection bag, is the world's most beautiful wedding dress.

My dress.

It does wonders for me, giving my boyish figure curves. I'll be wearing it in exactly one week. The wedding will take place at my fiancé Chris's gorgeous vacation ranch in Brazil, where I'm heading right now.

I've made this flight numerous times before, but it's the first time I'm traveling in Chris's private six-passenger jet without him, and it feels empty. When I next board this plane, my last name will be Moore, Mrs. Christopher Moore. I sink farther down in my seat, enjoying the feeling of smooth leather on my skin. The emptiness of the plane is accentuated by the fact that there is no flight attendant tonight.

I couldn't bring myself to ask Kyra, Chris's flight attendant, to work tonight. Her daughter turned three today, and she's had the party planned for ages. No reason for her to pay because I decide on a whim that I absolutely have to return to the ranch tonight instead of tomorrow so I can supervise the wedding preparations.

The poor pilot, Tristan, wasn't so lucky—he had to give up what would have been a free night. But he'll forgive me. I've found people are willing to forgive many things—too many in my opinion—from a future bride. I'll have to find a way to make it up to Tristan. Maybe I'll buy him something he'll enjoy as a token of gratitude. That might be a challenge since I don't know Tristan all that well, though he's been working for Chris for a few years. Tristan is very guarded.

I've gotten pretty close to Kyra, who seems beside herself whenever I travel on the plane.

I suspect Chris and the business partners he usually flies with aren't as entertaining as the endless discussions we have about the wedding. But all I have managed with Tristan is to get him to talk to me on a first name basis and crack an occasional joke.

Three hours into the flight, Tristan's voice resounds through the speakers.

"It looks like there will be more turbulence than usual tonight.

It'll be safest if you don't leave your seat for the next hour. And keep your seatbelt fastened."

"Got it," I say, then remember he can't hear me.

The plane starts jolting vigorously soon after that, but I don't worry too much. Tristan Bress is an excellent pilot, even though he's only twenty-eight—just two years older than I am. I've made this flight often enough. I'm almost used to the occasional turbulences. Almost.

I peek out the window and see we are flying over the Amazon rainforest. The mass of green below is so vast it gives me goose bumps. I gulp. Even though I'm not scared, the continuous jolts do affect me. An unpleasant nausea starts at the back of my throat, and my stomach rolls, somersaulting with each brusque movement of the plane. I check the seat in front of me for the sick bag. It's there.

I grip the hem of my white shirt with both hands in an attempt to calm myself. It doesn't work; my fingers are still twitching.

I put my hands in the pockets of my jeans and try to focus on the wedding. That brings a smile to my face. Everything will be perfect. Well, almost everything. I wish my parents could be with me on my wedding day, but I lost them both eight years ago, just before starting college. I close my eyes, trying to block the nausea. After a few minutes it works. Even though the flight isn't one bit smoother, my anxiety loosens a bit.

And then an entirely new kind of anxiety grips me.

The plane starts losing height. My eyes fly open. As if on cue, Tristan's voice fills the cabin. "I have to descend to a lower altitude. We'll get back up as soon as possible. You have nothing to worry about."

An uneasy feeling starts forming inside me. This hasn't happened before. Still, I have full confidence in Tristan's abilities. There is no reason to worry, so I do my best not to. Until a deafening sound comes from outside.

I snap my head in that direction. At first I see nothing except my own reflection in the window: green eyes and light brown, shoulder-length hair. Then I press my forehead to the window. What I see outside freezes the air in my lungs. In the dim twilight, smoke paints black clouds in front of my window.

Black smoke swirls from the one and only engine of the plane.

"Aimee," Tristan's voice says calmly, "I would like you to bend forward and hug your knees. Hurry." The measured tone with which he utters each word scares me like nothing else. "We've lost our engine and I am starting the procedure for an emergency landing."

I barely have time to panic, let alone move, when the plane gives such a horrendous jolt that I bang my head on the window. A sharp pain pierces my temple, and a cry escapes from deep in my throat. Sharper pain follows. Piercing. Raw.

My body seems to have moved on its own, because I'm bent over, hugging my knees. Horrible thoughts wiggle their way into my mind. Emergency landing. What percentage of emergency landings go well? My heart races so frantically, and the plane drops so fast it's impossible to imagine it's very high. Another thought grips me. Where will we land? We were over the rainforest last I looked. We couldn't have made it very far since then. My palms sweat, and I grit my teeth as the plane inclines, feeling like I'll be ripped from my seat and propelled forward.

The temptation to raise my head to look out the window is suffocating. I want to know where we are, when the inevitable impact will arrive. But I can't move, no matter how much I try. I'm not sure if it's the plane's position forcing me to stay down or the fear. I tilt my head to one side, facing the corridor. The sight of the protective bag with the dress inside sprawled on the floor makes me forget my fear for a moment, leaving one thought stand out. Chris.

My wonderful fiancé, who I have known since I was a small child and with whom I practically grew up.

With his round, blue eyes and stubborn blond curls, he still looks boyish, even at the age of twenty-seven and dressed in expensive suits.

I'm thinking about him when the crash comes.

Chapter 2: Aimee

I wake up covered in cold sweat and something soft that might be a blanket. I can't tell for sure, because when I open my eyes, it's dark. When I try to move, a sharp pain in my temple makes me gasp.

"Aimee?"

"Tristan." The word comes out almost like a cry. In the faint moonlight coming in through the windows, I see him leaning on the seat in front of me, hovering over me. I imagine his dark brown eyes searching me worriedly.

"Are you hurt?"

"Just my temple, but I'm not bleeding," I say, running my fingers over the tender spot. I assess him next. It's difficult given the dim moonlight. His white uniform shirt is smeared with dirt, but he appears unharmed. I turn my head toward the window. I can't gauge anything outside in the darkness.

"Where are we?" I ask.

"We landed," Tristan says simply, and when I turn to look at him he adds, "… in the rainforest."

I nod, trying not to let the tight knot of fear in my chest overtake me. If I let it spiral out, I may not be able to control it.

"Shouldn't we … like… leave the plane or something? Until they rescue us? Is it safe for us to be inside?"

Tristan runs a hand through his short, black hair. "Trust me, this is the only safe place. I checked outside for any fuel leaks, but we're good."

"You got out?" I whisper.

"Yes."

"I want—" I say, opening my seatbelt and trying to stand. But dizziness forces me back into my chair.

"No," Tristan says, and he slumps in the seat opposite mine on the other side of the slim aisle. "Listen to me. You need to calm down."

"How deep in the forest are we, Tristan?"

He leans back, answering after a long pause. "Deep enough."

"How will they find us?" I curl my knees to my chest under the blanket, the dizziness growing. I wonder when Tristan put the blanket over me.

"They will," Tristan says.

"But there is something we can do to make it easier for them, isn't there?"

"Right now, there isn't."

"Can contact someone at base?" I ask weakly.

"No. We lost all communication a while ago." His shoulders slump, and even in the moonlight, I notice his features tighten. His high cheekbones, which usually give him a noble appearance, now make him look gaunt.

Yet instead of panic, I'm engulfed in weakness. My limbs feel heavy. Fog settles over my mind.

"What happened to the engine?" I whisper.

"Engine failure."

"Can you repair it?"

"No."

"There is really no way to send anyone a message?"

"No." As if in a dream, I feel Tristan put a pillow under my head and recline my seat.

I close my eyes, drifting away, thinking of Chris again. Of how worried he must be.

Chapter 3: Aimee

285

It's daytime when I open my eyes; weak sun rays illuminate the plane. I've slept with my head in an uncomfortable position, and it's given me a stiff neck. I massage my neck for a few minutes, looking around for Tristan, but he isn't anywhere in sight. I try to breathe in, but the air is thick and heavy, and I end up choking. Desperate for fresh air, I look up and discover the door at the front of the plane is open. So Tristan must be outside. I stand slowly, afraid the dizziness from last night might return. It doesn't. I avoid looking out the windows as I walk through the aisle between the two rows of seats, running my hands on the armrests of the three seats on each side. If I'm about to have the shock of my life, I prefer to face it all at once, through the door, not snippet by snippet through the windows.

I stop in front of the door, my eyes still on the ground. The metallic glow of the airstairs—the stairs built into the door of the plane—throws me off for a second.

I clench my teeth, pick up my courage, and step forward into the doorway, looking up.

And then I wince.

The view outside the door does not disappoint. It is as terrifying as it is beautiful. Green dominates. The vivid, shiny kind that seems to flow with life. It comes in all shapes and sizes, from lush, dark leaves the size of a tennis racket to the moss covering trees. There is no pattern to the leaves of the trees. Some are heart-shaped, some round. Some spiky, and some unlike anything I have seen before.

Rays of sunlight lance shyly through the thick canopy above us. Trees block a good chunk of the light. Many trees. Tall trees. They tower over us, and I have to lean my head all the way back to see the canopy properly. I frown.

How did Tristan land this plane here unscathed? One look at my right tells me he didn't. I gasp, my grip on the edges of the doorway tightening. The right wing of the plane is a complete wreck. I assume the other wing isn't much better.

Two gigantic trees have toppled over the right side of the plane toward the back—with such force they have carved a very deep dent in the plane. Glancing back inside the plane, I see they have fallen right over the only bathroom. I realize with horror the bathroom is probably unusable.

Shuddering, I decide to get out of the plane. When I step off the airstairs, my feet get wet. It must have rained a lot recently, because the ground is fluid mud that engulfs my feet right up to the shoelaces of my running shoes. Each step sloshes, spraying muddy water in every direction as I walk. I inhale deeply.

Or at least attempt to. The air is thick with suffocating moisture, but it's not excessively warm. It's been warmer in L.A., where I've lived my whole life.

But never this humid. My shirt and jeans have already begun to stick to my damp skin.

"You're up," Tristan says, appearing at the front of the plane.

His hands are darkened with dust, and he wipes them with a cloth. His white shirt is unbuttoned at the neck and soaked, molding to his muscular frame. The air seems to get thicker by the minute, and I'd rip open my shirt—or skin—if that would help me breathe better.

"Engine still good?" I ask.

"Still dead, just checked it. There's no risk of anything blowing up; don't worry."

"And the communication system?"

"Also dead. The entire electric system is."

"I know it's unlikely they work here, but how about checking our phones?"

"I checked mine last night after the crash. Yours, too; I hope you don't mind. I found your purse. Your tablet, too. No reception, obviously."

I nod, but the sight of the damaged wing unnerves me, so I turn to look at the jungle instead. The wilderness unnerves me even more.

"Beautiful, isn't it?" he asks.

"I'd prefer to view it on TV. I feel like I've stepped into a documentary."

Tristan steps in front of me, eyeing my cheek. "You have a scratch here. I didn't see it last night. But it's very superficial. Nothing to worry about."

"Oh, well..." I raise my hand to my cheek and my voice trails away as I stare at the diamond engagement ring on my left hand. Chris. The wedding. My beautiful, perfect wedding that should take place in less than a week. I shake my head. It will take place. They will rescue us in no time.

"I'm thirsty," I say, turning away from him so he won't see the tears threatening to fill my eyes.

"There are some supplies in the plane. Not much, though. Four cans of soda, which are nothing given the rate at which we'll dehydrate in this climate."

I raise an eyebrow. "We're almost ankle-deep in water. Surely we can find some clever way to have clear water."

"I don't have anything to make a filter good enough to turn this"—he points at the ground—"drinkable. Our best bet is rain."

"How about the water tank in the bathroom?" I ask half-heartedly, thinking of the trees that fell right on top of the bathroom.

"The water tank ruptured—I suspect the moment the trees fell—and the water leaked out."

"Is the bathroom usable at all?" I ask.

"No," Tristan says, confirming my fears. "Everything is wrecked. I crawled inside, and those are the only useful things I could retrieve." He points toward one of the trees that's fallen over the plane. At first I'm confused, but when I look closer I notice there is a pile of what looks like shards of a broken mirror just in front of the tree. "Mirror shards?"

"They are good for signalling our position, among other things."

We both walk toward the pile. I shudder at the sight of the pile of uneven shards.

Most are the size of my palm, a few even smaller. If those trees had fallen over my seat, or the cockpit…

I notice there are a few other things lined up next to the mirror shards. A pack of Band-Aids, eye pads, a pair of scissors, a whistle, needles, thread, a pack of insect repellent wipes, and two multifunctional pocket knives.

"These are part of the supplies from the survival kit," Tristan says. "I brought them out to make a quick inventory."

"Why just a part? Where's the other part?"

"Part of the survival kit was in the cockpit. It contained the things you see here. The other part was in a compartment at the back of the plane, next to the bathroom." He gestures toward the point of contact between the fallen trees and the plane. "It was crushed."

"Great." I debate for a second asking him what items were in there but decide against it. Better not to know what we're missing out on.

My stomach rumbles—I'm growing hungry.

"There are also some peanuts, chocolate sticks, and two sandwiches," Tristan says. "Peanuts and chocolate will make the thirst worse, so I suggest avoiding them." The scant supplies don't surprise me. Chris and I flew to the ranch two weeks ago to oversee the final preparations for the wedding. Since he didn't need the jet while at the ranch, he had it sent for its annual technical inspection. A lousy job the technicians did too, considering the crash.

My boss at the law firm I work for unexpectedly asked me to come back to work the third day we were at the ranch, saying he needed help with a case. I flew back to L.A. on a commercial airline. My boss promised it would take less than a week, so I would still have a full week before the wedding to get things ready. The private jet was supposed to take me back, since the inspection would be done by then. I worked day and night, finishing a day early, and told Chris I wanted to return immediately.

The plane had been emptied of all supplies before the

technical inspection and was supposed to be restocked the day before taking me to Brazil. Since I insisted on leaving a day earlier than planned, Tristan did some quick supply shopping for this trip.

"We're good," I say. "The supplies should last until they rescue us."

Tristan doesn't answer.

"Won't they last?" I press, turning to him. He's bent on one knee between the pieces of the wrecked wing, inspecting something that separated from the plane and lies on the ground.

"They might last," he says.

"I've read about emergency location transmitters—"

"Ours is defective."

"What?"

"Useless."

"But the plane just had the technical inspection…"

"They did a terrible job," he says angrily.

For a few moments, I am too stunned for words. "The flight plan…" I mumble.

Tristan stands up, his dark brown eyes boring into mine. Somehow I know, even before he opens his mouth, that what he is going to say will kill the last hope I'm clinging to. "We did file a flight plan. But I deviated considerably from it last night when I was looking for a place to land. We lost communication before I deviated, so there was no way I could inform anyone."

"What are you telling me, Tristan?" Desperation strangles my voice. "That there is no way for them to find us?"

"It's not like that. They can still guess how we—"

"Guess? We're in the middle of—" I stop, looking around wildly. "Where are we? Is the Amazon River nearby?"

"No."

"How do you know?"

"I've climbed that tree to look around." He points at one of the giant trees next to us. "The river isn't anywhere in sight."

"I don't believe that," I whisper. "I don't..." Swirling on my heel, and sinking about an inch further in the muddy earth, I head to the tree.

"What are you doing?" he calls after me.

"I want to see."

"You'll hurt yourself."

"I don't care."

Driven by rabid determination, I curse the overgrown roots around the tree for blocking access to it, but once I find my way through them I'm grateful for them because they help propel me upward until I reach the first branches. I'm not an outdoors girl, and it shows.

I'm panting when I'm only halfway up the tree. In my defense, this tree is higher than a three-story house. Once or twice I slip, which may be because I can't bear to look too closely at where I'm putting my hands.

The entire surface of the tree is covered with a mushy moss, and by the creepy tingles on my fingers every time I grab a branch, I have the uneasy feeling there are plenty of tiny, multi-legged animals I don't want to see lurking inside it. I've never been a fan of animals with more than four feet.

When I reach the top and wedge myself between two branches, I breathe relieved, happy I made it.

And then I taste bile in my mouth as I take in the sight in front of me. Nothing but green tree-tops. Everywhere. Dense, and stretching as far as I can see. The tree I'm in isn't even high compared to the ones I see in the distance, which makes me think we are on some kind of hill. No sign of the river, or anything that might indicate there are human settlements nearby. If we leave the plane, there is nowhere to go. I make a full turn. From what I can see, in a radius that seems like a few hundred miles, there's no sign of civilization, or a path.

Our best bet is to find the Amazon River and walk alongside it. Human settlements are most likely close to the water. But there's no saying how many miles there are to the river or which direction is the right one.

And the jungle isn't a good place to set out on foot, hoping for the best. No… Our hope will have to come from the sky. Which is empty. No planes or helicopters. Not even a distant sound.

A knot forms in my abdomen, and I start another full turn but stop when my head starts spinning. I rest on the branch, closing my eyes. Chris will come looking for me. He will. Determined not to lose my faith, I start climbing down the tree. I cringe as nameless small creatures crawl on my fingers, but I keep my eyes on my destination and manage not to panic.

Until I only have one set of branches between me and the roots, and my hand touches something cold, slimy and far softer than a branch could be. In the fraction of a second it takes me to register it's a snake—a large snake—I instinctively withdraw my hand, which throws me off balance. I hit the roots with a loud thump, landing on my right ankle and twisting it slightly, then stumble forward until Tristan catches me.

"What—?"

"Snake," I mutter, fisting his white shirt, seeking refuge in the warmth of his arms as cold sweat breaks out on every inch of my body. Right. Legless animals have just surpassed multi-legged ones on the list of creatures I despise. Strands of hair stick to my sweaty face, and as I push them away, my engagement ring comes in sight again. And I start crying in earnest, with tears and sobs that wrack my body.

As much as I tried to convince myself Chris will find us when I was on top of the tree, down here that seems an impossibility. Tristan is saying something, but I can't make out what.

"I am so glad Kyra isn't with us," I say between sobs.

"Yeah, me too," Tristan says, his arms tightening around me. At least neither Tristan nor I have any children. He has parents, though. Strangely, I feel relieved that my parents aren't alive anymore. I can't imagine what a hell they'd be going through if they knew their only daughter was lost in the Amazon rainforest, most likely dead.

"Chris will do everything to find you, Aimee. Don't doubt that for a second."

"I don't." I say, his words giving me strength. That's true. If I am certain of one thing, it's that Chris will do whatever it takes to find me. Being the heir to his father's multimillion-dollar empire, he has the resources to do it. I don't know how long I stay curled against Tristan, overwhelmed, weak, and sweating. He tries to soothe me, his arms embracing me with an awkwardness groomed over years of spending hours at a time in each other's company, the silence between us interrupted only by polite requests. Our relationship has always been stilted, so different from the relationship I have with the other employees in Chris's household.

Well, his parents' household—the Moore's have an enormous villa with an even more enormous garden just outside L.A. Chris and I live in a spacious apartment downtown with no employees at all. But we're at his parents' house so often, it's almost like a second home.

We were there three weeks ago to celebrate my twenty-sixth birthday. Their staff has been with them so long they are like one big family: the cook, the maids, the gardeners, and my beloved Maggie—the woman who cared for Chris and me when we were kids. Our parents were close friends. Since my parents' work took them away from home for months at a time, and Chris and I were the same age, I spent most of my childhood at Chris's home, with Maggie babysitting us.

Chris's parents kept her as housekeeper after we were grown, because she had become like family. I am very close to her and on friendly terms with the other staff. Tristan is the only one who actually works for Chris, flying him around the country about once or twice a week to visit the company's subsidiaries. I see Tristan often, because when Chris doesn't fly out, Tristan is my driver. But we haven't grown any closer because of it.

Still, his presence is like an anchor for me. I rest my head on his hard chest, my cheek pressing against his steel muscles.

His heartbeat is remarkably steady. I want his calmness and strength to overpower my despair. I stay in his arms until I've cried out my weakness. Then, with a newly found determination, I stand up.

"Let's walk until we find a river—any river, then we can continue downstream. It must flow into the Amazon. They can find us easier if we're on the river. And if they don't find us," I gulp, "we have a better chance of finding a settlement along a river."

Tristan, his shirt so soaked from the humidity he looks like he's been walking in pouring rain, shakes his head. "For now our best course of action is to stay here, near the plane. It's easier to spot a plane than two people. They might be able to figure out where we crashed. The first forty-eight hours after a crash are when the search missions are most intense."

Relief ripples along my skin. Forty-eight hours minus the ones when I was knocked out. Then we'll be going home.

"I want to start a fire," I say. "If they send planes over, they will see the fire, right?"

He hesitates. "I doubt they can see a fire down here with the canopy so thick." He's right. The rich canopy weaves itself in a dome above us, allowing slim strings of light to drip through it here and there, drawing loops of light that illuminate the humid cloud-like shadow surrounding us.

"I still want to start a fire."

"We will. There's a way to build it so it's safe even with so many trees nearby. We need a lot of smoke. That'll rise up far above the canopy. It'll be an excellent indicator of our location. It'll be tricky finding dry wood, though. Almost everything here is wet."

"But that's good for smoke, right? Wet wood?"

"Yeah… but we need dry wood to start the fire."

"Can't we start the fire with one of those mirror shards? I don't know much about it, but I saw that on TV once."

"It's not necessary to use a mirror; I have a lighter. But we still need wood."

"We'll find something," I say, undeterred. But Tristan seems hesitant. "What?"

"You stay inside the plane," he says. "I'll search for wood."

"No, I want to be helpful."

"The jungle is a dangerous place, Aimee. I'd rather you were unharmed when Chris finds you. Us."

"Well, if we don't search for the wood, we won't be found. It'll be quicker if we both do it. Besides, we won't go too far away from the plane, will we?"

"No, we won't," Tristan says. "I'll get a can of soda. We have to take care not to dehydrate."

The moment he mentions it, my thirst returns full force, my throat dry and raspy. Tristan disappears inside the plane, returning with a soda. I take the first sip, and it's all I can do not to drink the entire content. I pass the can to him, and he takes a few sips as well.

"Why did you bring just one can?" I say, my throat aching for more.

"We have to be careful not to run out of it."

"But this is the rainforest, right? It should rain soon."

Tristan puts the can on the ground, goes to our supply line-up, and returns with the two pocket knives. "It hasn't rained since we crashed last night. But it's the rainy season; we should have some soon."

"Well, let's look at the bright side, if there's no rain, we can start a fire."

He hands me one of the knives, saying, "Use this to cut any branches that might be useful. Take care where you step."

With that, we head toward the tree nearest to us. It's not the one I climbed earlier. I intend to steer clear of that one, though I'm sure other trees are full of snakes as well. I recoil at the memory of its cold skin. It was a very large snake, though not large enough to be an anaconda. I watched a few documentaries about the Amazon a few weeks back, because our honeymoon was supposed to be in a tourist resort in the rainforest, and Chris wanted to make a safari inside the forest.

The documentary told about the millions of things that could kill one in the forest: animals, contaminated water, poisonous food, and a lot more. In fact, the only thing that seemed harmless was the air. It put me off the safari, and I managed to convince Chris to drop it.

Despite being surrounded by trees, finding dry wood turns out to be just as problematic as Tristan predicted. We even search inside hollow trees, but what the rain hasn't touched, condensation has turned unusable for starting a fire. We advance very slowly, the thick plants making our task cumbersome.

"Damn it. If we had a machete this would be easier," Tristan says, walking in front of me. After a while, sweating like a pig, I start losing concentration; the little soda I drank earlier long having left my body.

Tristan appears to be feeling just as bad. The path beneath us slopes slightly downward, which confirms my suspicion we are on a hill. The more we descend, the muddier the ground becomes. It's almost fluid.

"Let's stop for a bit," I pant. I buckle forward, my knees trembling, and I put my hands on my thighs to steady myself. I keep my eyes on the forest floor, which is covered in mud and leaves and has a red hue. I'm grateful I'm wearing running shoes and not sandals, because they protect me from the creatures crawling on the rainforest floor. I notice a myriad of insects, and decide to close my eyes to stop from giving in to panic. But closing my eyes seems to make my ears more sensitive, because the sound of a thousand beings breathing all around me hits me. Angry chirping birds, sinuous slithering, and howling I don't even want to think about. They're ominous, all of them.

"These will do," I hear Tristan say, and with great effort, I stand up straight. He's carrying a bunch of twigs with one arm. "Can you hold these?" I nod and take the twigs from him, holding them tight against my chest with both arms. He returns a few minutes later with another bunch in his arms.

"Are you ready to walk back to the plane, or do you want to rest a while longer?" he asks, eyes full of concern.

"I'm fine, let's go." Tristan puts one of his hands protectively at the small of my back, and I'm grateful, because my legs wobble. My breath skitters as I try to propel my feet forward, and I press the twigs so tight to my chest they crinkle. The walk back takes forever. I pull myself together when I see the plane again. Tristan goes inside and returns with a lighter and a can of soda. We each take a few sips, and I rest against the airstairs, strangely reassured by the feel of the metal against my skin. It's something familiar in this otherwise alien place.

Though overcome by a tiredness that has crept into my bones, I move to help Tristan start the fire, but find he's already done it. He placed it in a spot under a wide hole in the canopy so the smoke can rise high in the sky.

"Lucky you had that lighter," I say, standing next to him.

He smiles. "I can start a fire without a lighter anyway."

"That's an... interesting skill to have." I notice he used all the dry wood to start the fire, and now he's putting the less dry branches on top. Smoke comes in a matter of seconds.

"I must say, after your encounter with the snake, I thought you'd want to avoid the forest," Tristan says.

I chuckle. "Give me some credit, will you?"

He bends over the wood, fumbling with the twigs, rearranging them. Though the fire is weak, swirls of smoke rise up to the sky. They're not strong enough to be visible from a distance though.

"We should gather more wood," I say. "Better wood. We need more smoke."

"No. What we need is water. We have two soda cans left. That's a more pressing issue."

I don't argue. He's right. "Where do you suggest we look for it?" I ask.

Tristan eyes me. "You go inside the plane and rest for a bit. I'll look for a stream nearby."

"I want to come too."

"No." The firmness in his voice takes me by surprise. "There's no need for both of us to waste our energy."

"I don't want to just stay here, doing nothing."

"Then bring out everything in the plane that can hold water, so if rain comes, we can collect it."

"Got it."

As Tristan leaves, making his way between the trees, armed with his pocket knife, fear grips me. "Be careful," I say.

"Don't worry about me," he calls over his shoulder. There is no tremble in his voice, no hesitation in his steps. The forest doesn't seem to scare him at all. I scout the inside of the plane for anything that might collect water, but I don't find much.

I line empty soda cans outside, then start peeking around the wrecked wing to see if there's anything I can use. I scout through the shredded metal, doing my best not to cut myself.

No luck. I give up the search when nausea overwhelms me, reminding me my water level is low. I walk over to the airstairs, resting against it. Where is Tristan? How much time has passed since he disappeared into the forest?

I stare at the empty soda cans, when an idea occurs to me. A few trees around me have leaves as huge as a tennis racket. They must be of some use. I drag my feet to one whose leaves have an edge that curls upward, perfect for holding water. I use the pocket knife Tristan gave me to cut the leaves. Though they come off almost effortlessly, by the time I cut off about twelve leaves or so, I feel like I'm going to faint. I wobble back to the plane, trying to bind the leaves in some form that will hold water. They end up looking like tightly woven baskets. I suppose we'll see if they're tight enough to hold water. I keep my ears strained, hoping to hear a plane fly over us. Nothing.

When I'm done with the leaves, I collapse on the airstairs, exhausted. I'm tempted, oh so tempted to grab another soda can from the plane and drink it…

It's almost dark when Tristan's voice resounds from the trees. "I didn't find anything. Oh, great thinking," he says, pointing to the leaf baskets I laid out in front of me. He looks terrible. His skin is glistening with sweat, and he has dark circles under his eyes. "These should collect a healthy amount of water."

Somewhere in the back of my mind, the implication gnaws at me. We won't leave this place as soon as I thought. But I can't find the energy to worry about that. Probably because of the thirst. "Let's just hope it rains."

"It will be pouring soon," he says with reassurance. "Let's get inside the plane, it's almost dark. It's dangerous to be outside in the dark."

"Beasts?" I ask.

"And mosquitos. They're more dangerous than beasts."

We each use an insect repellent wipe from the survival kit. Then Tristan grabs the contents of the survival kit he laid out, as well as the mirror shards, and we proceed to the airstairs. Even with Tristan's help, I climb very slowly. He helps me to my seat and shuts the door of the plane. We each eat a sandwich and share the last two cans of soda, which do nothing to still my thirst.

Afterward I lie on the seat I slept on last night. I didn't bother putting it upright this morning or removing the pillow and blanket Tristan gave me last night, so it's already resembling a bed.

"I'm going to the cockpit," Tristan announces.

"Why?"

"To sleep."

"You can sleep on one of the other seats. It'll be much more comfortable than—"

"No, I prefer it that way."

I shrug. "Fine."

Acknowledgements

There are so many people who helped me fulfill the dream of publishing, that I am utterly terrified I will forget to thank someone. If I do, please forgive me. Here it goes.

First, I'd like to thank my beta readers, Jessica, Dee, Karen and Janet. You made this story (and those before it) so much better!!

I want to thank every blogger and reader who took a chance with me as a new author and helped me spread the word. You have my most heartfelt gratitude. To my street team. . .you rock !!!

Last but not least, I would like to thank my family. I would never be here if not for their love and support. Mom, you taught me that books are important, and for that I will always be grateful. Dad, thank you for always being convinced that I should reach for the stars.

To my sister, whose numerous ahem. . .legendary replies will serve as an inspiration for many books to come, I say thank you for your support and I love you, kid.

To my husband, who always, no matter what, believed in me and supported me through all this whether by happily taking on every chore I overlooked or accepting being ignored for hours at a time, and most importantly encouraged me whenever I needed it, I love you and I could not have done this without you.